LESSONS FROM THE VOID

Book 2 of the Lessons Saga
JONATHAN E. FURNEAUX

I0677420

Lessons from the Void

Copyright © 2021 by Jonathan E. Furneaux

Cover illustration by Rachel Smartt © 2020

Independently Published
ISBN: 978-0-6487696-3-7

www.jonathanfurneaux.com

For Wendy.

As a babe I thought only of my need for comfort.

As a child, I longed for love.

Now as a man, I wish to find joy.

How lucky I am, to have found all three in you.

Dramatis Personae

Royalty
Prince **Du Mon** (Male). Youngest Martian Prince.
Commander **Kaya Plessis** (Female). Duchess of Mars.
Crowned Prince **Ju Tin** (Male). Crowned Prince of Mars.
The Emperor **Liu Wei** (Male). Third Eternal Emperor.

High Command
Admiral **Abdul Heydari** (Male). Admiral of the Navy.
High Consul **Maevin** (Male).
Captain **Soona** (Male). Captain of the *Montessori*.
Consul **Barclay** (Male). Disgraced, former Consul.

Military
Lt. Commander **Tam Sunter** (Male). Pilot Ace.
Lieutenant **Jenna Whit** (Female). Pilot.
Lieutenant **Ivanov** (Male). Marine *6th Division*.
Lieutenant **Joe Shiwa** (Male). Marine *6th Division*.
Lt. Junior **Sheree Wagner** (Female). Marine *6th Division*.
Lt. Junior **Mav Tarigan** (Male). Marine *6th Division*.
Snr. Ensign **Vishan Walsh** (Male). Tactical Officer.
Snr. Ensign **Gum Snyder** (Male). Marine *4th Division.*
Ensign **Kyuri Kim** (Female). Computer Systems Officer.

Civilians
Harmony Xu (Female).
Peace Xu (Male). Twin brother of Harmony.

Prologue

53ME (Mars Era). Five Years Ago.

When she saw Mars from orbit, Harmony's breath caught in her throat. She sat. Handcuffed. Surrounded by mountains of waste in the space elevator's cargo hold. As the red planet rose from below to greet her, Harmony shifted in her harness. Two rows of marines flanked her on either side.

The ship's warden had dressed Harmony Xu in the clothes she had worn when she boarded the battleship *Socrates*. Her floor-length cerulean dress cinched around the waist with a maroon sash. The clothes of a companion. She tried to ignore the long sleeves that scratched her skin. Her navy veil fell to a sharp point at her sternum, obstructing her view of Mars. Several long pins in her high hair bun held the cover in place.

What an elaborate insult, she thought. *I'm dolled up in my concubine clothes, and they're unloading me with the ship's garbage.*

Harmony felt the pinpricks of terror on her fingertips. Her stomach rose inside her as the space platform continued to plummet. The sensation of falling didn't seem to bother the dozen or so spacers who milled about her. Many of them had spent years alternating between gravity and weightlessness.

"How long since you were on the surface?" one spacer asked another, who was busy lashing a container of human waste to the bulkhead. It was now labelled as *biomass.*

"I reckon it's been a decade," replied the other. She scratched her scalp roughly. She bit into her fingernails and spat something crusty into the air. "I earned a lot of extra loyalty credits by doing back-to-back runs out to the mining colonies."

"Hey. That's not a bad idea," the male spacer replied. "I always spend my loyalty before shore leave is over."

The spacer's locked his gaze on her while he spoke. She felt his eyes as they wandered along the thin cleft of her skin visible between the dress bodice and her veil.

What a creep.

"You reckon that's the traitor?" the spacer said, not bothering to lower his voice.

"Aye, I reckon so."

"I like the outfit. Wonder which pleasure house wears that outfit?"

"Don't look at her Jeorge. The warden might think you know her."

"But look at that long dress thing around her ankles. It's strange seeing a lady riding the platform."

His friend was picking something out of her teeth. She wiped it on her dark overalls. "What are you saying? I'm not a lady?"

A ring of crash seating ran along the space elevator's circumference. A large space sat in the centre, reserved for cargo. The warden sat a few seats away, facing Harmony. He was an enormous man: thickset and hairy. He sat, whistling, as he polished a rifle across his lap.

The gravity continued to increase, crushing Harmony after months in space. Her vision went dark and splotchy. When she opened her eyes again, Mars was much closer than before.

Much closer to death.

The outcomes of the secret royal courts were never released to the public. One could guess, however, the fate that awaited traitors.

Death, or something worse. My mother told me about the secret rooms hidden in pleasure houses. Then there's the water mines. Dark corridors under the planet, that aren't on any map. I could be put to work at either of them. I'd vanish forever.

A tear fell behind her veil. It caught on the fabric. A tiny drop of moisture on the expensive material.

I want to see mother. Just one more time before I die.

Harmony looked up. The spacers could now stand without floating away. Like a colony of insects, the uneducated labourers swarmed over their crash seats. In unison they strapped themselves in, laughing and jostling with each other.

"Why do you reckon they always do that?" the marine on her left asked. The name on his breast pocket said that his name was Wagner.

"Showing off," the marine on her right replied. His nametag read Smit. "Only thing they've got going for them is their aptitude for space. Poor wretches."

Wagner raised an eyebrow. "You almost sound sorry for them."

"Not me," Smit said, backpedalling. "They could always join the military if they wanted to move up in society."

"See, you've walked straight into my trap." Wagner gave the other marine a wink. "My parents were actually spacers, so I would have got you either way. I haven't seen you around the elevator before. Recent transfer?"

The marine on the right tightened his crash netting some more. His eyes were the only thing visible from behind the sheen on his helmet's visor. "Is it that obvious?"

"Smit? You've been sweating the whole time." Wagner seemed to be older than the other marine. His voice sounded wiser, aged like a fine wine. "I'm surprised it hasn't condensed and formed a cloud."

Harmony recognised the name Wagner from the *Socrates*. She tried to recall his face from the brief glimpses she would have had. She shook her head.

I spent half the journey in the prince's chambers to keep my cover in check. Now I don't know a friendly face. Perhaps if I'd made more friends while I was with the prince, they could have... She shook her head. As soon as she'd been labelled a traitor, all of those friendships would have ended immediately. It was self-preservation. It was natural. *And then I'd be feeling abandoned by them as well.*

"The trip upwards was a lot worse," Smit said. Through the tinted visor, Harmony could see a faint smile.

Is he looking at me?

"The trip upwards was a lot worse," he reported. "I keep thinking about what would happen if this whole platform broke free from the guide rail."

Harmony leaned back in her crash chair. She could taste bile on her tongue. *They're talking as if they're out on a delightful holiday.*

The passengers aboard the platform could watch their descent on the console projections above them. Even from this distance, Harmony could see the population domes that dotted the equator. They were immense—unforgiving structures of tessellated steel and leaded glass. Below the domes sat entire cities, replete with gardens and parks.

She looked beyond the dazzling domes. Large factories spewed gas into the atmosphere, fed by thermal vents. Liquid waste from factories pooled into artificial seas of algae that bubbled. Beyond the factories and thermal vents was Harmony's real home: the Artemis dome.

My birthplace in the darkness.

The surface of Mars rushed up to greet them. Now the aerospace port was visible at the end of the platform's guide rail. Olympus Mons cast a black shadow across the desert wastes. A terrible yellow cloud of dust was building across the equator, heading for the tiny point where the space elevator touched the planet.

Harmony began to feel normal as the gravity lifted. The warden stood, slung his rifle's strap across his shoulder and aimed it towards her. "Let's get a move-on. You've got a date with the High Court tomorrow."

The marines that flanked Harmony ripped her from the crash seating, and thrust her through the platform's exit. The loud gossip of spacers rang in her ears.

The aerospace terminal was a squat concrete bunker. Its low ceilings ended in sloped walls. Uniformed men and women ran through its hallways pushing cargo on gravity prams. Others were carting inventory that would travel back up to *Plato*. Spacers stood, gossiping with their crates of goods. They scattered as a squat officer started shouting instructions.

Harmony felt the crowd examining her. The officers on either side frogmarched her, each holding onto her arms to prevent escape. The warden walked behind her. His rifle was pointed at the small of her back. She thought about running, or slipping away into the public, or hijacking a vehicle. But the marines held her biceps firmly.

The warden probably gave them strict instructions beforehand.

"Make way, make way," called the warden. "It's a left up ahead."

They descended inside the terminal and stopped at a guard station. The warden waved his digital badge in front of the guard's face. "Prisoner transfer."

The guard pulled the badge away from his nose and waved it atop his console. Wagner was looking at the vehicles lined up behind the guard's station. Smit, however, released his grip slightly on her bicep. "Your veil is slipping," he said. He reached up and adjusted one of the pins. "There you go."

"Thanks."

As they stood close to one another, Harmony caught a glimpse of his eyes through the dark visor. They were grey and glassy.

Something about those eyes...

Harmony felt his arm hold her bicep again, but this time it was much gentler. Something sharp pressed into her palm.

Smit didn't want the warden to see. She remembered something from long ago: a memory as she chased her brother through an alleyway. She could remember laughing as they ran. *Back before I knew any better.* Her stomach tentatively unknotted itself, little by little. In its place, a small flicker of hope had ignited.

Is that you, Peace?

The guard waved them through. "Vehicle T-376 is on the right."

The warden led the way, confident now that another guard blocked Harmony's retreat. They passed rows of personnel carriers. In the far corner were two anti-aircraft launching stations mounted on treads. The warden stopped beside a small transport that seated eight. It sat on large metre-wide tires with enormous threads.

"This one's us."

Harmony clambered into the back of the truck. Four seats sat facing each other in the rear, with a driver and passenger sitting up the front. The grey-eyed marine Smit sat in the back next to Harmony, with his rifle out of reach. The warden sat across from them, next to the doors. A gun rested on his lap but kept it pointed in Harmony's direction. Smit fastened her cuffs to the arm rest between them.

"We good to go?" Wagner said from the driver's seat. His voice sounded muffled through the thick perspex that separated them.

"Close the doors," the warden replied. The group of marines who had escorted them through the terminal visibly relaxed.

I'd relax too. It's a short ride to the military base.

The rear of the transport hissed shut from the driver's command. Harmony's ears popped as the interior pressurised. Oxygen hissed through a vent in the ceiling.

The Wagner hesitated as the space elevator's transport airlock cycled open. Then he punched the throttle forward. There was a sickening lurch as their vehicle dropped out onto the flat plains of Mars.

My trial is tomorrow.

The thought was enough to wind her stomach back into a coiled spring of panic. News of her crime had been public enough that the crown had decided to host a public trial. Many who threatened the royal family were not so lucky. The warden was staring outside at the red dunes. He sighed deeply.

"Good to be back."

Harmony glanced at the sharp object in her hand. A key. Small enough to fit her handcuffs. The warden looked back at her, and she closed her hand tightly.

Smit gave her a slow, almost imperceptible nod in her direction, then he reached up, tapped on his temple, and his visor became transparent.

Peace!

Her twin brother's face had changed drastically in such a short period of time. His jaw was much longer than it had been when she left the planet. The cheeks were sunken craters.

Surely the warden can see my heart beating through this dress.

Harmony forced herself to walk normally. She took calm, even breaths. Inside, however, she wanted to throw her arms around Peace and embrace him. She wanted to sob and thank him for finding her. For risking his life to be here. *He's here to save you. Hold it together. Get the warden away from his gun.*

"I hear that the crown is bringing in the best to prosecute you," the warden said. "You know what you're accused of? A lot of things. Conspiracy to kidnap and extort the prince. Treachery that jeopardised one of His Majesty's vessels. Treason for leaking military secrets. High treason for plotting against the royal family. Seduction of the prince."

Harmony laughed at that. "Seduction? Please. Du Mon— His Highness, just wanted to feel like he was in touch with the common person."

I wanted him to run away with me, though. That part was true. To throw it all away for me. How did it go wrong?

The warden stood up in the back of the truck, balancing easily as it jostled him about.

The plan was simple: disable Socrates, *get 'captured' by the Earth-Lunar Mining Guild, and then the resistance would dismantle the Martian government, while the Martian military was off trying to rescue Du Mon.*

"The prince said he'd marry me," she looked the warden dead in the eye. A smirk found its way across her mouth. "Can you believe that?"

The warden didn't reply. Instead, he backhanded her across the face.

The blow was a gunshot inside the tiny cabin. Harmony clutched her face as the white-hot pain ignited from just below her eye. One of the armoured knuckles from the warden's uniform had just avoided blinding her. Harmony balled her fists through the pain, and realised that the tiny key was now gone. Bright, painful spots of light danced in her vision as she scanned the floor quickly, searching for it. Her eye had started weeping uncontrollably.

The warden raised his hand to strike her again. "How dare you speak about the royal family that way!"

Peace caught the warden's fist as it swung. There was a pause, as the warden stared, mouth agape at the officer who had stopped the blow.

"What are you doing? I'll court-martial you for touching me."

"Go ahead," her brother replied.

Harmony lifted her dress with her free arm and lashed out with a heeled boot. The warden's gun flew across the cabin. The three of them watched it bounce once, before coming to rest next to the rear doors. Harmony's eyes found the key for her cuffs. It lay on the floor, halfway between the gun and her seat.

The warden licked his lips.

"Mutiny, is it? How disappointing. I've had to put down a few prison riots in my day." His eyes glanced between his own rifle and the one that Peace had propped up next to his chair. The three of them waited for an unspoken signal. Then, instinctively, they collided in a sea of limbs.

Harmony scrambled towards the key on her elbows and knees, her shackled wrist pulling her back painfully, as she desperately stretched across the floor of the truck. The warden leapt towards Peace and landed a punch directly between Peace's grey eyes. Then another. The marine managed to catch the warden's wrist on the third strike. He kicked. The warden exhaled rapidly as the boot connected with his gut. He was puffing as he swung again. Peace ducked.

Harmony felt like her wrist was going to snap as she strained forward. Her fingertips brushed at the keypass.

Peace was fumbling blindly for his rifle, as his left hand shielded his face from the warden's blows. The young marine managed to curl his fingers around the barrel of the gun, but the warden had reached across and grabbed the rifle as well. They both tugged, like children fighting over a toy.

Harmony felt her fingers close around the tiny keypass. She turned, nearly dropped it again, and buried it into her handcuffs. She turned the key.

The Warden held Peace's shoulders and sank a square kneecap into the smaller man's chest. There was a loud crunch. Harmony stood, but a giant hand enveloped her face, and she was forcefully pushed back into her chair. Her veil caught on the fabric of the warden's ring, yanking the hairpins out. Harmony grabbed at the material and held it close to her.

"Can't flirt your way out of this one." The warden pulled the rifle free from her brother's grasp. Peace's fingers were clawed as he desperately tried to cling to the weapon.

Puffing, Harmony watched the warden sink his steel caps into the side of Peace, who screamed.

"What's going on back there?" the marine driving asked. He peered back through the connecting window and saw the warden kicking an officer on the truck's floor.

The truck lurched to a stop, causing the warden to sway, before overcorrecting and falling forward towards Harmony. She held a hair pin firmly between her thumb and forefinger. It was about the length of her middle finger. She sank it into his face. It glanced off his cheekbone and plunged deep into the warden's eye.

"Call for backup!" the warden screamed, clutching his eye.

Through the glass, Harmony saw Wagner hit the alarm on the vehicle's radio. He looked back at the warden, writhing on the floor, and kicked the driver door open.

Peace scrambled to his knees, coughing and spluttering. He crawled over the warden's writhing body and tossed a rifle to Harmony. They pointed the barrels at the door as it depressurised, and the precious, oxygenated air of the truck trickled outside. Peace kicked the door open, and heard the satisfying *bang* as it opened like collided with Wagner's helmet.

Wagner flew back as the doors swung open. His visor was wet with condensation when he spotted Harmony and Peace. Both had their rifles trained on him. The marine paused, and then dropped his gun onto the red dust. It landed with a soft *thud.*

"Can you drive?" Peace asked, as he started to choke on the Martian air.

"A long time ago."

Harmony's vision was beginning to blur. She gasped, but couldn't draw enough oxygen from the air. She slipped from the rear of the vehicle and staggered around to the front. Lethargically, she managed to pull herself into the front seat and heaved the driver's door shut behind her. A woman's voice on the radio was speaking quickly. Reassuring her that air support was being mobilised. Harmony switched the radio off. She sat, panting as the air scrubbers hummed loudly.

Nearly a thousand years of terraforming, and we can still only last for a few minutes outdoors without oxygen masks.

Outside, Harmony heard a gunshot. In her mind's eye, she saw her brother with his big, grey eyes. A terrible sadness washed over her, as though she had just witnessed the death of that memory. *That little boy grew up a long time ago. It's time you did as well.*

A minute later, Peace climbed into the passenger's seat. The oxygen rushed out as he climbed back in. Harmony's head began to throb painfully.

Peace touched his temple and then examined the bright red blood that slicked his fingers.

"That could have gone better," he said.

"Absolutely," Harmony replied. "You could have stopped the first slap, for instance."

"You could have stabbed him in the eye from the get-go."

"Why didn't you just shoot him?"

He shrugged. "That box would have deafened us both forever. Plus, you know, the ricochet. Yeah, the ricochet would have gotten us."

"Shame the younger one had to die."

"Such a shame. Had to be done."

"Did you go through their pockets, Peace?"

He nodded and sank back into his seat with a wince. "Ripped off their rank and names as well, to delay any investigations. I saw a dust storm from the space elevator that was rushing this way. If we're lucky, it might cover them for a few days."

Harmony checked the sky. "Wishful thinking."

"That's why we joined the resistance," he replied. "Wishful thinking."

Harmony was still carefully scanning the red planet's horizon. "The Artemis dome is that way."

"Good memory."

"I couldn't forget it. I've tried to." Harmony sighed deeply and rubbed her tired eyes. "It's so good to see you, Peace. What's the plan?"

Peace ripped the fake name Smit from his uniform. He grinned. "It's good to see you too, sis. That's it."

"What's it?"

"My plan was to get you free, and then if we weren't both dead, I figured we'd go on the run. My contact from the resistance got me onto the space elevator with a fake identity. That was it."

Harmony's eyes widened. "So, what? Were you planning on us waltzing up to the Artemis dome and expect them to let us in?"

"No. I figured we'll need to lie low for a few months in the space corridors."

Harmony took one last look at the Artemis dome. "Is mother still in the temple district?"

"Yes."

She turned the wheel away. Building along the horizon was a dust storm the size of a small mountain. It curled backwards, swirling around, and mixing with itself in a swirl of yellows and browns, like milk added to coffee.

Harmony pushed the throttle to its max. "We'll lose them in that storm."

Peace smiled without any joy. "No, we're going to die that storm."

Tiny pellets of sand pattered against the front windscreen as they drove straight for the mouth of the storm. There was a flash, and lightning erupted through the clouds of dust.

1

High Consul Maevin was a very particular man. It said so in his record, to which he had the highest level of read-write clearance. If Maevin spoke into his office desk, intricate machinery inside it would perform live updates to everything the Martian government knew about him.

At precisely eight o'clock, his receptionist brought in his breakfast tea, suspended in a red terracotta cup. Maevin's new receptionist was much more careful than the last one had been. She gave a small bow at the waist, right arm stretched at a 45-degree angle from her body, her hand opened, palm facing towards him. Maevin realised he'd forgotten her name. It was possible he'd never asked for it.

A banner stretched over his door. 'All Martian Life is Sacred,' it read. He'd studied those words each day. It was his duty to protect the quality of each life on the red planet.

Yet I always seem to find displeasure with my receptionists. It can be anything. An unconscious gesture. An oversight. A knowing glance. These were all things that had led to the receptionist's predecessors being quietly reshuffled to a lower floor of the consulate.

Perhaps I find fault with them on purpose, to prevent any attachments clouding my judgement. I might retain a sub-

optimal receptionist if I became too fond of them. Again, he studied the words on the banner. *It is better to care for people you don't know.*

Maevin studied the view outside his office's window. The consulate was a reinforced ziggurat, adjoining the royal habitat dome. Unlike the royal palace, the consulate building was a self-contained piece of architecture that didn't require a habitat dome. Instead, the consulate joined the palace dome via reinforced walkways and vehicle bridges.

Outside he could see the Martian cliff faces that provided a degree of protection from the howling winds and biting sandstorms. The cliffs resembled black and red walls, forged through some unknown tectonic catastrophe. As the old consul watched, the clouds billowed overhead. They rolled backwards, surged, and then retreated, like those old videos of Earth's oceans. He could almost smell the sizzling, electromagnetic field of the artificial ozone.

With a sudden start, Consul Maevin realised that the receptionist was still standing there, waiting.

"Rise."

The receptionist stood upright. Her cheeks were now rosy from the blood that had pooled there while she waited. If she was upset at being made to wait, she didn't show it.

"You have an appointment in five minutes with His Royal Highness, Du Mon," she said.

"Could you read my itinerary for today?"

The receptionist's face was smooth and detached, perhaps artificially so. Looking at her was like watching one of those cheaply animated dramas, where an AI with no human supervision, generates the visuals of the show just from scanning a script.

Maevin was aware that many beauty clinics now offered such a service: voluntary facial paralysis. If this was the case, her surgeon was outstanding. There were none of the telltale slurring of the earliest attempts at the surgery. Some claimed that it slowed the signs of aging, because the skin across your face no longer stretched or bunched. Others did it for professional reasons. A soldier might find it very helpful having a look that masked expression, which could push them towards an early promotion. Maevin, however, decided that he didn't want a reception who could perfectly mask her emotions.

He thought about the word *memo* and how much he wanted to remember this particular topic tomorrow morning. There was a moment's resistance, and then he felt the tiny tendrils of electricity inside his head. The sensation tingled along the contours of a memory chip embedded in his frontal lobe, just below the skull. The chip was the size of a child's fingernail, nanometres across, that probed the folds of his working memory. It would communicate with his desk, and tomorrow morning the memory would be presented back to him when he sat down.

If only every new invention from the beauty clinics were as wholesome. There were some surgeries that High Consul Maevin had deemed 'useful' and 'healthy'. Brain chipping, for example, held so many benefits, particularly for assisting memory. High Command had approved it unanimously after reading his report. *It was an excellent report.* He'd had it framed on the wall of his office. Now it hung against the polished concrete backdrop behind his desk.

Other technologies that had crossed his desk had been quickly met with roadblocks from his department. Iris or fingerprint reconstructions, for example, posed risks for some of the outdated security systems dotted around the planet, as well as many off-world mining frigates.

Usually, it was just rich kids wanting to have the eyes of a cat, or celebrities who wished to have fingerprints that swirled with their actual signature. In those instances, he'd made sure only a handful of clinics on the planet were permitted to perform the procedure, and only after the surgeons, the patients, and the exact reasons for the procedure were carefully vetted and documented. So far, only three procedures had been officially permitted.

The old consul smiled, half-listening to the receptionist as she continued reading down the list. Reading an itinerary was something his computer could do, and with much defter skill. His chief reason for keeping the receptionist here was so it could cause the prince a moment's hesitation when he arrived and had to knock, instead of being buzzed through by the receptionist without breaking his stride. *Someone could demand plenty of things if they're the sort of person who can be buzzed through on sight. Better to cause some hesitation, before the prince comes barging in with another request.*

'Is there anything else, sir?' the receptionist asked.

Maevin waved her over. 'There's a dull pain in my left shoulder, I was wondering if you could see to it?'

Without hesitation, the receptionist crossed behind his desk. She rested her muscular forearms on the top of his chair and began kneading the muscle tissue of his neck. The receptionist had begun a confident pulling motion—stretching his head one way while guiding his shoulder in the other—when there was a brisk knock at the reinforced office door.

Prince Du Mon of Mars would have been an average-looking person, if not for all the clothing and finery that indicated his position. He was much shorter than his older brother, the Crowned Prince Ju Tin. Du Mon was also thinner. Less handsome. His beard grew in patches. As he closed the door behind him, the prince bobbed his head in an acknowledgement and dropped his gaze, electing to slink into the room instead of barging in.

Maevin indicated the empty seat across from his desk. "To what do I owe the honour, Your Highness?"

The prince gave Maevin a polite glance and then looked out the window at the approaching storm. His face was soft, exactly halfway between a man's and a teenager's. The baby fat still refused to leave his cheeks. The prince wrung his hands, playing with the soft skin on his ring finger, where the marital tattoo was etched. Maevin inhaled, and could faintly detect the smell of spices that clung to the prince: a strange mixture of paprika and mint.

"I've come to request command of Project Tortoise." The prince had a softer voice than his brother. Less confident. Less commanding.

"If you don't mind me saying so, Your Grace, you look like you've had a long week. We could always reschedule this morning's meeting."

Heavy bags hung beneath the prince's almond eyes, darkening the tan skin by a few shades. Du Mon shook his head, but the movement looked like it took more effort than steering a capital ship.

"I've heard whispers that High Command will be selecting a captain for the *Black Tortoise*'s maiden voyage. I'd like to be that captain."

Maevin's receptionist was doing some stellar work with her knuckles. She hammered the sides of her fingers into the tender tissue like a jackhammer, her fingers clicking as the space between each digit connected. Maevin indicated the prince.

"How rude of me, please see to the prince as well."

The receptionist paused, then abandoned the consul's knobbly shoulders.

Du Mon sat straighter in his chair, leaning away from the receptionist's outstretched digits, as if they were the legs of some monstrous spider.

"Don't trouble yourself."

"I insist," Consul Maevin said. He allowed a faint smirk to tease the left corner of his mouth. His sources suggested the prince was still recovering from his injuries five years ago.

The prince managed to bear the pain for a few moments, tears welling in his eyes as the receptionist grabbed a fistful of flesh on his upper shoulder.

So, Maevin thought, *the injury is far worse than the royal family is letting on.*

Du Mon pushed the receptionist away, a little more roughly than necessary, and blinked several times to dispel the tears. "Don't touch me."

"That's quite enough," Maevin said. He made sure his voice conveyed urgency and sympathy. "You've upset His Highness."

The receptionist backed out of the room, bowing a thousand apologies as she went.

"I apologise again, Your Grace." Maevin offered a cup by picking it up from the tray the receptionist had brought in. "Tea?"

"I'd rather not."

"I believe I understand Your Highness' desire to leave the planet," Maevin said, choosing his words very carefully. The prince's personnel file sat in the background of the consul's computer. It listed his temperament. *Impatient. Short-tempered. Prone to emotional and violent outbursts.*

"My sources tell me that you hardly ever leave military buildings, or their cordon zones. You always take several officers with you when travelling between secure locations. May I ask why?"

Du Mon screwed his eyes into a squint. "If you've taken the trouble of gathering all that information about me, you probably already know why."

"You are afraid of the terrorists? The rumoured resistance?"

"I'm most at risk here, planet-side. In space, I can sleep peacefully, knowing the sensors will detect an enemy within ten thousand kilometres."

Unless the enemy is in your crew, Maevin thought. "No word on the arrest of that traitor, Harmony Xu?"

A tendon strained along the prince's neck as he ground his teeth together. "You, of all people, know the answer to that question. There haven't been any sightings of her in five years. She ventured into a sandstorm and vanished. Now, either you're trying to antagonise me, High Consul Maevin, or your department isn't keeping close-enough tabs on wanted fugitives."

Maevin smiled as warmly as he could. Beneath the prince's feet was a textured metal floor, painted to resemble timber. *You'd talk different if you knew that connected to this metal floor, is a security system controlled by my brain chip.*

Maevin lifted his feet off the floor, so only the rubber wheels of his chair anchored him to the ground. His mind danced around the word 'electrocute'. It was a gentle flirtation with the concept, as opposed to a thought-command. His mind felt like fingers dancing across a big red button. *One imperative thought from my brain and the prince would die, just like that. He'd even do a little jig, twitching on the ground as the life ebbed from his body. It would be high treason, of course.* The thought of that control, however, sent tingles of delight along the consul's spine.

"I'm merely making conversation, Your Highness. However, as you've said, there haven't been any sightings of Ms Xu, ever since she disappeared en route to the courtrooms. Is it true that you threatened her before she disappeared?"

A crack appeared in the prince's expression, a small twitch of the mouth. A slight sagging of the shoulders. "I threatened her on the *Plato*, because I figured I'd never see her again."

You'd make a terrible diplomat, Maevin thought. "And now," he continued aloud, "you're in quite the predicament. Always looking over your shoulder, just in case she's still alive, and wants revenge. Perhaps you feel like you can never relax again, until she's taken out of the picture?" The older man shrugged by widening the distance between his palms and tilting his head at a jolly angle. "I understand your eagerness to go back to space, Your Highness, but as royalty you could simply commandeer the next vessel leaving for the asteroid belt. Why come to my department, asking for the special project?"

The prince chewed his bottom lip and let out an exasperated sigh. "I want to do something more than just ferrying cargo back and forth, and I can't approach High Command's chambers directly."

"You could talk to Admiral Heydari and make the request officially."

"I've tried that. He told me he has another candidate in mind."

"But your father could present your case again, on your behalf."

There was a pause, as the prince looked out the window once again.

Maevin pretended to wipe some dust from his desk. *So, you aren't talking with the old man. Or maybe you just don't want him having control over your military career.*

"I can always put in a recommendation with my peers when we meet next week," the consul said. He studied the pretend dust on his finger. "Doubtless, Admiral Heydari has your name on a list of potential candidates somewhere. Perhaps, if he knew you had my support, it would persuade him?"

Du Mon blinked, surprised. "You would do that?"

"Of course. I'll just have to convince the Admiral it's a favour for me. We have quite a close working relationship, you know."

Du Mon stood. "I'd appreciate that a lot, High Consul."

"Although," the older man scratched his nose absently. "Your brother has also put forward an expression of interest.

Two princes, huh. It might be *difficult* for me to choose a better candidate."

There was a subtle tightening of the muscles along the prince's jawline. Maevin controlled his own expression perfectly. *The prince might benefit from some facial paralysis surgery. What's he wrestling with? Fear? Anger? A mixture, betrayal?*

The consul remembered his tea and blew the steam from it. His personal cup was made by a craftsperson named Mi'lle, according to the stamp etched into the cup's underside. The red terracotta was perhaps one of the most dangerous cups in existence.

The prince sank back down to his chair. When he broke the silence, Du Mon's voice was terse, holding back a flood of emotion.

"What can I do, to help convince you that I'm the better candidate?"

Maevin peered into his tea, searching for any tell-tale flakes of red dust suspended in the green liquid. The cup's walls were poisonous. It was a luxury item: carefully glazed and baked to prevent any of the toxins from seeping into his beverage. Death was almost a guarantee if a small scratch were made to the inside of the cup.

Once he was satisfied that today's cup of tea wouldn't cause him intestinal pain and then death, Maevin took a sip from it.

"I happen to know some particular officers in the military. I'd like them to join your program. You've met Lieutenant Ivanov from the secret service?"

"I've heard of him. The news isn't good: he's a thug."

"Indeed, but he's a thug who I owe a favour. In exchange for his unit's inclusion, I'll ensure that you are captain of the *Black Tortoise*. He's loyal. As long as you dangle a treat in front of him, he'll make an excellent shock trooper. Raw, explosive power."

Du Mon held up an index finger before they shook on it.

"Only if I'm captain of the *Black Tortoise*."

Maevin smiled. "Of course. Leave it to me."

2

Buried under the surface of Mars, the training facility and adjunct barracks were a well-kept secret. Prince Du Mon's boots clicked against the polished concrete floor. His almond eyes carefully surveyed his marines while they trained.

"Nice place you got here," said Tam Sunter. The pilot wiped a gloved finger along the walls and inspected it. "Does your cleaner do home visits?"

"The junior officers do the cleaning."

Through the windows that lined the cold hallway, Tam saw a patchwork of young men and women sparring, studying, disassembling weapons, building explosives, laughing, and eating.

"So, this is your team?"

"The pool of soldiers, yes. The enlisted officers will get selected at the end of the next training retreat." Du Mon paused to watch two soldiers, fists raised, exchanging swings. The shorter one ducked beneath a punch and swept the legs out from his opponent.

As they watched, Tam snuck a sideways glance at his friend. In the reflection of the hallway's windows, the prince appeared like a phantom. Du Mon's skin was pallid, hidden away from the sun for at least a week. Acne had broken out along the prince's hairline. His eyes drooped heavily.

Du Mon nodded appreciatively at the marines. A slight smile was etched on his tired face. "My office is this way, lieutenant commander."

The prince led them through an automatic door, past the showers and sleeping quarters, and into a small office where the centralised hallway terminated. The office was packed to overflowing. Du Mon waved Tam to a seat facing his desk, and began shifting piles of equipment and trinkets from his desk.

"Sorry, I wasn't expecting company."

An old, lumpy roll-out mattress lay sprawled in the corner of the room. The walls were decorated with paintings and diagrams. One was a topographical map of the now-destroyed mining colony on Ceres. Another was an artists' depiction of spacers leaping from a corvette into the vacuum of space.

An enormous display shelf sat behind Du Mon's office chair. Trinkets and trophies were arrayed inside the glass on small stands and podiums: a red ceremonial dagger, military medals of valour, jars of liquid, a framed picture of Captain Dav'i, and a scale model of the capital ship *Socrates*. In the centre of the display was an immense sculpture of the Elder Seeker. Tam felt his stomach lurch.

The Elder Seeker resembled a giant, worm made of crimson chitin that had been cut at staggering angles. Its maw was broad, with thousands of stub-like teeth spiralling down inside its throat.

The thing that destroyed the Ceres mining colony. Many good Martians died as a result.

The space-faring creature had entered their solar system five years ago, controlled by an alien race that the Martian scientists now referred to as the Outsiders.

Tam shook his head. "Why do you keep that there?"

Du Mon's face blanched as he acknowledged the sculpted Elder Seeker sitting high on the shelf.

"It's a reminder."

Tam began to recognise some of the more obscure objects on the shelf. One of the jars of liquid contained an actual shard of the worm's red carapace, about the size of a finger. Tam shifted in his chair. The rest of the room was filled with weaponry, database drives, as well as sim gear.

"Wait, is that a real head?"

In the rear corner of the office, an Outsider's head was suspended in a clear fluid. Two round, milky eyes stared blindly at Tam. The mandibles were covered in a luminous jelly, preserved perfectly, even after all these years.

"I requested it for educational purposes, to show the officers." The prince stood up, then paused, unsure of why he stood up. Then he sat back down again.

Tam gave a theatrical sigh. "You need a holiday, Du. A haircut wouldn't be a bad idea either."

"Don't call me that, and I don't have time."

"I could get Mith to come by and help out. She did my hair last week. Plus, she could bring little Jace along. He's starting to look just like me, Du. Keeps on asking when you'll visit again. Hey, they could probably help you clean up in here. Heck, you could probably look ten years younger if you took a shower."

The prince's eyes finally locked onto Tam with clarity. A smirk played at the corner of his mouth.

"I saw a picture of Mith recently. She's lost...ten kilos since pregnancy?"

"Something like that."

"And it seems you managed to find them just as quickly."

Tam clutched at his heart weakly, and nodded. "Generally, I only take lifestyle criticism from people who can remember seeing the sun."

Du Mon nodded in a slow and deliberate fashion. "What do you want, Lieutenant Commander Sunter?" Du Mon dropped into his chair. "I doubt you snuck in just to criticise me about my Feng Shui."

Tam kicked his boots off and planted both feet on Du Mon's desk. His hoisted his arms back behind his head and laced the fingers behind his neck. "The emperor sent me."

"Why?"

"For Phobos sake, you need help!"

The prince opened a drawer in his desk and retrieved a ruler. He tried, unsuccessfully, to prod Tam's feet off the table with it. "Why didn't my father send a message?"

"Apparently that hasn't been working. The emperor wanted a more personal touch, from an old friend." Tam pointed a thumb at himself and clicked his tongue twice. "So that's why I'm here."

"Does he have an update on who's been chosen to captain the *Black Tortoise*?"

Tam measured his words while studying Du Mon's face. "Not exactly. He wants you to go home to see your wife."

There was a visible twitch beneath the prince's left eye. "I see. Why doesn't His Highness give me a direct order, in that case?"

"She hasn't seen you in a week, Du."

"Don't call me that. It's not my father's business, or yours. My task force has picked up a lot of momentum in these final stages. In fact, I'm going to begin my final round of recruitment for the rank-and-file of this special unit."

Tam raised his eyebrows in surprise. "You don't have enough soldiers?"

Du Mon leaned over and successfully pushed his friend's feet from the table. "I have enough soldiers and special officers. If we get selected for the mission, I'm going to need a ship's cook, a warden, comms officers, and a helmsman."

"Why not lodge a request to High Command? There's no need to interview for them yourself. You're giving yourself weeks of unnecessary work."

Du Mon laughed. "The team has to be perfect, lieutenant commander. No more casualties under my command."

Tam's eyebrows furrowed. "What do you mean, no more casualties?"

"This time, we'll be prepared. I won't have another Ceres on my conscience."

Tam looked up. The model of the immense space worm hung above Du Mon. The black and terrible maw was open. From where he sat, it looked as though the Elder Seeker was about to eat through the prince's head.

"Ceres was a success. We killed the Elder Seeker and repelled the Outsiders."

"Too many losses," Du Mon replied cheerily, with a wave of his hand. "Ceres showed me how ill-prepared I was for leadership. Please tell my father I respectfully decline his invitation home. I'm needed here. We're doing zero-g combat simulations next week."

"Your Highness, I'm afraid the emperor gave strict instructions for me to bring you home to Kaya Plessis. Go home. It's an imperial order. You're leaving this filthy office and having a decent night's sleep."

Du Mon smiled and shook his head. "My squad can't be left behind."

Tam stood. His chair reeled backwards. "You mean that squad of highly-trained and over-qualified marines out there? Delegate. Who's your second-in-command?"

"I haven't chosen."

"Choose now."

"I can't. I need to run more exercises with them."

"Drilling doesn't make a leader. Choose."

"No."

"In that case, Your Highness. Pardon me." Tam leapt across the table, barefoot, and tackled the prince around his middle. Du Mon's chair tipped up and over, and they both tumbled backwards. Tam hit the display shelf with his shoulder. Pictures, medals, and trinkets all crashed inside the glass display.

"Stop!" Du Mon yelled. He pushed his hand against Tam's face, trying to pry himself away as Tam kneeled on his torso.

"Why do you want to be a martyr? You're coming home, and you're apologising to Kaya."

"Help!" Du Mon hollered at the closed office door. "I'll shoot you for treason Tam!"

The prince pulled back his fist and swung, but it glanced off Tam's temple without seeming to slow him.

"That's a weak punch you got there, Du!"

"That's because I ruined this arm saving your worthless life!"

Du Mon bucked, chest heaving with the effort, and managed to pull his good arm out from underneath Tam's body. With both hands, he grabbed his friend by the throat and squeezed.

"Du—" Tam's eyes went wide, and his own hands went to pry the prince's hands away. "—starting to hurt." His face went bright red, and his mouth stretched downwards like a frog's as he tried to breathe.

The prince pushed the thumb of his good hand deeper and then stopped. He released his grip.

Tam collapsed on top of him. They both lay gasping. A greenish fluid dripped from the display shelf above. Du Mon waited for Tam to collect his breath.

There was a polite knock on the door, and a marine entered. Several jagged scars ran from her left eyebrow, all the way up, dividing her blonde crew-cut in half. Tam had seen friendlier-looking street brawlers on the theatre circuits.

"Excuse me, captain? I heard a commotion." She glanced across the damaged office and found them both lying on the floor. A deep cut ran along Du Mon's cheek. The marine tilted her head far to the side, so that she could make level eye contact with the prince. "Do you need me to shoot your visitor, sir?"

"No thank you, Wagner. But I appreciate it all the same."

"Very good, sir. There's a complement of the royal guard here to escort you home."

Du Mon groaned. "My father sent the royal guard too?"

Tam climbed off the prince and held out a hand to help him up. "Just in case you refused."

The prince accepted the offer and scrambled to his feet. The golden half-cloak fastened to his shoulders had come loose on one side. The prince looked around at the piles that littered his office. "I might need a hand taking some of this home."

Tam put a firm hand on his friend's shoulder. "I refuse to help you take work home. The guard is waiting. I gave them orders to come in with shock batons and taser everyone, if you didn't come out in ten minutes."

"Ha." The prince straightened his back out and limped towards the door.

"Actually, I'm not kidding." Tam winced apologetically. "You'd better hurry."

"I don't believe you," Du Mon called over his shoulder. The clicking of his boots, however, grew in urgency as he turned the corner at the end of the hallway. Tam waited until the prince was out of ear-shot before rubbing his throat and grimacing in pain.

"What was your name again?" Tam asked. His voice sounded squeakier than usual.

"Sheree Wagner," the marine replied.

"You seem like a no-nonsense type of person." Tam Sunter threw a lazy salute before he left. "Congratulations. You're in charge until he gets back."

3

The Artemis temple was constructed of sandy masonry and sat in the heart of the artisan precinct. It was lit by spotlights from below so that the eye was drawn upwards. The skies of Mars appeared distant through the heavy dome that protected those who looked upward: a reminder of the divine protection all Martians experienced.

The last hour of the day-shift had just ended. Outside the temple, hundreds of people hurried home, or to one of the theatre rings dotted about that side of town. A steady trickle of men and women broke away from the crowds of foot-traffic to ascend the temple's steps.

The Artemis dome was the most populous habitat dome on Mars. What it lacked in wealthy residents, it more than made up for with a breadth of culture and art. It was a well-known fact that many high-ranking dignitaries, council members, and even royalty visited the Artemis dome and its temple.

From the crowd, a tall man also peeled away from the crowd and began the short ascent to the temple, assisted by a lady who held his arm. He was dressed in the modest finery of a dome engineer: his long, yellow overcoat stood out clearly against the temple steps. He teetered to one side, overcorrected, and nearly fell down. At the last minute, he was caught by the lady at his elbow. The engineer's laughter echoed through the chilly evening air.

As they ascended, a small dot appeared in front of their faces. It spread, then coalesced into a bright patterned mask, that sat across each of their faces for the sake of anonymity. It was a courtesy of the anonymity system built throughout the temple.

The lady deposited the engineer on a lounge sofa at the entrance, and then approached the row of eight attendants by herself. Each attendant wore the spiralled white and gold eye masks that denoted their importance inside the temple. They stood in a semi-circle, barring access to the sweeping double-staircase that curled towards the upper balconies.

The young lady studied the attendants as she approached. One of the attendants at the far edge caught her eye: she wore the golden sash of a companion who had retired with grace from His Majesty's employ. Judging by the colours of the glass embedded in the sash, this particular attendant had borne six sons and two daughters during her tour of duty.

The young lady was stooped over when she greeted the attendant. "My master is a patron here."

The attendant looked up, and saw the nose-ring of a household servant: a large, golden piece that pierced the cartilage of her nose. It was a symbol that she was in the service of the engineer, in an attempt to pay off some form of debt or crime.

"Of course, my dear child," said the attendant. "Which companion does he support?"

"Xu."

The name caused the attendant to wrinkle her nose in

disgust. She licked both index fingers and rubbed them into the corners of her eyes. Once again, she examined the engineer who the servant had brought in.

"*He*'s the one keeping *Xu* on retainer?"

"Is there some sort of problem?" the servant asked.

"No, nothing wrong, *per se*. Just, it's strange. He's just young enough to be Xu's child."

"My master's been paying for her services for some time. He's always been very particular about visiting her. You know how men can get."

"Yes, yes, I'm sure. Pardon the idle talk of an old lady." The attendant blushed. "I would never say this to a patron's face. However, as someone who has his ear, perhaps you can persuade him to stop seeing her."

The servant lady leaned towards the attendant. "Why do you say that?"

"She's the mother of the companion who betrayed—" she lowered her voice to a breath, "—who betrayed *Mars*. Same surname, doncha' know?"

The servant's eyes widened. "I see. I'll have to address it as soon as he's in a more...sober state."

In a corner of the foyer, the engineer was eyeing one of the potted plants. His fingers wandered down to his trousers.

"Very well," the attendant waved the servant forward to the payment console. "Please show him to the bathroom suite beforehand."

The servant woman pulled out her master's credentials and waved them across the attendant's console. There was a digital hiccup before the console flashed a red prism into the air.

"I'm very sorry," the attendant replied. "It seems that there's an issue connecting to your master's account."

The servant woman shrank back from the flashing symbol, trembling, and threw a wary glance over her shoulder at the drunk engineer.

"No, that can't be right. Everything was working just this morning."

The attendant nodded. "These things happen occasionally. Our system is very secure. It has a straight connection to the Treasury's database. If your master has even slightly overdrawn his loyalty credits, or if he's visiting locations that don't match his credit history..." she threw up her hands in a helpless shrug. "I'd suggest contacting the Treasury tomorrow morning."

The servant woman hadn't stopped trembling, however. She fell to her knees, feebly clutching at the attendant's plain robes as she did so. Her brilliant chestnut eyes were slick with tears. "Please, there must be something you can do."

A few temple patrons paused in the foyer, watching. The other attendants paused their conversations and watched with intrigue.

"If you correct the account, you can return tomorrow evening," the attendant added in a hurry. Her eyes flicked across the foyer as the servant began making a scene. The poor soul collapsed onto the floor, sobbing and sniffling. A rope of snot trailed across her cheek.

"Please stand up, dear."

The wailing grew in intensity. It echoed across the foyer, drawing attention from some of the more lucrative patrons in the upper balconies. The attendant was about to call for the guard when the servant's scarf fell away in the commotion.

Two scars ran along the underside of her jaw. They began an inch below her ears and met at the tip of her chin: a cursive letter *M* carefully carved into the underside of her face.

The attendant had seen it before. She felt a strong urge well up inside her.

A pretty girl, she thought, *and she's afraid.*

The dome engineer was becoming irritated. He paced back and forth, casting meaningful glances in their direction. He sighed dramatically and came plodding over.

Certainly, he's drunk. I could have him thrown out. But he's here to see a companion. What will happen to this woman if I refuse him?

She mentally toyed with the panic circuit installed in her skull. The royal guard, five of them, would burst through the door behind her. *We could detain the engineer for public indecency.* Except she'd seen this scenario often enough to know that wouldn't help things at all. *The courts have ordained this arrangement between them. At the moment, he hasn't committed a crime. He's here because his first impulse wasn't to take out his frustrations on her.*

"Enough! Stand up." The command from the attendant bounced across the stone easily. It resounded across the balconies above. The servant woman's cries vanished into fits of shivering. Slowly, she struggled to her feet.

"I can open a line of credit for this evening. Short-term. Payable within two days."

The servant sniffed and nodded.

"Failure to pay will mean both your master and his estate—that includes you dear—will be indebted to the crown."

The servant smiled through the wet tears streaming her cheeks. She planted a strong kiss on the forehead of the old attendant.

"Whas' going on?" asked the engineer as he approached. He placed an arm around his servant's shoulders, who stood very still. "Ish she making trouble? Ma'am?"

The old attendant bowed cordially. "I'm afraid our system has had some problems today, Mr Patron."

His face was flushed and irritated. "Does thath mean no lady tonight?"

"Not at all. However, I've had to open a line of credit. You'll need to pay it tomorrow. Do you understand?"

The drunk engineer nodded. The servant lady passed the credentials across the console again.

"I'll send you three reminders before lunchtime, so you remember." The attendant waved them through. "If you don't pay, then I'm not responsible for the debt you'll accrue."

"Thanks." The dome engineer went to give her the customary kiss, but the attendant pulled back from the stink that wafted from him.

As she waved them past, the attendant caught a glimpse of the engineer's glassy grey eyes. "Next time, please avoid any pre-drinking before you arrive."

The engineer and the servant ascended the steps carefully. Once the engineer was out of earshot, one of the other attendants leaned across. "You've gone soft."

"Perhaps," the old attendant replied. "She reminded me of myself."

"Except prettier."

"Hush now."

The temple's architecture resembled that of a bank or government building: squat and square, with imposing pillars and a high-vaulted foyer that ran from the ground floor to the top. Each pillar was carved to resemble thickset workers, each bearing a pot or tool to serve their planet.

A large pendulum hung from the centre of the ceiling, nearly two stories tall. The immense pendulum rod was also engraved and painted. Its carvings depicted many Martian animals: giant red hens, algae crabs, and cave boar, all dancing on their hind legs around its circumference. The dunes and mountains of Mars were depicted as well, with Deimos and Phobos etched above them. It was an impressive circular display, in the centre of the perfectly square building.

"So, the architect envisioned Mars and Heaven combining here, in the emperor's whorehouse?" the servant said quietly, concentrating on each step.

The engineer's head spun around with animated excitement. "It's *so* lovely!"

The servant rolled her eyes. "Don't overdo it."

"No such thing, Harmony," replied the dome engineer. "People are uncomfortable around a drunk. The *more* attention we draw, the *less* people will suspect that we're trying to draw attention."

A group of companions stood on the second balcony, giggling as they watched Peace pretend to stagger. The youngest one called out. They arrived at the first balcony level as a middle-aged companion descended the steps. She was trying to estimate the spacing of each step beyond her rotund, pregnant belly. She paused as they passed. Her mirthless eyes lingered on Peace's antics.

"Everyone has a limit, Peace."

Harmony's brother took out a flask from the pocket of his coat and raised it to his lips. Harmony could hear the starch wine slop back into the flask as Peace lowered it.

"The system rejected the credentials, then?" he asked.

"The engineer had a marriage tattoo," Harmony said. They'd found him stumbling home drunk in the upper quarter when they'd swiped his credentials. "Most-likely he'd never been to the temple before."

"What a troubling time we live in," said Peace with a sigh. "Remember back in the glory days? A drunk could go missing for a week before they'd cut off his loyalty."

"You can only fake bio-credentials for so long. I'm just surprised they aren't running retina scans here yet, like they do at some of the other temples."

"That's because retina scanning is invasive." Peace made a face of disgust and mimed crying. "As is finger pricking, or mouth swabbing. The clientele doesn't want their buzz destroyed by something unpleasant before they meet with a companion. Besides, the whole point of coming here is anonymity. Doesn't matter how safe the system is. If you had a database leak of bio information, well. A lot of marriages might end."

Harmony allowed her fingers to dance along the balcony's rail as they walked. She imagined her fingers were two little legs of a person running. The fingers leapt over the tig welds of the balcony rail, narrowly avoiding death. Below, people milled about in the foyer. Harmony closed an eye. The finger-person leapt from head-to-head.

You're nervous, she realised. *How long has it been since you saw her?* Peace, on the other hand, took advantage of his drunken alibi to upturn a waste bin and knock an abandoned wine glass from a cocktail table.

"You'll get us kicked out."

"But they're so very accommodating here," Peace replied with a sneer. "Cool down. I've done this plenty of times before."

They arrived at the door marked 136 and knocked.

"Yes?" a voice called. The security system must have interpreted it as consent because the door swung open with a soft beep. Inside, the room was only lit by the tiny orange glow of an emergency bulb above the door.

"Is that you, Pea?" came the sing-song voice.

"It's me, mother." Peace entered the room confidently and knelt down in the shadows. Harmony could just make out the faint lines of a cheap bed frame in the corner of the room. She closed the door behind her. Hanging from the inside of the door was a white sash: the banner of a companion who hadn't served her time yet. Only two of the available eight slots were filled: the first slot was coloured a masculine yellow, which symbolised a son. The second slot was Harmony's, a feminine blue.

"It's disgusting in here," Harmony said. The room smelled as though it hadn't been cleaned in years. Her shoes stuck to the floor, as she crossed the space towards her mother.

"Who's there?" called her mother from the darkness.

Harmony dug inside her bodice and withdrew a small tube. She depressed the button at the top of it, and suddenly the mask across her face vanished.

"When did you build that?" Peace asked, helping his

mother sit up on her bed.

"Last week. It jumbles holo-surveillance systems for a small radius."

"Who's there?" her mother asked again.

Peace stood and fiddled with the switch on the wall above the bed. The lights remained dim, but became just bright enough so that Harmony could make out the shape of her mother's face. The faint light sketched the rims of her mother's eyelids.

Something's wrong.

Her mother's pupils darted about, as though she were in the fits of REM sleep. Despite the fear in her mother's voice, her face was a picture of serenity.

Harmony slapped a trembling hand across her mouth. "She's using tranquillity?"

"She started taking it a few months after you left for space." Peace's voice was thick with emotion. "She said it helped her forget about work."

"You didn't stop her?"

"Stop her how? It's provided *pro bono* by the temple. As soon as I started supporting her as a patron, she became eligible for it. Would you rather she kept seeing other gentleman visitors?"

"Of course not."

"Besides, if she's ever pulled in front of the court to testify against us, nothing will stick."

Harmony made a noise of disgust and reached out to hold her mother's hands.

"Who are you?" Harmony's mother asked.

"I'm your daughter."

"No. My little Harmony looks completely different."

Peace crouched down again to their mother's eye line. "This is my sister, mother. Look at her eyes. I used to be really jealous, remember?"

Their mother nodded, but it was clear she didn't understand.

"Harmony just graduated from the officer's academy. Under a different name, of course. She's turned into a real whiz with computers and stuff. Remember how you smuggled money to us, so she could have lessons?"

"Mother," Harmony began. "I came by because I had to tell you that all your sacrifices paid off. I guess I always felt so awful because you couldn't have any more children after us twins, and so you're stuck here in this place."

Harmony saw the flitting pupils of her mother wash over her, but there was no trace of recognition.

"I'm sorry ma'am. Forget about it." Harmony stood, and wiped a stray tear. "Goodbye." She clicked the device, and the mask reappeared over her face and the face of her brother.

Peace shook his mother's shoulder lightly. "Hey. We don't know when we can return. But we're going to find a way to get you out of here, soon."

Mother Xu's brow furrowed. "Go somewhere else? I'm getting too old for manual work. I never really learned to read or write well either." She patted Peace's hand and smiled into the darkness. "Thank you, Pea, but I'm quite content just sitting here. Bring Harmony along next time."

Anyone watching the footage from room 136 would have seen a young dome engineer leave the companion's room, with his arm around a servant who was sobbing.

"Have you considered extracting her?" Harmony asked. She wiped her eyes as the tears continued to flow. "Between the two of us, we might be able to manage it."

"We had to wait a long time—" Peace studied his sister's face, "and go through a lot of pain, to reach this point. Right now we can move about around Mars unobstructed. If we pull mother out of the temple, then they'll know something suspicious is going on. Even coming out here, five years after you disappeared from custody, is still taking an immeasurable risk."

Harmony wrapped her arms across her middle and nodded. They waited for a small machine as it ran along the balcony's bannister, polishing as it went.

"Look," Peace began to sway again as they approached the staircase to the ground floor. "They haven't hurt her yet because of you. Even the emperor wouldn't condone hurting a parent for a child's crime. It sets a bad precedent."

"I hope you're right."

"Of course I'm right." Peace paused at the top of the balcony and cast a furtive look for any eavesdroppers. "Mother will never be safe as long as things stay the way they are. If we topple the emperor, we write a history where we're the heroes. Mother gets liberated and can live freely."

"So we follow the resistance?"

"For now. Until we have our own ship."

"Okay then." Harmony wiped her eyes once more.

"Hey, I know what would make you feel better. There's this great crushed ice place around the corner."

"I haven't eaten crushed ice since I was six, Peace."

"Is that a no?"

Harmony grabbed her brother's elbow, so she could pretend to support him. "I didn't say that."

4

The palace guard stood at attention as Du Mon marched through the front gates and into the palace compound. A curtain of concrete walls, watchtowers, and gunneries surrounded the central palace tower and its adjoining wings. As he followed the Eastern Wing towards the palace tower, Du Mon saw the gardeners and botanists cutting, mulching, and occasionally arguing. Twisting citrus trees sagged under the weight of their fruits. Rows upon rows of vineyards grew, like green-ribboned fences. Bunting hung from each corner of the palace's tower, covering the sky in a colourful web.

As the prince crossed the gardens, he heard the sound of children laughing and playing. A herd of Du Mon's nieces and nephews spilled around the corner of the tower, screaming in pretend terror.

"Quick, to the battleship!" cried the tallest child. He barrelled ahead of the others, and turned around just in time for his forehead to connect with Du Mon's stomach. The young nephew hit the grass, and rolled backwards nimbly. "Pirates! They've laid mines ahead!"

The carousel of children twirled and flowed past him like a fluid made of limbs and giggling.

"Save us!" one of his nieces squealed. "Save us again, Uncle Du!"

From around the corner, Du Mon spied the small head of the Elder Seeker as it rounded the corner, chasing the young children.

The worm-like puppet had been hastily assembled from a stocking, and was held aloft by Du Mon's older brother. The crowned prince cackled like a madman as the children turned and fled in renewed terror.

The children were spared from the terrible wrath of the Outsiders, as the Elder Seeker paused to converse with the prince who had devised the plan to kill it.

"Oh, welcome back!" said Ju Tin. He grinned, and the Elder Seeker puppet rose up between them. "Have we met somewhere before?" asked the puppet in a squeaky voice. "Didn't you kill me?"

Du Mon pushed the puppet away with his bad arm. "I'm delighted to see the children using the death of Captain Dav'i, and my crew, as the backdrop for their games."

Ju Tin pulled the puppet off his hand and stuffed it under his elbow. "Still having nightmares?"

"Not at all."

"Right. Whatever you say, little brother." Ju Tin wrapped an enormous forearm around his brother and escorted him towards the tower. The crowned prince studied the wrinkles etched between Du Mon's eyes. "Playing games is how children learn to cope with the difficulties of life. Don't begrudge them for trying to understand some of the horror they've heard about."

The older prince pushed open a side entrance to the main palace. Inside, stringed music floated in the air. They crossed the gilded ballroom, past the adjoining conference chambers.

"Is father home?"

Ju Tin readjusted his round spectacles thoughtfully. "I'm sure he'll be here by evening. He had a few things to attend to before the festival."

Du Mon stopped dead. "The festival starts tonight?"

"You've really forgotten what day it is?" Ju Tin shook his head. "I suppose it can't be helped. I'm glad you're here. The people will want to see you at the festival. You understand, don't you? Your victory at Ceres has become legend."

"It was hardly a victory."

"Believe what you will. You should get some rest before the parade. Kaya is waiting in your sitting room. See you tonight."

Du Mon realised that his brother had steered him to the door of the sitting room he shared with Kaya Plessis. With a sharp slap on the back, his brother once again pulled the puppet of the Elder Seeker onto his forearm. "Now, if you'll excuse me." He raced away in the direction of the gardens, giggling.

The prince stood alone at the chambers, examining the door. *It's been painted red since I last came home.*

He turned the handle, then stopped and knocked instead. *No response.* He turned the handle slowly, and pushed the door ajar.

The sitting room was brightly lit. Heavy, crimson curtains along the western wall had been thrown wide. Natural sunlight through the tinted windows reflected from the polished floors and walls, giving the illusion that the room and its furniture was floating in the middle of a desert's mirage.

A simple room, for the lowest-born of the emperor.

Despite this, the room was still decorated with all the finery Mars could offer. The legs and armrests of the sofas, for instance, were made from real wood. The set of three matching sofas could seat up to nine people, and would have probably cost nearly as much as an *Interceptor*-class fighter.

Plessis reclined on the sofa that faced the doorway. Her hands were folded in her lap, with a tablet discarded beside her. She was dozing quietly in the sunlight, allowing its beams to brown her skin.

Her tan is much darker than I remember.

Du Mon closed the door with a quiet click. He removed his shoes and satchel at the entryway, crossed the room, and opted for a seat in the sun beside her. Plessis' legs were crossed at the ankles and angled away from the doorway, betraying her status as the daughter of an aristocrat. Her sky-blue dress was carefully tucked beneath her legs. A navy shawl was modestly draped around her shoulders. To complete the look, Du Mon would have expected her head to be tilted slightly to the side, implying gentleness while she dozed. For Plessis, however, her posture was a soldier's. Perfectly straight.

As Du Mon sat, Plessis must have felt the shift of weight on the sofa. She opened her eyes.

"Welcome home, Your Grace."

"It's been some time. My apologies Plessis."

The prince settled between the soft, warm pillows. A stiffness in his shoulder loosened a little. Plessis tucked a bleached-white strand of hair back behind her ear. Her hand reached out and touched his wrist delicately, before retracting. "How are your preparations going?"

"Fine, thank you." Du Mon permitted himself to sink

lower in the sofa. The beginnings of a headache throbbed at his cheekbones. "There's still so much to do. Scenarios, briefings, practice combat, final recruitments for the non-combatant personnel. High Command keeps sending weekly requests for updates. I've spent two days writing up reports instead of training my people."

Plessis reached over to the tablet she had left between them and skimmed through its contents. "The *Black Tortoise* is sitting in orbit as we speak: a new era of space-faring technology. Earth is going to find out about the ship sooner or later. They might even be planning to sabotage it right now."

Du Mon sighed. "It's inconsequential whether Earth knows about it, or not. They won't be able to scratch us now that we have the Elder Seeker's self-repairing chitin as armour."

"You don't need to lecture me on its credentials, I helped design it." Plessis stood. She crossed the room to a small table recessed against the northern wall, and prepared the tea in a flat, glassy teapot. "And it's because I designed it, that I'm worried. Civil unrest is growing in some of the more...colourful districts of Mars. Did you see the report on increasing attacks in the artisan district? Quality royalists are getting mugged in quiet alleys."

"High Command will have a plan to deal with any dissent."

Plessis returned with the pot. The room sensed what she was doing, and a small plinth rose from the floor, so she could rest the teapot. "What if a group of terrorists were to break aboard the vessel and take it? We'd be unable to do much without committing extraordinary firepower to destroying our own vessel. Five years of development would be wasted."

"I agree. The *Black Tortoise* will be safest when it is mobile, and away from the port."

"So why is High Command dragging its feet? Why have they given you a task force without officially assigning you to the ship?"

Du Mon's headache was growing steadily. As he sat there, he felt the exhaustion that he'd been suppressing for months finally catching up to him.

Plessis retrieved two small cups that were recessed underneath the plinth and poured the tea.

Du Mon accepted the cup with both hands and took a sip. The brew was fatty and tasted faintly of mushroom. "The Admiral must have a reason."

"That's what I'm trying to warn you about," Plessis replied. She pursed her lips and blew gently across the surface of her own cup. "I think a few people in the higher ranks are dragging their feet on purpose. They may decide to give command of the ship to someone else."

The prince felt the words strike him like a physical blow. "No, High Command wouldn't have me slave away at a project for years, just to reassign me. Surely. As a logistics officer, they'd have given you some indication about it..."

Plessis shrugged. "I'm just reading between the lines. High Command is made of many competing forces."

Du Mon rubbed his cheekbones, silently urging the headache to leave before it became worse. "They can't give it to someone else. I've already made arrangements to make sure it's me."

"Made arrangements?" Kaya put her cup down on the

plinth. "With whom?"

"Maevin." His headache was worsening.

"Why would you indebt yourself to the High Consul? You know he's going to twist your arm for something in return?"

"It seemed like the fastest path to the *Black Tortoise*. It still seems that way."

"That's the problem, the fastest path." Plessis reclined against the sofa's cushions. "For all we know, Maevin could be responsible for the delays in the project. Holding things in check, hoping that he'd get some leverage over you."

The thought of some other captain coming in, and taking control of the ship and my crew. Perhaps I lost track of what was important. Negotiating? Begging for help? Captain Dav'i would've kicked down the door of High Command and demanded to speak to the Admiral. He did it on two occasions and got what he wanted.

Another, smaller voice inside the prince piped up. *Yes, but Dav'i was an excellent Captain. The Admiral couldn't afford to lose him. What have you done that's noteworthy?*

Du Mon's head was now a fog of pain. "I'm going to rest up before the festival," he said.

"I'm just looking out for you, Du."

Du Mon returned his cup to the table and planted a half-hearted kiss on his wife's forehead.

"Thank you for your work, Plessis. I'll see you at the festival."

The bedroom was hidden at the rear of the sitting room. Du Mon approached the space where he knew the door should be. There was a buzz, and the door slid inwards.

Plessis waited until the door had closed behind the prince. She counted to twenty.

"Okay, you can come out now Ju Tin."

One of the heavy curtains jostled. Plessis poured another cup of tea as the heavy-set man entered through the panic hallway.

Ju Tin joined her on the sofa. "One positive thing about the palace, is that there's no shortage of secret passageways and panic rooms. It makes eavesdropping a breeze."

"But did listening in help?" she asked.

Ju Tin raked his curly beard with slow, deliberate strokes, from his chin down to his pectorals. "What a fascinating relationship you have. You seem very guarded around him."

Plessis' bottom lip trembled as she relaxed her face. "His Grace doesn't seem particularly fond of big displays of emotion. He loves me. He just struggles to show it."

Ju Tin nodded as he accepted the offered cup of tea. "Thank you. Was it always this way?"

Plessis shook her head. "He actually used to be quite doting. Things changed after he received his commission to train his team of anti-Xeno soldiers. He's under incredible pressure."

"From High Command?"

Plessis laughed bitterly. "Himself, but you know what he's like."

Ju Tin smiled broadly between sips of tea. "How delicious. Yes, I'm quite familiar with the situation. Father was very candid about what has been happening in Du Mon's professional life."

"The issue is his perfectionism. High Command has been called in to conduct three separate audits of his training techniques. They're brutal and calculating."

"Not exactly the sort of thing you imagine when you see the little prince on the theatre circuits, heroically fighting aliens. I have a working theory about what has soured here. The issue isn't your marriage. Not really."

"That doesn't change the fact that our marriage is in shambles. It's not *passionate* in the slightest. I've offered him children, many times. He doesn't seem interested at all."

Ju Tin shook his head with careful, solemn shakes. "Du Mon isn't looking for a connection with you if you'll pardon my frankness. He's frustrated and isolating himself because he can't build a connection with someone else."

Plessis drew her silk navy shawl around herself. "Who is he trying to build a connection with? Another woman?"

The crowned prince set his cup down. He picked up Du Mon's discarded cup and examined its contents. "Who does His Grace respect the most in the world?"

"His father, I suppose. Oh, and Captain Dav'i. Du received special clearance from the consulate to read the late captain's reports. He said it was for the purposes of career development."

"My understanding is that Dav'i had a somewhat *unique* relationship with your older sister?"

"Yes, they were very close."

"Was it a romantic relationship?"

"I don't think so." Plessis closed her eyes, trying to recall fragments of conversation, bits and pieces she'd managed to ascertain from going through her dead sister's things. "It was more than that. Judging by my sister's diary, he was the only one she felt truly understood her."

"Would you call it passionate?"

"No, it was professional. Sometimes it even bordered on

co-dependent, but it wasn't what you would call romantic. Respectful, perhaps. Deferential. She missed many birthdays in the line of duty. They served back-to-back assignments together tirelessly."

"Did they have children together?"

"No why would—oh," Plessis clasped a hand to her mouth. "I see."

Ju Tin waggled his eyebrows. "I suspect that Du Mon idolises the relationship between Dav'i and your sister, rest them. Thrust under considerable pressure, and without a living mother whose marriage he can emulate, he is playing the role of Dav'i."

"And I am my sister?" Kaya's eyes winced in disgust.

"You met Du Mon while he was wrestling with the loss of two superior officers, as well as the death of a friend. It makes perfect sense. You even resemble her."

"Stop." Plessis nearly dropped her cup. She placed it back on the table with trembling hands. "You're telling me that my entire marriage is some sort of role-play?"

Ju Tin's thick eyebrows drew together above his round spectacles. "Not at all. Just because you were thrust together through circumstance, doesn't mean you can't have a healthy and happy marriage. It might take some work, but no. There is something else that we're all missing, which is causing His Highness to revert."

A tear spilled over Plessis' cheek. She wiped her eyes with the corner of her shawl. "Can you do anything to help?

"I have a plan," Ju Tin replied. He finished examining his brother's cup and returned it to the plinth. The crowned prince stood, and bowed to the lowest duchess of the royal family. "If I might entreat you, please don't mention me being here to Du. The processes of healing can be painful. No need to cause him any unnecessary distress. He might worry about us conspiring against him"

Plessis nodded. "Thank you for your time, Your Highness."

5

Peace and Harmony waited on a concrete bench nestled between two large oaks. Above them, the craggy skyline of a Martian lava tube faintly reflected the artificial light from cheap chemical lamps that littered the poorest district of Mars. The Spacer Corridor was well-known for its illusion of being in perpetual night. It was an entire subterrestrial city, built alongside underground glaciers.

Peace checked over his shoulder twice. The park where they sat was roughly ten square metres of filthy faux grass, in the centre of a quiet intersection. A bar was the only building receiving foot traffic at this time of night. It was perhaps the most well-kept building in his eyeline, followed closely by the Treasury Depot beside it. Many residential blocks rose up into the darkness around them. Harmony scanned the windows of tradespeople, spacers, urchins, and all manner of other denizens who the emperor deemed unworthy of surface real-estate. A few curious residents watched her back.

"The Treasury says twenty percent of us live down here," Harmony said. She spoke in a low, breathy whisper. Her teeth had started to chatter.

Peace coughed, and his breath was a plume of smoke that matched his eyes. "I'd wager it's at least forty percent, in that case. Forty percent of us are living down here like rats."

The only other building of interest was a smaller residential home. An unskilled painter had sprayed the words 'beauty clinic' on the front of it. The term 'beauty clinic' now meant black market chop-shops: places where someone could alter their body in any number of ways.

Have a cranial implant inserted on your lunch break. Lose twenty kilos the day before your wedding. Transplant your face for a nicer one. The rare beauty clinic down in the Spacer Corridor was far cheaper than the regulated ones in the domes. More private too. *The dirty ones don't keep very detailed records for the Crown to sniff through.*

In bootleg shops like that one, a Martian could save even more loyalty credits by opting to undergo their surgery without any painkillers and just have a whiff of the drug tranquillity instead.

Peace stifled a shudder as it ran down his spine. *I still have nightmares about my face being peeled open and a masked doctor pinning my tongue to one side. It felt like he was trying to scoop up an egg yolk inside my skull...*

He blew into his hands, and was grateful for the heaters that were always failing down here.

At least Harmony won't wonder why my hands are shaking.

"—Did you hear anything I just said?" Harmony hissed.

"I was just thinking about mum."

Harmony's eyes softened. "Okay. Focus. I can spot two face scanners. There's one affixed to the Treasury Depot, next to the bar. The other one is glued to a private residence."

"I guess it can't be helped then." Peace drew his cargo boy's hood tightly around his face, then he activated the chip planted underneath his tongue. In his mind's eye, he imagined a squarish face for himself. There was a pause, and then Peace felt his cheekbones slip sideways. His nose grew from a gentle slope to a more pronounced tip.

His skin was like the ocean, hiding the shifting motions of tectonic plates. His vision blurred for a moment as his eye sockets recessed more deeply into his skull. Small silicon pouches in his lips inflated. When Peace looked up, he had a new variation of his face. He also looked about ten years older.

When his contact from the resistance told Peace that his sister was going to be tried for treason, they had offered him enough loyalty credits to get the procedure. A changing face.

I can't believe they couldn't scrape enough together for the general anaesthetic. Peace pushed down the disgust and terror he'd felt in the filthy beauty clinic. *The Crown is responsible*, he told himself again. The anger he'd felt for his entire life came back to him, washing over him. *Anger is familiar. My hate is comforting.*

Harmony gasped as his two front teeth descended and clicked into place. "Eww. Don't use that setting again."

"Ugly, isn't it? I figured this was a good setting to burn once, and never use again."

"I kind of wish I had one of those," Harmony said. She touched her face, prodding it roughly. Even after all these years, she wasn't used to it.

She wants a transplant like yours, so she can see her old face again. A small part inside him regretted it. *But, if I hadn't asked the resistance to pay for her surgery, she would have spent the rest of her life, living in a tiny room buried down here. Unable to leave, in case one of the scanners spotted her.*

Peace gave her a playful knock under the chin. "You don't want one of these old things. Have you ever left the house and forgotten your credentials? It's like that, but with your face."

"Well, it's not like I could afford one anyway. You're lucky."

"I'm not. I just have someone high up in the resistance who likes me."

On the other side of the plaza, a giant of a man ducked underneath the bar's door and entered.

"Barclay's here." Harmony said, her voice sounded worried. Her chest rose and fell quickly with her rapid breathing. "Are you sure about this contact? I have a history with him. If he works out that you're with me, he might decide to turn you in."

"Deimos!" Peace stood and stretched languidly. "As if I'd go in there and drop your stupid name. If my resistance contact is correct, and they usually are, then Goliath over there is a perfect recruit for the resistance."

Harmony placed her hand on Peace's forearm. It was a warning. "That man will never betray the emperor."

Peace nodded.

"However," she added. "Barclay might betray the prince."

"That's what I'm counting on."

Peace slipped away from his sister. He walked directly towards the Treasury Depot and then hooked around, approaching the bar via the sidewalk.

The Spacer Corridor boasted a varied collection of bars, pubs, and watering holes. This particular pub had been recently renovated—the sign at the front described it as *The Tiered Palace.*

Inside, pillars made from modern tables towered across the main floor space of the bar, exponentially increasing the number of patrons who could fit inside the bar during busy nights. A person could sit at one of the upper tables by climbing up to it, and have their feet dangle above the heads of those below them, and so on. The walls and floors had been left faded and stained, perhaps for their rustic charm.

Or maybe the cost of those tables and seats blew the bar's budget.

At the entrance, a man who looked like he'd been picked in beer swiped Peace's credentials. "What's yer drinking budget?" he asked.

"Two drinks."

The man grunted, returned Peace's credentials, and handed him two tokens that he could redeem inside.

"New restrictions?" Peace asked.

The man rolled his eyes. "Gotta' pre-order your drinks now. They say it stops people from falling. Or drinking themselves into oblivion."

Isn't that the point of such a place?

As Peace watched, waiters moved between the tables, taking orders, and accepting the small tokens tossed down to them as payment. Staff approached the towers of the clientele and passed up the drinks using devices that hoisted the drinking mugs up into the air on a retractable rod.

Peace walked through the bar confidently. His entrance attracted the attention of very few. Most of the bar's customers were content with staring into their drinks, or having loud conversations with their drinking buddies. A local butcher sat at one of the ground-level tables. His apron was splattered with blood and viscera as he picked his teeth with a thin filleting knife.

My kind of people, Peace thought. *All squashed by the weight of the emperor's riches. People who have paid for new battleships with their health and happiness.*

There were two exits that he could see. The entrance he'd come through, and the service door that the staff flowed through. There were no windows, but then again, there was no view worth seeing in the Spacer Corridor.

Peace spotted Barclay sitting in the far corner of the bar, three tables in the air. The tall man was facing the doorway. As Peace approached, the old man's head swivelled to follow him. His head nearly scraped the roof.

He's like a red turkey up on its perch.

Peace climbed a ladder that was welded to the stack of tables. As he slid into the seat opposite the old man, he realised that he didn't have a proper excuse to strike up conversation.

"Hello friend." Peace pulled the most genuine smile he could manage. *That was terrible.*

"Friend?" came the slurred reply. "That's terribly suspicious, because I don't have any."

Up close, Barclay's resemblance to a beaked predator was even more uncanny. The man was as gaunt as a skeleton, and his nose was long and hooked. He wore a noble's cape, attached to a cotton blouse with puffed sleeves, which he hadn't bothered to tuck in. The clothes were now wrinkled and dirtied. A permanent neck-brace held his head in place. The matted tangle of hair that jutted out from above his ears, combined with his rapidly receding hairline, further completed the image of a strange owl.

"I wasn't expecting company this *fine* evening."

When Barclay spoke, it was the voice of a predator who was satiated and had decided to entertain a creature he would typically eat. A tin mug rose up in the air beside the disgraced consul, lifted up on a pole with a special-built grip for the mug. Barclay screamed when the mug appeared in his periphery. He recovered quickly, pulling it free and drinking greedily. The rod lowered again.

His voice isn't slurred because he's drunk, Peace realised. *He's had some kind of nervous stroke.*

While the consul was distracted, Peace leaned over the side of the table and dropped two tokens into the waiting basket of a waitress below. He held up two fingers and pointed to Barclay. The waitress scurried away.

Barclay swirled the cheap vodka in his mug and watched the liquid stir. Peace permitted a pregnant pause to linger between them. The old consul sniffed at the drink. He took another long sip. Due to the neck brace, he had to lean his entire torso backwards. When Barclay corrected himself, a trickle of vodka ran from the lazy side of his mouth. He smacked his lips several times, and then wiped them with his sleeve.

"At the palace I used to sip federation wine. Can you imagine that? Wine older than me."

"It sounds like you've fallen a long way, Barclay."

"I have indeed, mister..."

"I could give you a name, but it would be fake. I'm here to speak to you about Prince Du Mon."

Barclay spat over the edge of their table, which caused a groan of dismay somewhere below them. "I don't have anything to say about that runt."

"Then, don't say anything. Just hear me out."

"Are you a journalist?"

"No."

"Debt collector from the Treasury?"

"Not even close."

Two more mugs rose up into the air. Peace took a mug for himself and placed the other in front of the consul.

"My understanding is that you served the royal family for the better part of your life."

"And the worse part as well."

"You tried to protect the Prince from a companion, who was trying to kidnap him."

"That's right."

"Then the prince hit you, a geriatric, in the back of the head with a rifle butt. Now, I'm not privy to what occurs in the courts of High Command. However, somewhere along the line, you went from consul liaison of the royal family, to spending your evenings in an underground bar. It doesn't exactly follow, does it?"

"I suppose not."

"I want to know what happened."

"So much for just hearing me out," Barclay said with disdain. "*Who*, precisely, is asking?"

Peace allowed his facial features to arrange themselves into the approximate shapes and dimensions that he'd been born with. In response, Barclay drank the rest of his wine with a quick backwards tilt.

"I recognise that face. There's a steep price on your head, terrorist." Barclay reached underneath his tattered jacket and scratched himself roughly.

"And so there should be. I paid a *lot* of money for this head." Peace concentrated once again, and his face returned to the features of someone ten years his senior and from a different lineage. "Or at least someone did."

"You know, I could turn you into the authorities." To illustrate his point, the old man retrieved a thin dagger from beneath his jacket. Barclay's face sneered. "If I turn you in, I'd be able to live out the rest of my days comfortably."

"And how many days might that be, realistically?" Peace forced every muscle in his body to appear relaxed. "Wouldn't you rather have a high seat in the New Order?"

Barclay moved his blade just beneath the table to keep it hidden from the other drinkers who might glance in their direction. His other hand was placed on the edge of the table. The gesture looked harmless, but Peace knew it would help the old man launch himself up and divide the distance between them.

This isn't going well. He's distracted by the sparkle of his old life.

Peace felt his own blade press against the skin of his ankle, where he'd strapped it. He'd be faster than the old man. Slice the neck, catch the body, and pull the torso atop the table. Slide down the ladder. Exit through the front entrance before the blood dripped onto the people below.

Instead, Peace held his hands up beside his face, palms empty and facing the old man.

"What's it going to be? I hear they're working you pretty hard on an assembly line these days."

"What's this New Order business?" Barclay asked.

Peace smiled. "By joining the resistance, you'd be promised a position of respect and importance once the Crown is overthrown."

Barclay raised an eyebrow. "And all I'd have to do in

return is commit treason?"

Peace gave a sheepish smile. "Well, that's certainly a finer point than I would have used."

Barclay lowered his voice to barely a whisper. "I have some very fond memories of Liu Wei. I told most of his children, you know. I don't want the Emperor to die."

"The resistance isn't interested in a bloodbath," Peace said. "We want a simple transition of power, to a system where every Martian life is treated equally."

Barclay mulled it over while staring into the dregs of his mug.

Peace switched tactic. "You served in the palace and consulate for a long time. I heard that you know how a planet needs to be run."

"That's what *I* told them!" Barclay said, a little too loudly. "They tried to wipe my mind regardless."

"I also heard you designed the Emperor's memory wipes, so it stands to reason you'd have to get around that problem."

Barclay smiled wistfully. "That's correct. The memory wipes didn't take like they should have. Why did the resistance wait until now to contact me?"

Peace thought it over. "I'm not privy to the plans of the higher-ups."

"Your best guess then? Why leave me to rot on an assembly line all this time?"

"We all need time to learn what it is we truly desire. If the resistance had sent someone to meet with you the first day after you'd been pushed out of the consulate, you probably would have stabbed them with that knife."

Barclay nodded. "They were waiting for me to become

truly desperate."

"They were waiting, until you understood what the New Order could give you."

The old consul belched. "Good wine?"

"We need you in the New Order. It will be a time of difficult transition. The more experience we can have, the better. Yes, you can sip on fine wine again. More importantly, you can have your dignity again."

Barclay thought for a moment, and then pushed the mug away. "What do you need me to do?"

* * *

Peace had a small skip in his step as he returned to the park outside. Harmony stood, and they both made their way deeper into the tunnelled rock of the Spacer Corridor.

"So it went well then?" she asked.

"Another happy recruit," Peace replied.

"I'll miss this sort of work. It reminds me of growing up." Harmony looked across at the glowing lamps, and the lights that pooled out from the homes that were dug into the rockface. She wrinkled her nose. "I won't miss the smell though."

"There's something pleasant about recruiting," Peace said. "But if I'm honest with you, I'm more excited about the front-line sabotage and fighting."

Harmony took a deep breath of the stale air. "The resistance will move us into position soon. When that happens, you might miss these quiet moments."

"I think I will," Peace said. The blade strapped to his ankle itched.

6

The emperor forbade himself from smiling, so instead he drew an infinitesimally small curve on the tabletop with his index finger. He sat at the head, and the table stretched out before him, bisecting the two rows of High Command that faced each other. Military and peacekeeping personnel sat to the left of the emperor, and the civil service to his right.

Consul Maevin was shouting. A small tendril of saliva clung to the old man's chin, fed by more spittle that spilled out over the edge of his pale, cracked lips.

"We are sitting on the culmination of five years' of Martian research. Outsider technology that has pushed us twenty, no, thirty years ahead of Earth's military, and you want to send the *Black Tortoise* on her maiden flight out to the belt?" Maevin beat the table with both fists. A vein pulsed between his eyes. "The orbits of Earth and Mars grow closer each day. In a month, the Lunar Shipyards will be closer than they have been for the past 700 days. We lost the Ceres mining facility, and now the Earth-Lunar Mining Guild is slowly pushing us out of the asteroid belt. All because our *Fearless Admiral*, our *Commandant-in-Residence*, *Defender of His Majesty's Red Soil* is so useless a strategist, so *stricken* with terror at the thought of aliens dropping on top of us, he won't destroy an enemy's capital ship if it means he'll lose a single *Invigilator* fighter!"

Maevin flapped his elbows like a big, dumb bird and started squawking.

Admiral Heydari wiped absently with his handkerchief at Maevin's spittle, which was now splattered across the table's waxy surface. "You sound upset, High Consul."

The emperor ran his fingers through the wiry net of curls that was his beard. "Perhaps, High Consul Maevin, you could express your dissatisfaction in a more civil manner? Or do we need to have a recess?"

Maevin fell back into his chair. "Such a wasted opportunity."

The other Consuls either side of him nodded in unison.

Admiral Heydari gestured above his tablet and examined the diagrams and lists that appeared. "I've read over your *suggestions*, High Consul. You might *believe* combat is the best testing ground for a prototype vessel. However, we need to test the capacity of the *Black Tortoise*'s hull in regular spacefaring conditions first. Throwing a new vessel into a warzone would not only jeopardise the crew. If the ship were lost to the enemy, we would also lose that technological advantage you were just touting."

Maevin nodded slowly. "Prince Du Mon could do it, though. He's proven himself before."

The emperor sat up slightly.

Admiral Heydari frowned. "An inexperienced captain, commanding the prototype into battle. How does that make sense?"

Maevin closed his eyes with great exaggeration and massaged his temples. "I don't know why you need me to champion your own officers to you. The prince is the most celebrated captain in the entire fleet."

"You've been listening to your propaganda machine for too long," the Admiral replied. "The crowned prince Ju Tin is a far more capable officer, *and* a more beloved public figure. Du Mon's mission out to Ceres was commendable, but he was learning as he went. Quick wits can give an advantage in battle, but self-discipline is what forges a warrior."

"You'd rather send the *crowned prince* onto a prototype vessel?" Maevin asked. "The first fruits of our people?"

"If it had to be one of the princes at all." Heydari smoothed the tip of his black, oiled beard between his thumb and index fingers, curling it into a point. "I don't think we should be sending any of the royal family away from home at this point."

"It *has* to be Du Mon," Maevin hissed the words like a spit adder. "Public opinion of the royal family is at an all-time high, thanks to the dramas of Du Mon's heroic deeds against the Elder Seeker. People are afraid. They need to pin their hopes on a figure. The younger prince is a suitable protagonist. If he launches a daring raid against the Lunar shipyards and succeeds, he will be a champion for Mars. If he dies, then a martyr is born for the people to rally behind."

"Your patriotism is laudable, Maevin," the emperor interjected. "In the future, I'd like you to refrain from talking about my youngest as though he were a chess piece. My inclination would be to have a staged mission: a stress test of the ship, followed by refuelling, and then a tentative skirmish against the Lunar Shipyards."

"With all due respect," Heydari said softly, "I think the entire exercise of a Lunar raid is ridiculous." It was now the

Admiral's turn to stand. The Sub-Admiral beside him also stood, and reached out both hands to steady the ailing man. Heydari began an arduous circling of the table.

High Command was seated so that the most-senior staff were sat closest to the emperor. The Admiral used the backs of the chairs to assist him, as he made his way slowly towards the junior officers and administrators at the far end of the table.

"We have received a gift. Technology beyond our means. Regenerating chitin from the Elder Seeker that we can line our hulls with. We haven't even scratched the surface of their other technology. While I appreciate the eagerness of the consulate to push our advantage, it is an advantage we can just as easily lose. I won't have my legacy jeopardised by launching a rushed attack. Mars and Earth will reach oppositional orbits again in another 700 days or so. We will be better prepared by then, and the prince will be too."

Maevin made a signal, a drumming of the fingers in a complex pattern, thumb extended. At the far end of the table, a junior administrator stood, bowed, and exited the room.

"Perhaps I've been too quick to argue," Maevin said, his palms separated in a dignified shrug. "We can send the *Black Tortoise* on a stress test, as you suggest, and hash out the finer points regarding the raid on the Lunar base while that mission is underway."

"Why are you so eager to launch Project Tortoise?" the Admiral asked.

Maevin's long eyebrows met together in the middle of his forehead, like the closing curtains of a drama. "A fair point. Perhaps I'll tip my hand then. This month we've noticed increased terrorist activity across the board."

"That's usual for this time of year. The occasional anti-royalist usually wants to disturb large events on the royal calendar."

"This week alone we've had to confiscate a tonne's worth of smuggled contraband. A protest erupted in the Tharsis mines. Our media teams spun it as a celebration that got out of hand."

The emperor nodded solemnly. "Whatever works."

"We're noticing patterns of terrorist activity. While the protest was going on, the checkpoint guards at the Temple district arrested four men who tried to enter the habitat dome. Each was carrying a gauss-assisted rifle, which had been stolen from a military caravan two weeks ago."

"How quickly things are slipping out of control," the Admiral said absently. "Perhaps the government requires some...judicial assistance from the military?"

Maevin's chair tipped backwards as he thrust a knobbed index finger at the Admiral. "If the emperor wasn't watching, by Demois I'd pluck that beard out and feed it to you."

"Gentleman," the emperor stood, signalling the end of all other discussion.

The pretence of collegial banter has long since evaporated.

Heydari gave a respectful nod of the head, and made his way towards his seat. Maevin inhaled and straightened his robes. He licked his lips, eyes scanning the faces of the other men and women gathered there. The junior administrator returned, carrying a glass of water for Maevin. The High Consul accepted the glass, and signalled for the junior to correct his chair.

This is happening too frequently, thought the emperor with a rueful purse of his lips. Beneath his tall collar, his neck was growing warm and itchy. *Two old men arguing as though their emperor wasn't seated before them. Perhaps they've already crossed the boundary of rudeness.*

Both men sat, reluctantly.

Maevin is used to getting his way. Administrators are such an unfortunate necessity for the royal family. The Crown needed them to carry out regular business. However, with every policy passed, and every project overseen, Maevin had slowly convinced himself that he was indispensable. *My father trusted him, and yet...*

Admiral Heydari, on the other hand, was a dear friend of the emperor. The old man had once been a laughing captain, who had taught a certain young emperor what it meant to be a military man. Heydari laughed a lot less these days, and had replaced his quick wit with a sly cunning that seemed solely directed at annoying High Consul Maevin. *Perhaps our friendship needs to be put back into context for him. He might also believe he is indispensable.*

It had been this way for too long. The push and pull of personal politics beginning to interfere with the sanctity of High Command's processes.

"We'll close the cabinet for today," the emperor said. "High Consul Maevin and Admiral Heydari will adjourn privately, and will arrive tomorrow with an outline for how to test the *Black Tortoise*. An outline," he added with a disdainful sniff, "that satisfies both the military and the Martian Culture Project. If this cabinet meets again without an amicable outline, I'll expect your resignations."

Heydari's eyes blinked, and were suddenly wide and glistening. Maevin's body froze with a shudder, but he recovered quickly. The assembly of officers and administrators stood and bowed in unison.

The emperor gave an imperceptible bow in return. "All Martian life is sacred." The words reverberated throughout the chamber.

"Bless the Red Soil," High Command replied.

The men and women filtered out through the grand doors that let downstairs to the palace gardens. As the enormous steel doors opened, the sounds of stringed instruments floated up from the foyer.

Admiral Heydari cast a distraught look in the emperor's direction. "Is the emperor's wish, then?" he asked.

"You know it is," the Emperor replied. He held the gaze of his old friend, until the Admiral turned away.

7

The Martian Independence Festival began with a parade. Enormous, decorated floats curled away from the academy, along the bustling streets and plazas of the royal dome.

Du Mon half-heartedly waved to the crowd from the royal float. The palace attendants had clothed him in the dress uniform of a Martian captain. His dress jacket was white, with wide cuffs and blue trim. The space above his left breast was decorated. A golden, full-length cloak hung from his shoulders. Above his head, a live projection of his own face was being broadcast into the air.

He smiled at a group of young ladies in the crowd below, who screamed and waved with excitement. Above him, the projection also turned in their direction and smiled. The emperor's face, however, dominated the parade: the projection was the size of a corvette above the crowds of people who had gathered to wave and cheer. The emperor came and stood alongside Du Mon as their continued to crawl. He placed his arm around Du Mon.

"It's good to see you interacting with the people," the emperor said. He glanced down at Du Mon's medal bar and raised an eyebrow, before returning his attention to the crowd. "You don't seem to be particularly proud of the medal I gave you."

The Emperor's Medal of Valour hung from the prince's pocket in miniature. Du Mon had instead chosen to wear the full-size *Research Excellence* medal from the military's science division.

"I just like the design more. It's nothing personal, father."

"You're angry at me."

"Not in the slightest. I'm just distracted, thinking about my work."

The Third Eternal Emperor of the Red Soil gave Du Mon's shoulder a firm squeeze. "Of course, but don't think of this festival as a punishment. This is a day that every Martian should celebrate with their family. That includes you. Today is a reward for good work."

Loud brass and strings, amplified throughout the dome, began the Martian anthem. The crowd buzzed and swayed, hands clasped over their hearts as they sang about their independence from Earth.

Du Mon dutifully placed his hand across his heart, but his mind wandered. The singing was all around him as the crowd thronged. Countless lungs expelled air.

So many eyes on me.

Ahead of them was a float that resembled the giant Elder Seeker. An image of Du Mon leapt upon the fictional projection. The stylised prince helped soldiers and spacers cut the creature open.

A complete fiction.

The crowd finished singing and began to wave and cheer again. Below the projection of the Elder Seeker, a small selection of spacers who had been on that mission waved shyly to the crowd from their own float.

"Father," Du Mon said quietly. "Do you think the people resent me?"

"Hmm?" the emperor scratched his gold-painted beard. "I don't see why they would. You single-handedly prevented the Elder Seeker from coming any closer to Mars. The people must respect you for that."

"I mean the spacers. The people on that mission. I don't want them to think I'm taking all the credit."

Ju Tin approached them, blowing kisses into the crowd, which sent waves of gasps from any lady lucky enough to be in the general vicinity. "That's very unlike you," his brother said. "Why are you worrying about what the spacers think?"

Du Mon let his hand drop from its dutiful waving. "You slummed it with the soldiers, Ju Tin. People respected you for that. You were in the thick of it. Me, on the other hand? I was safe in a battleship, giving orders when the Elder Seeker died."

"It died because you had a good strategy," his father corrected.

"And I was lucky."

"What's eating at you, Du?" Ju Tin asked. "It's beginning to sound like you regret killing the worm."

"Forget it."

The palace crept into view, visible above the grounds and gardened plazas.

"Father, do you believe High Command will take this assignment from me?" Du Mon asked. "Things keep getting delayed. No captain has been announced."

"I wouldn't worry," his father said. "I heard one member of High Command discussing whether they could use your soldier-centred training methods, in the main branch of the defence force."

"That wasn't my question."

The emperor's smile remained warm and kingly. "It's not up to me whether they remove you from the project."

"It *is* up to you! I only received this training assignment because of you."

His father's face creased slightly in confusion. "I didn't have anything to do with that. They thought you were the best person for the job, and I was inclined to agree. Let me make this clear: I don't want anyone thinking you or Ju Tin received accolades that you haven't earned yourself."

The emperor gave a broad and regal wave to the crowd with both hands. Du Mon saw something fall from his father's sleeve, straight into his mouth.

"Trying to keep the scurvy away?" Du Mon asked.

"You can never be too careful," the emperor replied, now with a pronounced lisp. Du Mon sighed. His father was smuggling candy in his sleeves. The emperor's smile grew a small dimple on one side, as he sucked on a citrus drop.

The floats snaked their way through each of the palace dome's major thoroughfares, before coming to a stop outside the palace. The crowd of Martians onlookers was the thickest here, and growing rapidly as many made the journey towards the outer palace grounds. In the distance, Du Mon saw people gathering with blankets and lanterns. Some pulled out instruments. The air was thick with shouting, laughter, and music.

As he climbed down from the float, the prince was cornered by a member of the royal press.

"Please Your Grace, take your recording?" came the cry from a pox-faced adolescent. The boy's chest was fastened with an expensive projection recorder.

The corners of Du Mon's face were aching from the constant smiling. "Where do you want me?"

"Right over here," the journalist gestured towards the giant worm float.

"Great."

The Elder Seeker loomed overhead, as the rabble of spacers waited beside their float. As the prince approached, their conversation stopped abruptly.

They hate me, he realised.

"Your Graceness," the lead spacer bowed low. "We've been enjoying your projections here."

In the air above them, the prince led the charge. He leapt through the void towards the Elder Seeker: one arm bloodied, in a sling, while the other held a rifle. Whoever had created the fictional events had even gone to the trouble of animating the condensation forming inside the prince's helmet, as he confidently barked orders to the mixture of soldiers and spacers around him.

"The old team reunited!" exclaimed the tiny journalist. He tapped the middle of his chest to activate the console-recorder strapped there. "How do you feel, Your Highness, seeing your old comrades again?"

Du Mon examined their scarred and weary faces. From the group of eight spacers, there were six missing limbs. One of them had gone blind from the bright flashes of laser drilling.

"It's great to see the old gang back together again," the prince said, slightly louder than necessary. Glancing from face to face, he realised that he didn't know the names of any of these men and women who'd wounded themselves under his orders.

All of them smiled broadly, and bowed at the waist.

"Your Grace," said the lead spacer. "It's so good to see you again."

Du Mon looked down at the dying skin on his bad hand. *So many died when I gave the order. I pretended to care about them, just so they'd sacrifice life and limb.* There was a flash as the reporter took his image.

"Let's try again," the tiny man said. "Your Grace? Could you please smile this time?"

Du Mon forced the corners of his mouth upwards. *I probably look unwell.* There was another flash, and the reporter stared down at the readout. Du Mon could see the tension around the small man's eyes. *He's struggling to decide whether it's rude to ask for another.*

"Excuse me," Du Mon said, bowing slightly at the waist to the spacers.

They gasped.

"I thank you all deeply for your service," the prince said, and straightened. "You must think me terribly rude, but I'm afraid the ride on the float made me slightly nauseous."

"No 'oblem," the eldest spacer said. He smiled, but there were no teeth.

Another stout spacer inhaled sharply. "What a treasure that young prince is. Fancy bowing his thanks to the likes of us?"

The crowd began to press in against the soldiers who held them back. The emperor was gesturing with poise as he spoke with another journalist. Ju Tin stood regally beside their father.

He looks every bit the model prince.

"Look at me, Your Grace!" yelled a young lady from the crowd.

"Quick, switch the recorder on!" called another, holding it above his head to grab some footage of the prince as he staggered towards the palace gates. As he scrambled away, the prince turned to see the glares of the spacers following him. His golden cloak twisted around him as he turned again, hurrying to the safety of a palace walls.

In his haste, Du Mon trod on the corner of his own cloak. He heard the fabric tear slightly, but hold. His bad shoulder jerked downwards unexpectedly. Du Mon landed on his rear in front of the royal press, the spacers, and the thronging crowd of onlookers.

The crowd, as one, made a sympathetic *ooh* sound through clenched teeth. The emperor turned and saw his youngest sprawled just inside the gates of the palace. The rear of the young prince stuck up from the crowd, pointed at the cameras.

Ju Tin was grinning like an idiot. Du Mon rose, and forced himself to walk slowly to the palace's tower, even though everything inside him screamed at him to run away.

He almost barrelled into Plessis as she descended the steps towards the festival. She was beaming. Her blonde hair had been professionally designed, shaped into one of those geometrically-perfect styles she'd always wanted to try.

"Your Grace," she curtsied and then dropped her hem to grab his arm excitedly. "I hear there's going to be a wrestling tournament tonight. Can we go and see?"

The prince forced his jaw to unclench. He inhaled, and it sounded ragged and broken. "I'm going back to the barracks."

"Du, don't."

"Don't call me that." The young prince broke away from her and marched up the stairs. Behind him, Du Mon could hear Plessis struggling up the stairs in her long dress.

"You only just got back! Your Grace don't abandon me like this! I don't want to go to the festival without you."

Du Mon opened their chamber door with such force that it crashed into the inside wall. "I've got interviews this evening," he called down the stairs. "Don't wait up for me."

8

Admiral Heydari had fallen silent as he watched Maevin across the consulate desk. The aging soldier had brought his cane to the High Consul's office: a stark piece of artisan craftsmanship, sharpened from the tall femur of some mammal. It must have been imported from Earth long before the trade wars began. The Admiral was joined by Captain Soona, an enormously fat man, who was sweating through his uniform and onto the consulate's fine furniture.

Maevin's receptionist sat on the corner of his desk, filing away at her nails as the tea steeped in the poisonous Mi'lle clay teapot.

"It has to be Ju Tin," the admiral said at last.

"I won't hear of it," Maevin waved the idea away with a flick of the wrist. "Du Mon has poured the last five years of his life into this project."

"And that's precisely why the responsibility of the ship shouldn't fall on his shoulders alone." The admiral shook his head and tapped the metallic floor with his cane. "He's too emotionally involved, not to mention impulsive and unstable. He needs oversight."

A small smirk played in the corner of Maevin's mouth. "I agree."

The Admiral looked shaken. "I'm sorry, what was that?"

"I agree with you."

"Oh." Admiral Heydari scratched his neck.

"In fact, I have several members of the consulate who would gladly take up the role of the young prince's mentor. He hasn't been overseen since the unfortunate incident with Consul Barclay."

The Admiral's eyebrows knit together. "The prince doesn't trust the consulate anymore. Not since Barclay went rogue and tried to take over command of the Ceres mission."

"He stepped outside his jurisdiction."

"You can say that again. It was practically mutiny."

"Which is why he was removed as a member of the consulate's inner circle." Maevin pursed his lips. "We had to set an example to the other administrators. There needs to be some distance between the consulate and the army. Otherwise we'd have martial law on our hands."

"Indeed."

The receptionist poured the tea. A single delicate finger held the teapot's lid down. The steaming beverage cascaded from the spout, filling the room with the scent of citrus and earthy mushroom.

"You want a military man," Maevin said, as he watched the receptionist pour. "Someone who has authority over the prince?"

"A clear chain of command is what's needed," the Admiral explained. "A sub-admiral could take the *Black Tortoise* as their flagship. That way the prince could remain captain, but would ultimately need to defer to the sub-admiral if things got out-of-hand."

"What a splendid idea," Captain Soona crooned, clapping his hands together in delight. "It's just what the young lad needs."

"Very well," said Maevin. "Which sub-admiral did you have in mind?"

"A new sub-admiral," Heydari said. The receptionist handed him a cup of tea, and he accepted it with both hands. The three men blew the steam from the tops of their drinks. "Tomorrow I'm promoting Ju Tin to the position."

Maevin's face registered shock and disgust, but the news wasn't revelation to him. *A logical choice if you wanted to frustrate me.* The old consul studied the leaves of his tea, checking for the tell-tale flakes of poison that might be lingering there. *Unfortunately for you Admiral, I anticipated this.*

"So that's how you want to play it?"

The Admiral traced his fingers around the rim of the cup, and then sipped his tea. "I'm afraid I don't have many years left in me High Consul. This is the only way I'd agree to have the mission head out towards the Lunar shipyards. If the emperor demands my position, it will be a sad day. However, I would retire gracefully. Don't look at me like that, I would. Are you willing to give up your position?"

Maevin did his best to look defeated. He allowed his shoulders to slump slightly as he pulled up a document on his desk computer. "I suppose I have no choice. We'll send both of the princes. Ju Tin will mentor his younger brother, and that will be that."

"I'm so glad you agree," the Admiral said. He downed the last of his tea, and placed the cup back on the High Consul's desk. "Does the computer have the documents ready?"

"Of course," Maevin replied.

A transcript of their conversation had been typed and formatted, down to the agreed terms. Heydari read it carefully. The *Black Tortoise* would embark towards the Lunar shipyards, captained by Du Mon. The young prince was to be overseen by Ju Tin as Sub-Admiral. After running stress tests, the ship was to conduct reconnaissance against the Lunar shipyards. If an opportunity presented itself, at the discretion of the Sub-Admiral Ju Tin, the ship would be given permission to engage with the enemy in an attempt to cripple their shipyards.

Heydari skimmed the document a second time, and then reached over with his credentials. He swiped his badge across the grey, oblong slate at the edge of the desk. The computer read his irises, fingerprints, and measured the capillaries in his fingertips. His signature appeared on the document, as well as his bio-code. Maevin reached over and did the same.

"There we go," Maevin said.

Heydari gave a wry smile. "And it only took us a year to reach an agreement. Is there any other business?"

Maevin scratched his chin thoughtfully. "Nothing comes to mind."

The Admiral got up slowly, and limped out from the office. Captain Soona bowed low several times as he backed out from the office. Maevin held out a hand, just before Soona disappeared around the corner.

"Soona?"

"Yes, High Consul?"

"Don't forget that you owe me a favour."

Soona froze, bent over mid-bow. He straightened, his sweaty uniform squelching as his rolls of fat shifted and jiggled. "Of course. I hadn't forgotten."

"Take the Admiral through the main street on your way to the palace."

When Soona left, Maevin collected the hand of his receptionist and kissed it.

"You were marvellous."

She blushed, and brandished her nail file. Then the receptionist collected the Admiral's cup from the desk: a cup that had a thin scratch from a nail file, which ran from the lip to its base.

Maevin allowed himself to grin widely. *Both princes in a prototype vessel. How deliciously perfect.*

Barclay had been too eager. He lacked the patience required to enact the plans of the inner consulate, which is why he was now a bum sitting in a bar somewhere below the surface.

Soon, the emperor will kneel and apologise, and I will graciously accept his resignation.

* * *

Heydari went into cardiac arrest when the armoured car was within sight of the Admiral's house. His hand shot to his shoulder, feeling a pure barb of pain, as though he'd been impaled. Then the pain spread slowly up and down his arm, like a wave of heat wafting in from the Martian deserts.

His other hand gripped Captain Soona's forearm tightly. Beads of sweat fell from the Admiral's forehead.

"Radio for a medical team!" Captain Soona yelled at the driver.

The driver's face grew pale, and he yelled through the truck's console, requesting immediate assistance.

Soona glanced across at crowds thronging through the streets, and clogging the main thoroughfares. In the rear seat of the armoured car, he held the Admiral upright. The old man dropped his cane, and it rolled underneath his chair.

"I think—" the Admiral swallowed with great effort. His saliva was a white paste across his lips and on the back of his tongue. "I think Maevin has—"

"Shh," Captain Soona said. "It's alright. The military will be in good hands." He reached into the Admiral's throat, and scraped away some of the paste that the old man was choking on. "I'm sorry you had to die."

Admiral Heydari looked up at the sweaty captain, who couldn't meet his eyes.

"Why?"

"They know about my visits to the temple. If my wife found out...well..." Captain Soona shrugged. "I never was a very good soldier. The consulate offered me a good position in the New Order. Things are going to be very different soon. No more royalty. Heh. Can you imagine that?"

A single tear welled in the corner of Heydari's eye. He was dead before it fell.

9

Du Mon poured through the digital files of ten applicants. His good hand smoothed back his hair as his eyes flicked back and forth across the cyan hue that glowed above his tablet.

Tam sat beside the prince, nursing his head in his hands. They both sat in Du Mon's office, facing the door. The prince was in his military uniform. Tam, however, was wearing the traditional garb for the Martian festival dance: a red pointed hat and a long, fasten-up jacket.

"Thank you for coming out," Du Mon said. "It's an emergency."

"How is this an emergency?"

"I need to fast-track the program," the prince replied. "I've decided to trust Maevin will come through, so I'm going ahead with the recruitment process."

"It's the festival tonight." Tam's voice was muffled through his laced fingers as he rocked on a stool. "We left the baby at my parents'. Mith and I were going to go dancing at the festival. Do you know how long it's been since we—" Tam closed his eyes and mimed a slow dance with his hands around his wife's imaginary waist.

"Exactly. It's the festival. When the recruits arrive for their interviews, we'll know they're serious about joining the crew. It also tests their ability to change plans at a moment's notice."

"It'll test their patience, Du. Are you sure you want to start your professional relationship with some of your crew by prematurely ending their holidays?"

The prince was squinting at his tablet. "Is the mess stool comfortable enough?" he asked. "The jar works wonders for my posture. I do some of my best thinking atop it."

Tam cast a wary glance at the tank where the preserved alien head floated. "I'm fine with the stool, thanks."

The prince put the tablet down and clenched his eyes tightly, trying to rescue his eyesight. "I'm planning on interviewing the marines that High Consul Maevin recommended."

"Even though you've decided to let them all in?" Tam asked.

"It's a formality, but it will start things off on the right foot."

There was a light knock at the door. Du Mon opened the bottom drawer of his metal desk. Inside, Tam spied four glass bottles of spirits and an officer's pistol that sat atop them.

The prince checked the pistol was loaded, and then depressed the button on his desk. He held the weapon against his leg. "Enter."

The door swished open, revealing a squinting man who had been escorted there by Sheree Wagner. Judging by her appearance, poor Sheree had also been dragged from the festivities aboveground. She wore makeup and a bright red dress over her muscular frame. To Tam, she resembled a painted battlecruiser.

The man she had accompanied threw a textbook salute.

"Senior Ensign Vishan Walsh. Reporting for duty sir."

"At ease. Thank you for coming at such short notice, Walsh. Please have a seat." Du Mon placed the weapon back in the drawer and closed it. The senior ensign moved between the door and the seat without breaking eye contact with the prince.

Walsh's hair was closely cropped. He wore the Martian Navy's uniform.

"I'm impressed that you managed to get changed so quickly," Du Mon remarked.

"I was at home sir," Vishan Walsh replied, deadpan.

"Well, I appreciate your dedication for coming out regardless. Did you have an opportunity to see the facilities?"

"Yes sir, very good sir."

"Do you have any questions about the special program before we begin?"

"No sir."

Tam shifted in his seat. "What drew you to requesting a transfer to this position for Junior Tactical Officer?"

"I believe it would improve my career outcomes, sir. I hope to begin a long career in tactical or logistics."

"I see," Tam replied. "Your military record is very impressive for someone so young. Exemplary organisation. No demerits for rule breaking."

"Thank you, sir."

Du Mon flashed what he hoped was a sympathetic smile. "No need to be so formal, Walsh."

"Yessir." Walsh retained his perfectly upright posture.

The prince and Tam glanced at each other before Tam continued. "While you have received a commendation from your current captain on the frigate *Descartes*, I noticed you haven't had any combat experience outside of training."

"No sir. My assignments have mostly been on routine runs from the belt and back, no trouble."

"How do you cope under pressure?" Du Mon asked.

"Oh." A glint appeared in Walsh's eye and then vanished just as quickly. "I'm not sure how my calculations would be affected. I look forward to finding out."

Du Mon intently studied the notes in front of him.

During the lull in the conversation, Walsh looked about the room, as if noticing it for the first time. "I quite like building models," the senior ensign said suddenly, leaning forward and breaking his posture. "Did you build that? The technique is fabulous! I can't see the joins anywhere."

The prince and Tam both followed his eye line to look at the Elder Seeker hovering over them.

"I wish I was that talented," Du Mon replied. "It was machined by a computer."

"Very good sir," Walsh said, settling back into his chair. "It looks very accurate to the data recorded from your voyage."

"Well," said Tam Sunter. "I don't have any further questions. Do you, Your Grace?"

Once the door slid closed behind Walsh, Tam let out a low whistle.

"What do you think?" Du Mon asked.

"A very qualified gentleman," Tam said. He examined the contents of his tin mug glumly.

"Yes, *qualified* is certainly the word I would use." Du Mon had become intrigued by the mummified alien head in the corner.

"A little bookish, wasn't he?" Tam offered.

"Monotonous too."

"I'm glad you said it, because that word was floating around in my mind as well."

"Still very qualified."

"Oh, he's definitely going places," Du Mon said with a nod.

Tam tried to hide a growing smile, by draining the remains of his mug.

"I'm curious to see how he handles the intensive," the prince said. "Do you think he liked me?"

"What?"

"He was formal the whole interview. Do you think he found it hard to relate to me? I'm worried he thinks I'm too aloof."

Tam threw his friend a grimace. "Who cares? You're his superior officer. *Order* him to like you."

"I just worry that this crew won't like me. Is that strange?"

Tam grabbed Du Mon's good shoulder and squeezed it. "You'll do great."

The prince's tablet summoned a green orb in the air above them.

"Yes, Wagner?"

Sheree's voice floated from the tablet. "The next transfer applicant is here. Ensign Kyuri Kim."

* * *

Ensign Kim hadn't stopped grinning with giddy excitement. From the moment she'd entered the office, her eyes had flitted, unresting, from the room's piles of equipment to the alien memorabilia. Du Mon had taken it upon himself to give her a tour of his collection before conducting the interview proper.

"Wow, do you think it can still see things?" Kim asked, her face pressed up against the glass container that held the alien's head.

"That Outsider's brain activity has been dormant for a long time," Du Mon explained. It was nice to have someone appreciate the alien head.

"The dramas don't really do it justice do they?" Kim said, with a visible shiver. "You get a real sense of malice from it."

"It was worse when you saw them move," Du Mon explained. "Like a sentient crab. They scoot along with their torso upside down."

Kim poked her tongue out and jumped back. "How horrid."

"The Elder Seeker was far more terrifying." Du Mon stared up at the maw of the worm that had ground Captain Dav'i and his ship to pieces.

"I can't imagine," Kim said. She stood beside him. Du Mon could hear her breathing rising and falling rapidly, as though she were secretly running. "It must have been terrifying. You were all so brave to fight it, even after so many others failed."

Tam nodded. "His Highness was certainly inspired by my bravery."

Kim giggled. It sounded melodic: a rising and falling scale. "Who's this?" she asked. On the back wall of the office, Kim had spotted a picture of Harmony Xu pinned to the wall.

"That's a terrorist," Tam said. "Used to know the prince. The picture is from her search warrant: generated by a computer to match what she might look like now."

Kim squinted at the picture. "Oh, she was very famous a little while back."

"Perhaps we should get the interview started," the prince said, quickly gesturing to the chair.

Kim sat and began swinging slightly on her chair again. Her feet barely touched the floor.

"When did you graduate from the academy?" Du Mon asked.

"At the end of the last cadet rotation." Kim pulled a hand through her hair nervously. It was black and silken. There was something inherently familiar and beautiful about the way she kicked her feet like a child.

"So why did you apply for this project?" Du Mon asked.

"I always wanted to do the heroic things I saw in those old military dramas. It sounds silly."

"Not at all," the prince reassured her.

"When I saw the modern dramas of you and the other brave officers fighting..." she clasped her hands over her heart and inhaled deeply. "I couldn't sign up to the academy fast enough."

Du Mon beamed.

"You've begun your military career a little later than most," Tam said. "I noticed that you didn't do your compulsory military service?"

"I was exempt," Kim explained. "Grew up on a mining frigate and helped with the communication systems out on the belt."

"So you've been to space before?" Tam asked, surprised. He looked over her records. "I was picturing someone who grew up planetside."

"Oh," Kim said with a giggle. "No, I've spent years on spaceships. I practically grew up in space. The details are filed under my previous employment history."

Du Mon scrolled through several documents on his tablet. There was a service record, signed by a Commander from the belt operations.

"Did you work closely under a captain?" Tam asked.

"I'm afraid my duties didn't bring me to the bridge very often. I was usually working on the machinery and automated mining drones, that sort of thing."

Du Mon looked at her files again with a raised eyebrow. "So you're a mechanic?"

Kim bit her lip. "Sorry. Not the machinery, per se. I worked on the digital systems and relay network. At the academy, I majored in communications and logistics. I'm a quick learner though. I do a lot of reading. I'm sure I could even pilot a fighter if I was given a few lessons."

Tam shrugged. "You're either very bold or stupid. I've never heard of someone applying for a role on a secret project straight out of the academy."

"I almost didn't apply for this position. I was afraid there'd be too many officers far more qualified than me. But I told myself, *what do you have to lose?* So here I am."

"I'm building a multidisciplinary team." Du Mon explained. "I don't want the *Black Tortoise* special project to be staffed with high-ranking soldiers who have ridden the coat-tails of others towards success. I want a range of officers and civilians, just like a regular starship. A crew who can learn from one another, and who have complementary skills. I don't just want specialists; I want generalists too. I think you might fit well into that role."

"It sounds like a very admirable goal," Kim replied. "I'm so excited I got to hear about it!"

Du Mon smiled. "Well, I've already made up my mind. Welcome aboard. I'll expect you to report here for intensive training after the festival."

Kim clasped her hands to her mouth in delight.

* * *

Tam's frown ate through his smile once Sheree had escorted Kim from the room. "Are you sure? She's sweet, sure, but immature. I know she's about your age, Du Mon, but she's inexperienced. Still got bright eyes and thinks the universe won't hurt her."

"She'll be capable."

Tam rubbed his eyes. "What I'm talking about is taking someone inexperienced and carefree, and throwing them on a project at the cusp of military progress! What if she cracks under pressure? What if the mission goes wrong and she sees friends and colleagues die?"

"She would have seen death on the belt."

"Are you certain about that? I think you're choosing to ignore the warning signs because you enjoy her company."

"She'd certainly be a good fit for the team. We've already got the battle-hardened special forces. It's important to have a mixture of personalities on a ship."

"You're going to damage her."

"I'm going to—?" Du Mon stood suddenly. "Excuse me, I need some air."

"Don't run away from me, Your Highness."

"Perhaps," Du Mon said, turning on his heel at the door. "You're the one who is ignoring the signs. She reminds me of your wife. Sweet, innocent Mith. Beautiful and carefree and thrust into terrible danger. Are you really trying to protect Kim, or are you afraid of feeling responsible if something were to happen to her? Did you rush to have Jace, just to keep Mith here, planetside?"

Tam pursed his lips. "I'm going to choose to ignore what you just said about my son."

"Take ten. We'll do the next interview when I get back."

Du Mon marched out of the office and straight into the sparring room. He walked confidently through the darkened room, his feet knowing exactly where to land. At the rear of the sparring room, a bag of sand hung, with the picture of an Outsider alien painted on it. Even in the dim light, Du Mon could see the white ovals of its cartoonish eyes glaring down at him.

He swung with his bad hand. The dead nerves in his knuckles registered pain as though it were lightyears away. The bag shifted slightly. Du Mon imagined his fist swinging through the target and out the other side. He pounded the mock alien, again and again.

The prince inhaled sharply through clenched teeth. Steam and spit crept from the corner of his mouth. A scream rose up from deep inside him as he continued to punch the sandbag with his bad arm, willing it to move, willing his fist to be strong again. His shoulder began to ache from the unprotected punches.

He stopped, and examined the palm of his damaged hand. The colour was yellow-blue and sickly. The digits kept twitching, no matter how much medication the royal doctors placed him on.

They'd saved his natural hand, remarkably. *Perhaps I should have let the physician just cut it off and mutilate me, instead of taking a cocktail of drugs and a carousel of surgeries.* He was still struggling to keep his food down. *Some sort of blood poisoning. How ridiculous.*

"You don't have the right to lecture me about protecting people, Tam. Saving your life, made my own hell." In the stillness of the sparring room, Du Mon examined the paper-thin skin of his hand. It had split across the knuckles and started bleeding.

* * *

Harmony vomited into the vac sink, and wiped her mouth roughly with the back of her hand.

Du Mon— she hurled again. There was more that she needed to expel, but Harmony's stomach held onto the bile instead, churning it in her gut. *Five years. Countless threats made against me on public noticeboards. But he keeps a framed picture of me on the wall?*

There was a polite knock at the door.

"It's open," Harmony said.

Sheree Wagner opened the door and poked her head through. "Ensign Kim? Are you sure you don't need any help in here?"

"I'm fine, thank you." The vac-sink screamed as she activated it.

Sheree looked concerned. "Did the nerves get to you, Ensign Kim?"

Harmony's eyes were bright red from crying. "Call me Kyuri."

The underground brawler smiled sympathetically, and it caused the scars across her forehead to bunch together. "Whatever you need, love. I felt intimated the first time I met the prince. He's very...intense." Sheree Wagner placed a protective arm around the smaller woman. "Don't worry, I'll keep an eye on you at the intensive training."

"Thanks." Harmony took a deep, ragged breath. "Is it...is it okay if I stay here for a little longer?"

"Anything you need. I'll be outside when you're ready." Sheree backed out of the toilet stall, and closed the door.

Harmony was left alone to stare into the wide mirror that graced the main wall of the bathroom. She lifted her head and examined the long, wicked scars that ran along the underside of her chin. Scars from the facial transplant she'd received, after Peace helped her escape custody. Harmony glowered in the mirror. She raised her eyebrows experimentally. It was the face she had known for five years, and yet it was still alien to her.

"Who are you?" she asked the reflection of Ensign Kyuri Kim.

10

Two days later, 'Ensign Kim' and Sheree Wagner stood at the Bradbury landing site. On the horizon lay the Bagnold Dunes, hugging the foothills of Mount Sharp. The mountain rose up from the blue-black gravel, fading from brilliant red to a soft pink.

It's beautiful, Harmony thought. Her stomach ached underneath her green combat suit. *Mother always wanted to see the mountains again.*

The sun glinted strongly from the transparent steel of Du Mon's helmet as the prince addressed the group of officers who had abandoned the festival in order to join the impromptu wargame.

"Humans landed a robot near this spot over a thousand years ago," Du Mon said. His voice was being broadcast to each of their helmet's speakers, via a console system that sat beneath an enormous recording antenna behind him. "This crater, and its surroundings, were called the Bradbury group, after the author who imagined Martians living here."

He gestured to the small group of officers gathered around him. "I can't imagine a more fitting location. We're here at the intersection of our planet's past, and its future. This was the place where people first began to explore Mars, and it is here that our team will be put to the test. Before we begin, let me make this absolutely clear: your performance in today's exercise could determine whether or not you will be included on the *Black Tortoise* project."

There were a few nods from the crowd. One person, however, raised a hand in objection. He was a mountain of a man, and his training suit was painted barn red.

"You say that, but surely there are some of us are guaranteed a spot?"

Du Mon shook his head. "As I've told you before Ivanov, your performance is always being assessed. If I think you are slacking off in today's exercise, or are making too many errors, I may pull you from the project."

A sideways glance was exchanged between Ivanov and another soldier in red.

Ivanov wasn't backing down. "What about our military records? Lieutenant Shiwa here is a decorated special operative. Do you really need to run this exercise to see how long a rookie can last against him?"

The prince clasped his hands behind his back and leaned forward on the balls of his feet.

"Absolutely. I place very little value on a person's record, compared to what I get to see with my own eyes. During my tour of duty out at Ceres, I met two very different men who'd reached the rank of captain. I can't even begin to articulate the difference in calibre between them. Therefore, I'll use your records to help weigh into any difficult decisions I might have, but that's it. Your performance during this activity, your ability to work as a team, that's what counts.

To the prince's left, five military flatbed trucks waited. Their wheels were two-metres in diameter, and each truck had been painted in a different colour: blue, red, green, and purple.

"Today we will be running a military exercise of my own invention. You have been placed in a team." The prince indicated the trucks. "Your team colour corresponds with the colour of the truck you are given. For the purposes of the military exercise, these trucks represent your space vessel. You must protect your space vessel from being commandeered by another team."

The trucks' cabins, which usually protected a driver from the elements, had been dismantled and removed so that whoever operated the vehicle was now just as exposed as the rest of the flatbed it pulled.

"There are shoe clamps attached to the flatbed so that your truck can transport your entire team easily. The battle arena is large, so you will need to use your truck to strategically position your team. You can commandeer an opposing team's truck if you want to."

Sheree raised her hand. "So, what is the goal of the exercise? To protect our vehicle?"

Du Mon shook his head. "You'll need your trucks for transporting your team. However, that's not the objective." With his good hand, Du Mon gestured to his belt pouch. It was a cheap pocket of sackcloth similar to the ones worn by market sellers. "Each of you will be wearing one of these pouches. There's a simple clasp at the front. They are designed so that one member of your team can easily, and secretly, carry your team's flag. Your main objective is to protect your team's flag. Your team's flag must be carried by a team member at all times. If a team loses their flag, they lose and must leave the wargame."

"So, it's like capture the flag?" asked a thin-looking officer with slicked-back hair.

"Exactly. If you are the last team to lose your flag, you win the exercise. This game is all about the ebb and flow of battle. As a team, you will need to switch between launching an offensive, to pulling back and defending. There is a wildcard, however: any team who manages to catch the jackalope, and carry him back here on their truck, will win the game immediately."

Du Mon landed a heavy slap on Tam's shoulder.

"Lieutenant Commander Sunter will be playing the role of the jackalope."

"Hello, all." Tam gave the group a little wave, and stuck two index fingers out from his helmet, like he had antlers attached to his forehead. His suit was painted a mottled orange and black, so that it could camouflage into the landscape.

"The jackalope is heralded as the most dangerous creature you will ever hunt. Indeed, those of you lucky enough to score its hide will become national heroes.

Tam's head whipped back to look at Du Mon. "*Its* hide? Hey, listen—"

The prince carried on, unimpeded. "—you will tell your grandchildren the tale, as you gaze up at its head, mounted in your dining room."

"Ha," Tam said through the radio channel. "Very funny. Your Grace, can I pull you to one side to discuss this?"

The prince smiled back warmly, and shook his head. Tam Sunter looked across the sea of assembled soldiers, and saw the hunger in their eyes.

"Oh." He turned, straddled the military-issue dune bike that he'd brought along, and gunned the engine hard. The nitrogen-cooled engine screamed as he took off, his front wheels wavering off the ground for a brief moment, before they came crashing back down into the dust.

Du Mon gave a short wave to Tam's back, and then returned his attention to the group. "You have three minutes to talk strategy."

Sheree Wagner ushered her team, including Harmony, away from the larger group. The broad-shouldered woman looked around at her team of five, all in matching green. She checked her wrist computer, and set it their radios to a secure channel.

"I vote Ensign Kim takes the flag."

"Wait, really?" Harmony asked. Her chestnut eyes widened in alarm. "I'm really bad at athletics, and fighting."

Sheree nodded. "They won't expect you to have it. See the red team over there?"

Twenty metres away, the red team were in a group huddle, slapping each other on their backs and rumps. There was a distinct difference in physical size between the red team, and the other groups.

The largest soldier from the red team, Ivanov, held the red flag high in the air, making sure the other teams knew exactly who held it.

"That's who we have to worry about the most," Sheree said. "The big grunt is Lieutenant Commander Ivanov. Wants to be the strongest and fastest. He'll come gunning straight for me. If we give the flag to Kim, it'll be the last place he'll look."

Sheree handed the flag to Harmony, who placed it in her pouch as the rest of their team crowded around to hide it.

"Why would Ivanov go straight for you?" Harmony asked. She studied the green scrap of fabric.

Sheree shook her head. "Don't worry about that now. Put it away, quickly."

Harmony tucked it into her pouch.

"I have a question about the teams," said Senior Ensign Vishan Walsh. He shifted from foot-to-foot in the suit, trying to adjust to its feeling. "It looks to me like some of the other teams know each other already."

Sheree nodded. It was difficult in her suit. "The red and blue teams are all made up of soldiers and officers who have been training since the first round of recruitment two years ago. Our team, and the purple team, are made of mostly new recruits who were transferred last week."

Vishan Walsh frowned. "It doesn't seem particularly fair. Why not spread the newcomers amidst the other teams?"

"The prince has his reasons," Sheree replied.

"In that case," said Walsh, "our first priority is probably to assign some of the team as defenders, and others as attackers. Communication could become strained during the exercise, and we can't afford to leave our flag undefended."

"I'll be a defender," offered Harmony. "I suppose that's a given, if I have the flag."

"I'll be a defender too," Vishan Walsh added. "I doubt I have the stamina to be out on the front line."

Sheree raised her hand, "I'll go on the offensive, as I've got the most combat training." She turned her gaze towards the remaining member of the green team. "So I guess that makes you our driver?"

The other officer tilted his head upwards slightly in reply.

Sheree frowned. "Are you sure you're okay handling a vehicle?"

The man nodded. His mouth was incredibly wide. "Can do. I'm Gum Snyder, Marine. 6th Division. Glad to assist." He was as thin as a missile, and despite his quiet nature, he stood confidently on one leg as he limbered up. The other leg had been amputated and replaced with a thin, motorised leg that protruded from his green combat suit.

"What method of victory should we aim for?" Walsh asked. "Take the jackalope, or take the flags?"

"There's another option," Sheree said quietly. Behind her, the red team were drawing lines across their necks: the universal gesture for death. "Incapacitate all the other soldiers."

"Wait," Snyder's wide mouth turned downwards. "I thought this was just capture the flag, or some big game of keep-away?"

"It is," Sheree replied. "However, I didn't hear any rules against physically harming each other."

Walsh gulped. "The jackalope is the fastest path to victory, which means several teams might go for it."

Sheree was studying the red team. "Ivanov will aim for eliminating everyone on the field. We follow the jackalope, stay clear of the red team, and try to pick our fights with the others carefully."

Vishan Walsh rubbed his hands together gleefully. "Depending on how the other teams respond, we can adapt our strategy."

There was a hiss of static, and then the prince's voice cut across all of their comm channels. "Time's up. Climb aboard your trucks. Wait for my signal."

"This is so exciting!" Harmony said, beaming. Her hands were starting to shake.

By the time they'd climbed aboard the green truck, the jackalope was just a trail of red dust in the distance.

"He's headed for the black dunes," Sheree said. She stamped on the floor of the truck's flatbed, and it magnetised beneath her, locking her steel combat boots in place. Harmony and Walsh both stamped on the floor as well. Snyder climbed up into the green truck's driving console.

From his spot underneath the giant antennae, Du Mon held up a hand, index finger outstretched. "You have two minutes of immunity. A buzzer will sound when you are allowed to begin combat." He dropped his hand with a flourish. "Commence exercise."

The trucks burst from their marks, in a shower of dust and pebbles. Harmony grabbed the safety railing that ran the length of her team's truck and held on, white-knuckled. She looked up, and found herself staring into the eyes of a woman who stood perfectly poised the blue truck. She was spider-like, rocking on the balls of her feet. The spider-woman held a staff as tall as herself, carved from a length of bone.

Gum Snyder swore as a rocky outcrop rose up ahead. He spun the wheel and the two vehicles parted. The blue truck carried on, relentlessly following the dust trail left by Tam.

"Who was that?" Harmony asked into her helmet's microphone.

"The blue team's leader," Sheree said. "Comes from an old family north of the capital. Her family is known for two things: breeding pilots, and fungi farmers. The prince put in a special request to have transfer to the *Black Tortoise* program as a pilot."

"Fungi farmers?" Walsh asked. His face grew pale. "Oh, dear. That explains the staff then."

"The prince doesn't hide his favourites." Sheree held a hand above her visor, and leaned over the railing to get a better look. "They're going to try and win by capturing Tam Sunter."

The black Bagnold Dunes spread along the base of the mountains for kilometres in both directions, like the walls of an ancient fortress.

"They're going to search for him in that?" Harmony asked. "If they can find him, then they deserve to win."

"Kim, be careful what you wish for." Sheree threw a practice jab in the air, straight-ahead, followed by a sharp uppercut. "You see Kim, those northern fungi farmers are great at tracking. She'd have grown up hunting actual jackalopes."

"That's what stinks about this whole competition," Snyder whined. "It was tipped towards combat-focused teams from the get-go. We've mostly got two support officers." He gave a polite wave in Harmony and Walsh's direction. "No offence."

Walsh shrugged. "At first glance, it certainly appears to be a combat game, but there's a subtlety to it as well. Why introduce the jackalope? I think it's to play to the blue team's strengths. Why include the trucks at all? So we can use them tactically. It gives a chance for the pilots to shine."

Two trails of dust were in the far distance to their right. The red dust rose like a smoking, volcanic fissure. Sheree shielded her eyes from the sun and watched as they vanished into the distance. "That's the red team, hunting the purple truck. At least they won't be an immediate problem."

"Do we chase blue?" Snyder called through his mic.

The blue truck had gained some significant distance on them. Further ahead, Tam Sunter had reached the black dunes. His bike easily carried him up the steep sandbanks, over and into the natural maze. Mount Sharp rose up on their right.

"Let's go around the dunes," Sheree said. "We'll try and meet the blue team with Lieutenant Commander Sunter in the middle. I think that will give us the best opportunity of catching him."

Gum Snyder spun the wheel.

The prince's voice came floating across their helmet headsets. "Commence combat."

Four metal rods extruded out of their truck's flatbed. Harmony bent down, and dislodged the rod closest to her. She examined it. The rod was black, and made from a reinforced plastic. At its tip, two metal prongs jutted out.

"I was afraid of this," said Sheree. Her voice sounded defeated. "Stun rods."

Harmony's thumb found a small indent halfway down the weapon. She depressed it, and nearly dropped it when an arc of blue-white electricity crackled between the two metal prongs.

11

The low, sultry voice of a computer made an announcement over the intercom. "Purple team, please be advised that you are now exiting the battlefield. Turn around immediately, or be disqualified." The message was being broadcast by the prince's console at the centre of the battlefield.

"Only one team decided to follow us," the purple leader yelled across the microphone. He was an aging marine, on his last tour of duty before retirement. "Spin around. We'll face them on that slope up there."

"Aye, lieutenant." The purple team's driver swung around, and was nearly side-swiped by the red team. Ivanov's truck matched the purple team's speed, as they both hurtled across the desert.

"Break hard, swing around on the inside of them," the lieutenant called into his mic.

The purple team's vehicle lurched as the driver anchored. The red driver had been expecting it, however, and matched their speed.

Ivanov unhooked his feet from the magnetic floor of the red truck. As the other marines whooped and hollered, he climbed the safety rail. Ivanov stood for a moment, teetering as the ground raced below him, and leapt the gap between the two vehicles.

In mid-air, Ivanov's left fist smashed into the purple leader's helmet, cracking the protective visor. The red leader then landed on the purple truck's flatbed, wobbling slightly as he gained his footing, and then drove his stun rod into the lieutenant's gut hard enough for the metal rods to puncture through the steel weave.

A deafening scream echoed through the purple team's headsets. Two of them instinctively slapped their hands to the sides of their helmets, trying to block the noise. Ivanov held the baton steady, as volt after volt was discharged into the lieutenant. The screams stopped abruptly, and the old marine was left twitching on the floor of the flatbed.

Both trucks had now slowed to a crawl. The other red team members leapt the gap, somewhat more cautiously than their leader had. The hulking Ivanov snarled a gap-toothed grin.

With shaking fingers, a purple ensign switched his mic to the open channel.

"Lieutenant Mull has the flag," he said, pointing to the twitching leader.

"So what?" Ivanov asked. He leaned back against the railing, and then lashed out with his foot: it connected squarely with the ensign's torso, launching him against the other railing and over it.

* * *

At the centre of the mock battlefield, Prince Du Mon could see a plume of dust as a vehicle approached. Reluctantly, the prince turned his back on the console projections that hovered above him, displaying the engagements taking place on the battlefield.

As the mysterious smoke approached, Du Mon could make out the details of a military APC. The armoured vehicle pulled up alongside him. The prince rested his hand gently on the officer's pistol at his belt. He masked the movement by placing his bad hand on his belt as well.

The passenger door opened, and his brother stepped out. The thick curls of Ju Tin's beard hugged his face closely, and pressed up against his helmet's visor.

"Good morning, Captain." Ju Tin's voice was slow and thoughtful, the opposite of how he'd been behaving around their nieces and nephews.

The back of the truck opened, and several soldiers emerged, carrying chairs and a giant parasol. "High Command has sent me to oversee today's military exercise. I trust I'm not too late to witness the spectacle?"

Du Mon caught himself grinding his teeth together, and relaxed his jaw. He held a palm open between them.

"Of course, who am I to refuse the crowned prince?"

Ju Tin pointed to a spot below the projections, and the soldiers set up the chairs. Another stood behind them, holding the parasol aloft. Ju Tin gave his brother a firm slap on the shoulder.

"Please, recline with me."

Du Mon hesitated, and then obliged. "I wasn't expecting a visit."

"High Command is curious about these activities you've been running for your soldiers," Ju Tin explained. "You've got quite a few admirers in the middle ranks, and so I've been sent to witness things for myself."

As he was talking, the watery eyes behind the tiny spectacles flicked quickly between the different projections that hovered from the console. Ju Tin was paying particular interest in the aftermath between the red and purple team.

"Do you always permit your soldiers to play so roughly?" Ju Tin asked. "I can see the vital signs for two people have dipped into the danger zone."

Du Mon shrugged awkwardly in his combat suit. "I have a medical team on standby. There are tolerances in place."

Ju Tin made a 'come hither' gesture in the air. The participants' vital signs grew larger in the air before him. His eyes skimmed the data being transmitted from the combat suits.

"There's a high probability that this Lieutenant Mull has sustained a punctured lung. He's going into cardiac arrest from the electrocution."

Du Mon nodded. "We've modified the combat suits to administer heavy painkillers and adrenaline. They can even defibrillate automatically. See?"

On the projection, Lieutenant Mull's chest buckled in the air, as his heart was remotely restarted.

"How very novel," Ju Tin said. "We should implement that into all our combat suits. Although, the painkillers could certainly be abused. And, if the defibrillator was faulty, it might stop someone's heart instead of starting it."

Du Mon's eyebrow twitched from the comment. "Something's been bothering me since the festival."

"What's that?"

"You're wearing spectacles."

Ju Tin waved the console's readout away, and settled deeper into his chair. "A small niggle with my eyesight. I wanted it corrected."

"Ah," said the prince. "I thought they might have been for show."

"The spectacles bother you, do they?" Ju Tin asked.

"Why not have the issue corrected, quickly and cheaply?"

"So that's what's bothering you?" Ju Tin asked. He swivelled suddenly to face his younger brother. "The emperor does prefer *all* his citizens to serve with able bodies. Since you've made a comment about my ableness, I hope you won't mind, Your Grace, if I make a small observation about your own?"

The prince nodded through clenched teeth.

"I find it fascinating that my spectacles bother you so much. Perhaps it's because you have a similar quirk of your own? Hmm?"

On the projections in front of them, the green team was about to career head-first into Tam Sunter, and the blue team who was trailing him.

"Don't think of me as an opponent." Ju Tin sat forward. His eyes eagerly anticipating the inevitable skirmish. "Instead, think of me as your mentor."

Du Mon flinched. "I don't need a mentor."

"I can understand your misgivings. However, hand on heart, I don't practice any strange throat warbling like your old Consul Barclay. Nor will I force you into any crusty history lessons or genealogies."

"Mentor or not, you're my brother."

"Which may cause our relationship some tension, but it has nothing to do with learning. Not really. You see, I believe in students teaching themselves. From today's exercise, I can see that's something we have in common. Father might be worried about you, but I'm really here to help you hear the lessons that *you* are trying to teach yourself."

On the projections, Du Mon saw the green team readying themselves on the back of their flatbed.

"And what, exactly, do you think I'm trying to teach myself?" Du Mon asked.

Ju Tin gave a knowing wink. "I choose to wear spectacles under my pressure helmet, for the same reason you've let your arm rot."

The prince grew sullen. "I don't know why I did that."

Ju Tin gave a contented sigh. "Then that's the first lesson."

* * *

The green team's flatbed skimmed the incline of Mount Sharp. The black dunes stretched away like a frozen ocean to their left. Out in the distance, Harmony could see the place upon the flat expanse where the red and purple trucks had stopped.

A few snippets of screaming floated over the open comm channel. Harmony checked her wrist computer. Someone on the purple team was broadcasting. The initial excitement she had felt, boarding the truck with the other members of her team, had quickly turned to gut-churning dread.

"Don't think about it," Walsh said. Harmony realised he'd been studying her expression. His own face looked pale, but there was a protective concern in his eyes, instead of fear. "We can get to the jackalope, before they get to us."

Indeed, from a distance, it looked as though a creature was hopping across the dunes. As the creature approached them, it became clear that it was Tam Sunter's bike. The small vehicle crested each mound on twin treads, before shooting him into the air. He vanished again, down the slipface, before launching himself over the next one.

"I'd be getting motion sick," Snyder said.

Behind Tam, the blue truck barrelled across the flatter section of the dunes. The larger vehicle's immense wheels spat sand in every direction. Sunter was nimbler. He was choosing to weather the hillier regions of the Bagnold Dunes, in order to evade the clumsier vehicle.

"Put us on a collision course with Sunter," Sheree said. "Through the rougher terrain."

"It'll be rough," Snyder called back. "Hold on."

As they hit the first dune, a collective groan went out from the green team as the rear of the truck slammed into the slope. The groan was replaced by white-knuckled silence, as the truck's flatbed tipped over the crest.

* * *

Tam cautiously checked the blue truck over his shoulder. It was a hundred-metres behind. On top of the vehicle, he could see the combat-clad figures behind the driver, waving and pointing at him.

He gave a cheerful wave back. *Cresting each dune feels terrible, but so far the wargame hasn't been too bad.*

A chill crept up Tam's neck. After years spent behind the controls of fighters, Tam immediately trusted the instinct. He killed his throttle and swerved. The green truck erupted through the top of the dune he'd been aiming for, narrowly missing his tiny bike. He overcorrected as he tried to steer away from the deluge of sand and gravel. A rain of detritus peppered his helmet and bike, spilling into his intake vents.

Three figures leapt from the green flatbed, stun batons at the ready. Tam recognised the lead figure as Sheree Wagner.

Is it just me, or is she even more terrifying? Probably the armoured combat suit, and the stun baton that will make me lose control of my faculties.

Sheree wielded her weapon with practised ease: down and away from her body, to prevent herself from accidentally touching herself with the baton while she ran. Tam didn't know the green team's driver: but the man was currently outstripping Sheree, even though his prosthesis was struggling on the loose dune gravel. Ensign Walsh was moving wide, trying to flank him. That left Kim.

Sweet, delicate Kim, who doesn't belong in a wargame. It was clear that she was puffing, as she waded through the shifting ground towards him. Tam gunned the bike towards Kim. *The sensible option.*

Despite his own justifications, Tam felt bad. It was clear she was the weakest member of the group. Tam felt the engine with a gloved hand. There was a hiccup from the gravel, but it would run. As he kicked the accelerator, Tam felt the ground rumble.

The blue truck is close. A feint towards Sheree and the other marine, and then swing out past Ensign Kim.

He gunned it. The bike's treads churned as he charged Sheree. He could see the shadow of the truck behind him banking, positioning itself to cut him off on the right flank.

Tam leaned hard, kicking gravel into Sheree and her teammate, and then swinging around. He almost tipped off the bike, but pushed out a foot and kicked himself off towards Kim.

As he lined up his approach past her, Tam gave a little salute. *Cheeky.* He grinned. *It's a straight path: past the green flatbed, then hang a sharp left, so the blue team have to go around the other truck to try and follow me.*

What Tam hadn't expected, was for Harmony stick her stun baton into his treads.

He saw the motion in his peripheral. The prongs connected with the steel tread plates.

There was a flash of white-hot light across his bike, and Tam bit his tongue.

Ouch.

His muscles clamped as the electricity left the baton and arced across his body in waves of silver agony. His fingers clenched tightly around the bike's throttle, causing it to release a burst of speed. The baton bounced off the treads, and then must have connected with the metal chassis again, because a second shockwave went through his muscles.

I can taste metal. Is my tongue bleeding? Or is that what happens when you get electrocuted?

The second, involuntary squeeze his fingers on the throttle tipped the dune bike up on its back wheels. Tam managed to force his hands open and lean forward, but it was too late. The bike teetered for a moment, its nose sticking straight up into the air. Tam released the handles, hit the sand, and rolled. The bike missed him by a hair as it came crashing down.

Tam lay on his back, staring up at the bronze sky above. He remembered to start breathing again. In the confines of his helmet, Tam could only hear the rasp of his breath. A bead of salty sweat rolled off the tip of his nose, and onto his top lip. Tam clenched and unclenched his hands experimentally. They felt numb. Above him, Tam saw the heavens move. It was a sudden, jerking motion. Tam closed his eyes and tried to breath normally. There was a strange sensation in his legs, like someone was trying to pull them off.

He tilted his chin down, and opened his eyes to look at his feet. Kim was there, tugging at his feet. Her feet duck into the sand, kicking as she tried to move him.

"You're too heavy!" she yelled over the open channel.

"I'm not that heavy," Tam said. He tasted a thick liquid pooling in his mouth and forced himself to swallow it. "There's no way those batons are safe."

The sun vanished, and Sheree Wagner was standing over him, red-faced. She dug her helmet into his armpit, and suddenly he was over her shoulder.

Tam bounced and kicked as she carried him towards the truck. "This is definitely worse."

"Quit squirming," Sheree huffed. "We get you onto the flatbed, and then no more electrocution."

"That's sweet of you."

Tam looked across the horizon from his perch atop Sheree's broad shoulders as she carried him. Flecks of blood and spittle were now sprayed across the inside of his helmet's visor. He started devising a way to install one of the stun batons in Du Mon's chair, so the prince would sit on it.

* * *

Harmony could barely keep up. Her breathing was coming in shallow bursts. Her knees felt like rusted machinery, barely capable of lifting her calves.

Sheree was struggling uphill under the burden of another person. The course, black sand of the Bagnold Dunes was tricky terrain, but had turned even more devilish under Tam's extra weight.

Harmony's feet sank up to her ankles with each step as she hauled herself towards the green flatbed. *Don't let them down,* Harmony thought. *Keep going. Keep going!*

The flatbed was twenty metres away. Snyder reached it first, and scrambled up into the driver's seat.

"Come on Kim!" Sheree yelled.

Don't let Sheree down.

Ten metres. Then five metres. *We've got it*, she realised.

Vishan Walsh stood atop their flatbed. His face was downturned in alarm, however, as his hands stretched wide to accept Tam.

"Move it! They're here!" he screamed across the channel.

"You try...carrying him," Sheree puffed. She grabbed Tam's hips and hoisted him, bottom-first, up to Walsh.

The blue flatbed cut the horizon behind Walsh as he reached out to take the jackalope. The blue team had mounted the dune at a dangerous angle. Their truck teetered sideways, threatening to tip over and crush the green truck beneath it.

Sheree's arms shook under Tam's weight as she tried to lift his body over her head. Snyder strapped himself into the seat, ready to go.

"Take him!" she yelled.

"Higher!" Walsh screamed.

The blue team's leader took a running leap.

In mid-flight, her foot planted itself atop green truck's safety railing. She pushed off from it, and went clear over Walsh, like he was a hurdle. Her other leg was outstretched, knee locked in a perfect martial art form. Her body was a triangle wedge, concentrated at the sole of her boot, which collided just below the base of Sheree's neck.

Sheree felt a bone in her chest resist, and then snap. She buckled at the knees and went down, spilling Tam Sunter backwards.

All three of them tumbled down the dune's slope. Sheree dropped to the ground, clutching her side. Tam rolled over two or three times, before coming to a stop, face-up. Across the open channel, a peal of gentle laughter echoed as the blue leader climbed to her feet.

Harmony could see Sheree was sucking greedily from the trauma whistle built into the side of her helmet.

"Well done for getting him this far," the blue leader exclaimed. "But I think you're forgetting who the real hunter is." She bent down beside Lieutenant Commander Sunter. "How have you been, Tam?"

Tam Sunter sat up from where Sheree had dropped him. "I've been better. Nice stick."

The blue team's leader sighed. She twirled the staff around her forearm and then held it at-the-ready, behind her neck. "I wouldn't expect *you* to understand or respect something so *sturdy* and *familiar*."

"Are we still talking about the stick, Jenna?" Tam asked.

Jenna Whit smiled through her visor, but there was no mirth in it. "I guess we aren't, old friend."

Walsh's ears tingled. The exchange below was flashy, drawn-out.

A diversion.

He spun around and saw the two blue team members who'd boarded the green truck while the rest of the team was distracted.

"Go," Walsh yelled into the green channel. He rapped Snyder atop his helmet to make sure the message got through. The green truck shot away, dropping one of the blue team members who'd tried to scale the side of it. One of the blue team members managed to keep his grip on the safety rail, his baton held confidently in his other hand, as the ground rushed past them below.

Vishan Walsh stared down the assailant. This blue soldier was fit, muscular and stood a full two heads taller than Walsh: that much was clear even through the suits. The blue soldier was also cocky. He swung a leg over the safety railing.

Walsh made sure his feet were secured by the magnetic flooring. He held a hand over his mouth to obscure his lips. "Brake!" he shouted and tapped his stun baton against the metal safety railing.

The blue soldier froze as his muscles contracted. He flew forward, smacking his head against the floor of the flatbed. He landed next to Walsh, who drove the stun baton into the other man's back.

"Just to be safe," Walsh explained with an apologetic smile. He bent down and checked that condensation was still pooling on the visor of the soldier's helmet, just below his nose. "Still breathing. Apologies for the headache you'll get later."

Vishan Walsh dragged the unconscious soldier from the flatbed and deposited him on the bank of a black dune.

12

Ju Tin had taken control of the console system again to check on the blue teammate who'd been zapped by Walsh.

"The medical team's been dispatched automatically," Du Mon said.

The crowned prince squinted through his spectacles at the displays. "Who was the greatest influence on your career, do you think?"

The younger prince raised an eyebrow. "Probably Captain Dav'i. Are you familiar with him?"

"Of course."

Du Mon sniffed dismissively. "His career has since morphed with legend. He wasn't exactly the hands-on type of mentor. Barclay was also there, which complicated things."

"Why did he have an impact on you?"

Du Mon realised the other man's magnified eyes were surveying him. The pupils were unflinching, as keen as a battlecruiser's sensor array.

"There were lots of things. He connected with everyone around him, even if it was in a small way. The spacers respected him. The officers did as well. That's rare in a captain."

"It is, indeed."

Ju Tin didn't offer a follow-up, so Du Mon filled the silence that followed.

"He died before he could teach me much. Most of it is what I learned from observing him. The way he walked, or the way he inspected every detail of his ship, for example."

"I can see why you train your soldiers in such a hands-on and free-flowing manner, then. I can understand why you are troubled by him dying." Ju Tin gave a single shake of his head, "However, you should be grateful."

"What?"

"There are far worse things a mentor can do, than simply die. It would have been far worse if you had surpassed him. He might have been proud of a student who outstripped him, but there would be no triumph for you. Instead, for you, it would have been a hollow moment: passing by him as you made it to Admiral, or as High Consul of Defence. You might one day send him off to die in battle, and then what would you feel?"

"At least I wouldn't feel...unworthy, like this. I could deal with regret."

"There's still a worse scenario." Ju Tin spoke evenly, and with a croak barely suppressed in his throat. "One day you might have seen Captain Dav'i betray his own principles. Perhaps he would have forgotten something that he had drilled into you. Then you'd be left with a mentor who could no longer instruct you, because each time he did, it would be accompanied by the resounding noise of doubt between your ears." Ju Tin cupped his hands to the glass of his helmet, mimicking an echo. "*Why am I learning this, if* you *don't use it?*"

Du Mon gave a thin smile. "I would've learned to deal with it."

"If you say so, little brother."

* * *

Sheree was sweating through the insulation in her combat suit. Her chest felt tight and painful, despite the chemicals she was huffing through her helmet's tube. Jenna Whit was arguing with Tam Sunter over the open channel.

Sheree kept her body still, and tried to turn her neck. The green truck was gone. A cloud of dust sat suspended in the air where it had been. Through the cloud, a blue soldier was being helped up by a teammate.

She caught the glint of Synder's green armour as he slowly approached Jenna from her left-hand side, flanking her.

Synder seems capable. Sheree pulled herself up to her knees and winced. *If I fight now, I might puncture a lung.* She saw Kyuri Kim, who was holding held her stun baton in front of herself, in both hands. *Not that I have much choice. It's three versus three.*

"I don't particularly want bloodshed," Jenna said. "We'll take Sunter to our truck, and the exercise is as good as over." A tall teammate joined her, stun baton drawn, facing down Gum Snyder who was circling. The tall one was handsome. His jaw was chiselled to a perfect square, and his cheekbones were strong and prominent. The other blue soldier was approaching, but stopped. His hand went up to his visor, blocking out the sun as he looked across the dunes.

"Someone's coming," he said.

Sheree struggled to her feet. As she rose, she saw the red flatbed. It was driving in a straight line towards them.

"They've spotted our truck," Jenna said, forgetting to switch to her own team's private channel. She sucked at her front teeth. "Just what we needed."

The ground rumbled, and the green flatbed loomed over them. Walsh waved from the platform.

The handsome soldier in blue clicked his tongue loudly. "The way I see it, there's no need for us to kill each other over the lieutenant commander right here and now. We've got a minute before the red team reaches us. I propose a temporary truce."

"I don't know about that," Sheree replied. "Temporary truces are easily broken."

"It's that, or we have a three-way scrap."

Sheree could faintly feel the pain in the centre of her ribcage where something had split. *I'll need to be carried out of here when this is all over.*

"Fine," she said at last. "You choose someone to guard the jackalope, and we'll do the same."

"I have a name," Tam Sunter said feebly.

Jenna nodded at the handsome fellow. "Tarigan, you guard the cargo."

Tarigan bent down to examine the jackalope. It was midday and the sun continued to beat down on them. Even in the heat haze, Tam could see that there was a gleam of malice in Tarigan's grey eyes.

"No running away now, little rabbit."

"I'll guard him as well," Kim offered.

Sheree felt a sinking sensation in her gut. Her command of the situation was being rapidly eroded. *It's poor strategy to leave Kim, our flag bearer, with a fighter like Tarigan.* Sheree realised Jenna was watching her. *I've already hesitated too long. I might as well tell them who has the flag at this rate.*

"You guard the rabbit, Kim. Once we stop the red team, we'll all fight over the jackalope, *fairly*." She made sure to emphasise the word.

Kim nodded, and Tarigan bowed low with a hand on his heart.

* * *

Ivanov sat on the front of the red truck, leaning forward. Particles of sand in the air sang as they pinged against his suit. He cackled, like a ghastly and possessed figurehead at the bow of an old water ship.

"I'm invincible!" he screamed into the open channel. He could see the green and blue figures scrambling to spread out. Ivanov lowered his voice to a breath. "Invincible," he cooed. "Indomitable."

"Criminally insane," Snyder added.

Sheree nodded. "Ugly too."

The truck swung wide, and Ivanov let himself be catapulted forward. He landed in a dead sprint towards Synder, who was on the fringe of the group.

"Come on!" Ivanov screamed. He slammed the handle of his baton against his helmet, causing it to ring. He struck himself in the head again as he barrelled forward.

Gum Snyder hesitated, and then widened his stance, baton ready as Ivanov charged.

Dodge the first strike, Snyder thought, *and you'll have the advantage.* He waited for the tell-tale flash of blue energy. *Dodge the first strike.*

Snyder's brain registered Ivanov's intention far too late. Something deep in the primal part of his brain had coaxed him to stay fixated on the weapon. If Snyder had been looking at Ivanov's eyes, however, he would have seen the blind violence directing the huge man.

Ivanov's arms went wide like he was going to embrace Snyder, then he dove low under the green soldier's guard. The steel bars of Ivanov's fingers close around Snyder's forearm, holding his weapon away.

Snyder was thrown over Ivanov's shoulder like a sack of cement. The smaller man tumbled backwards, but his elbow was being firmly held against Ivanov's shoulder. Snyder felt his elbow bend backwards, and then his shoulder dislocated. He screamed as a wedge of pain trailed up his neck and lodged itself squarely in his brain.

Ivanov dumped Snyder's writhing body on the ground. He made sure that Sheree was looking, and then stepped on Snyder's broken elbow with his full body weight. The lean man's screams stopped abruptly as he blacked out.

Ivanov licked his lips. "Wagner. No surrendering today, I hope?"

"Giving up never stopped you in the ring before," Sheree replied calmly.

Ivanov shook his head and chuckled. "It's stupid try and talk your way out of a fight." He tapped a bicep that managed to bulge from his combat suit, despite the layers of insulation. "Did it hurt you, when you saw your soldier get hurt?"

"Stop it." Sheree hoped that the glare from the sun would hide the tears that pooled against her eyelids.

Ivanov squinted in the sunlight. "Does it eat away at you like poison? It should. You're like some pathetic surrogate mummy, sweeping in to protect the weak. Ystopher wasn't weak. Maybe that's why he died."

"Enough—" Sheree's words couldn't escape her throat properly. A sharp pain ached in the middle of her chest that the painkillers would never be able to stop. The other red team members had finally caught up. Sheree scanned their faces.

There's no disgust or pride when they look at Ivanov. Just fear.

Ivanov put his fists up. One of them still curled around the unused stun baton.

"If you keep this up, you'll get us all killed, Wagner. That's why you signed up, isn't it? To get others killed."

"So that's your game, is it?" Sheree asked. "Settling your personal grudges, in a training match? Fine. I'll take you on, Ivanov." She reversed her grip on the baton and raised her other fist defensively. She began a wide and careful circle around her opponent.

"Self-sacrifice again? How noble." Ivanov took a few practice swings as he followed her movement. "Come and rescue your teammate then, coward."

* * *

At the back of the group, Harmony ground her teeth together. She took a step forward towards Ivanov and

Sheree. Even from this distance, it was clear that Sheree was walking with a limp.

"I wouldn't recommend getting involved," Peace said. His firm hand touched her elbow as a warning. "You'll only get hurt."

Harmony looked back as Sheree ducked a calculated swing from Ivanov.

"She's all alone."

"I think she prefers it that way. If you run in now, you might make her lose focus."

Harmony nodded and brushed the hand away. "Don't get too familiar now."

Peace laughed and shook his head lightly. His grey eyes were turned upwards in delight.

13

In the sun's heat, Jenna's sweat ran in rivulets down her spine, pooling at her belt. She could feel the heat of her breath, bouncing off her helmet's visor, and wafting back across her eyes and nose.

The red team was making headway, forcing the green and blue teams backwards as everyone zapped, kicked, punched and shoulder-tackled. She swung her staff overhead, and the soldier in front of her let it glance off his forearm. The red team severely outmatched them in muscle, agility, stamina.

I hate this sort of fighting.

Jenna took two steps backwards, feet planted parallel, as her opponent swung wildly with his baton. It was just her imagination, but she could feel the tendrils of electricity dancing across her ribcage each time she leaned away from the weapon, narrowly avoiding it. To her right, Sheree lashed out with an uppercut that connected with Ivanov's chin.

There's no dignity. No repartee. Her team's driver went down with a firm blow to the chest. That assailant turned towards her as well. *Two of them.*

She held her staff at the very edge, and swung it like a baseball bat. The sickled tip slammed into the shinbone armour of the red soldier on her right. Then she pulled, and his feet went out from under him.

The air crackled with light as a barb of electricity connected with her neck from behind.

How uncouth. A muscle spasm jerked her head away from the business end of the stun baton. Bright white spots filled her vision, like a poorly-recorded drama circuit. Jenna threw up in her mouth, and then swallowed. She lashed out without looking, and felt her staff connect with someone's gut. There was no skill left in this fight. Just pure luck and reflex.

This is just like Du Mon, Jenna thought. *Pushing us towards the impossible, and seeing how we fare.* There was a small comfort there, however. If the odds were stacked against her, it meant the prince believed she could succeed against them.

Vishan Walsh, one of the green officers, tried to rush one of her assailants. He went down, and received a kick to the helmet that cracked his visor. Sheree was driven backwards by two good punches in her gut from Ivanov. The gargantuan man was frothing at the mouth, eyes rolling lazily in their sockets.

Sheree collapsed onto her rump. She backpedalled across the sand, away from Ivanov. Kicking up a spray of grit as she desperately tried to put distance between the giant and herself.

So this is it then? Jenna thrust her staff in the direction of one red officer, and then made a feint at the other. Her arms were weak. The tip of her weapon dipped lower and lower as she struggled to keep the weapon moving, and hold her assailants at bay. One of the red officers circled right, and the other left.

Sheree crawled along the ground, gasping for air.

Jenna took two clumsy jabs at the soldier on her left, and barely managed to turn and threaten the other one with a backwards swing before he got too close. Both of the marines in red were grinning.

They can taste victory.

A flash of blue glinted off the sand behind one of them. Jenna Whit swung her staff in an exhaustive and intimidating arc. She was going to drop the weapon any minute now. The sunlight caught the glint of blue again. Tarigan was running towards them. Hunched over, arms behind his back, minimising his profile.

He abandoned Tam, and is coming to fight. She cast a quick glance in the direction where Tam Sunter was being held. The pilot was now sitting up, looking around, while Kyuri Kim's attention was directed towards the fight between Sheree and Ivanov.

Kim has the green flag. She's holding back.

Jenna watched the lips of the soldier in red on her left. He was shouting a warning to the other one. Jenna swung her staff at the one who was shouting a warning. It was reckless, leaving her back exposed to the other attacker.

She forced her exhausted body to cooperate, and centred her feet, one in front of the other. Her head swam. Two steps forward, jab. The soldier deflected the blow with the armour on his forearm and lunged forward. Two steps back, jab.

This is more like it. They were partners in the dance of death now, and Jenna knew all the steps. She chanced a glance over her shoulder, half-expecting to see the business-end of an enemy's stun baton. The other soldier, however, was dodging blows from Tarigan.

Jenna's opponent was trying to stay at the outer-limits of her reach. Each time she swung, his hand lashed out towards her staff, trying to grab the weapon so he could get inside her guard, without getting skewered by the sickle at its tip.

She felt a firm hand on her right shoulder, and flinched. The person was already brushing past her, however.

Tarigan.

Behind her, Jenna guessed she would see the writhing body of a red marine. She didn't look. Instead, Jenna focused all her energy in keeping the point of her staff upright, and trained on the red marine in front of her. The marine tried to circle away from Tarigan, so Jenna aimed her staff further left.

Two steps forward, jab.

The red marine spun away from the tip of the weapon, and suddenly his ribcage was acquainted with Tarigan's stun baton.

"Just Ivanov left," Jenna said, panting.

The giant was screaming over the open channel at Sheree. Jenna had tuned his frequency out to focus. As Jenna staggered towards them, she saw Sheree cowering from Ivanov, scuffling backwards through the dirt. Ivanov was completely fixated on Sheree. His baton jabbed at the air between them, not as a weapon, but in order to emphasise some choice words as he screamed. It was unintelligible, a cacophony of sounds that rolled into each other.

It was clear, however, that Sheree understood the gist of it.

Her cheeks were stained with tears. Scrambling there in the dust, she looked like a child being berated by their parent. She winced as Ivanov's volume grew.

He's winding himself up into a frenzy. He's going to kill her, right here.

Jenna looked over her shoulder at Tarigan "Get the flag from Kim," she said. "If Kim doesn't have it, zap her, and carry Tam onto our truck."

Tarigan hesitated. "I can take Ivanov."

"That's an order."

Tarigan's grey eyes squinted at her, assessing something. Then he turned, and ran in the direction of the trucks.

Jenna used her staff as a crutch as she approached Ivanov. He'd activated his baton. The electricity licked along the twin prongs, highlighting the contours of Sheree's face. When she was within a staff's reach of Ivanov, Jenna stopped.

I'm too exhausted to fight.

Strapped around Ivanov's waist was a thin belt with a small pouch attached at the small of his back. Jenna smiled. She reached out with the sickle on her staff, and neatly cut through the nylon that held the pouch in place.

Ivanov stood up as he felt something tugging on his waist. He spun around, baton swinging wildly. Jenna was well out of reach, however. Her sickle came down onto the pouch at Ivanov's feet. *Just like the dexterity games father made me play.*

Then, she pulled the staff towards her. Ivanov looked down. His brain ticked over stupidly, trying to understand why Jenna wasn't attacking him. Jenna opened the pouch just as Ivanov's body lurched into action. She pulled out the scrap of red fabric and held it aloft. A buzzer went off, and a computer's voice announced that the red team was eliminated.

Ivanov took a deep breath, and then hit her with his baton.

* * *

Jenna blinked, and then parried another bone-jarring blow with her staff. Her opponent was short and muscular. In order to emphasise his physical superiority, or perhaps merely to aggravate her, the tiny man took delicate sips of mushroom soup from a tiny bowl, as his own staff slammed into hers with a flurry of quick downward chops.

There were only two respectable occupations for a member of Jenna Whit's clan. You could be a pilot, just like her grandfather, or you became a terraformer like her great-grandfather. Jenna's father was the pride of the family: serving ten years in space and making his way to Commander, before returning to Mars to continue the terraforming tradition.

Her father took another dainty sip of his soup while he withstood her attempts to strike him. He didn't spill a single drop, despite the fact that Jenna's arms felt as though he was placing the entirety of his tectonic strength behind each swing.

The bone-like shafts of their staffs sang like wooden percussion as they circled each other. They were sparring in a natural clearing between the thousands of mushroom and fungi that grew like a forest from the sand around them.

Jenna glanced to her left. Her cousins were sitting on a fungi stem that had been felled that morning. Along the stem, which was just as wide as any tree trunk, other species of fungi clung to it, forming enormous, brown plates.

Through the windows of their clan omnibus, Jenna could see the untamed surface of Mars. Thousands of mushrooms and fungi grew like a forest from the red dust. She came to, just in time to duck underneath her father's strike.

Her cousins were throwing sticks of loyalty credits into a pile. Jenna doubted anyone would be foolish enough to bet for her as the victor. *Perhaps the wager is how many strikes it will take father to defeat me.*

"Focus Jenna," her father said. Jenna snapped back into focus again, and had barely enough time to leap backwards and avoid his staff taking her head off.

"That could've been nasty," her father said, and took another sip of his soup.

"I thought we agreed: no killing strikes," Jenna huffed.

"No harm done, my dear."

"My arms are nearly giving out," Jenna said, and lunged forward with an exhaustive thrust. Her father merely stepped aside lightly, and toasted his bowl of soup against the point of her staff with a faint *chink* sound.

Jenna saw the red in her father's eyes. The slight tensing of the mouth, and sudden concentration at the point where he intended to hit her. An image reached her in that split second: her stomach sliced open on the hook at the edge of his staff, and her entrails spilled across the floor of the omnibus. *He's aiming to kill me.*

Her father swung his polearm overhead in an arc of death, sweeping the sickle-like blade at its edge towards her middle, but Jenna had already side-stepped the swing. She planted her foot on her father's own, wedging him in place.

The sharpened point of her own weapon jabbing downwards to skewer her father in the knee.

Her father pivoted sharply on the foot that Jenna had trapped. Her blade caught in his baggy trousers, just above where they were bound to his pressurised stockings, but it missed the flesh.

Jenna stumbled, bringing her staff up quickly to protect her neck and head, but the ex-Commander had already reversed his grip on his weapon, and now had the staff tucked underneath his armpit. He reached out and caught Jenna by the scruff of her jacket before she ran into the blade. His sickle was centimetres from her temple.

"For future encounters," her father said, licking his moustache, "You should refrain from telling your enemy about when you are nearing the end of your strength."

"And I recommend you refrain from illegal moves," Jenna snapped back.

"In true battle, there is no such thing as an illegal move. A fact that I feel is often forgotten at the military academy." He gestured in the general direction of the sleeping quarters.

Jenna blew a stray lock of hair out of her eyes, and followed her father. "That sort of attitude is why you've never won a clan tournament. You would easily clean out every prize in hand-to-hand combat, if you obeyed the by-laws of terraforming combat."

Her father had a sudden, distant gleam in his eyes. "I just had an idea for a new tournament competition."

"Oh?"

"It would involve all the contestants entering a sparring ring simultaneously, and the last person standing would take the trophy. Perhaps we could blindfold everyone as well?"

"That seems like a difficult competition to adjudicate."

Her father's characteristic laugh boomed across the omnibus. It was the sort of laugh that drew the attention of everyone in his vicinity. "Precisely my point, Jenna! Why bother with all these trivial rules, when two champions can simply test their raw cunning against the other. Unadulterated. Unblemished by constraint. Let the clans witness the pure savagery of Mars: the spilled blood of their family."

They climbed the internal steps of the Whit clan's omnibus: a towering fortress on treads that housed their entire bloodline, and enabled them to scout the limits of their terraforming farms, without being too far from home.

At the top of the stairs, they sat down on facing benches, just outside the sleeping quarters. Jenna kissed her staff, and placed it in its bracket. She then began to unstrap the practice padding from her stiff body. Her father simply sat down on a stool and raised his arms. One of Jenna's little cousins approached cautiously, and began removing her father's armour.

Jenna ran a hand across her forehead, collecting the moisture there. She wiped her hand on her pants. "Every injury on the tournament ground, means one less terraformer or pilot for the emperor."

Her father sniffed disdainfully. "I would much prefer a child who was calloused and injured from real combat, instead of a child who can only fight when there's arbitrary rules. As it stands, His Majesty's navy is slowly being filled with soft, egg-like officers, who've been handed their leadership because they can use a pen better than a gun."

"Is that why you cheat in the tournaments, father?"

He raised an eyebrow at her, and Jenna studied the wrinkles that time had etched into her father's features. Deep furrows along the forehead. Beneath his oxygen scrubber, trenches ran along the corners of his mouth.

"I think sacrificing a trophy is a fair trade, for reminding the clans that real savagery exists in war, and out here in the desert wastes. We've had too many years of relative peace."

"Hopefully, it remains that way. Thank you for indulging me, father."

"Nonsense," her father replied with a chuckle. "I rarely have the pleasure of beating my children."

14

Peace ran up the black slope of the dune. Harmony had a foot placed delicately on Tam's stomach, preventing him from moving as she watched the skirmish through her the monocular built into her combat suit.

"Anything interesting happening?" Tam asked. His arms were crossed behind his head as he looked up at the sky.

"Shh," Harmony hissed. "Lieutenant Whit is trying to steal the red team's flag." She suddenly clasped her hands together in delight. "She did it!"

"Please be advised," came the computer's voice. "The red team have been eliminated."

"Kim?" Peace said quietly. His thumb played with the button on his baton. "We're the last two teams left."

"Hang on," Harmony pushed the monocular away from her visor and bit her lip. "Ivanov just struck down Lieutenant Whit after he was eliminated."

"Kim." Peace chose his words carefully. No doubt the prince was recording their performance today. "We're the last two standing."

Harmony looked at the face of the stranger Tarigan, and tried to imagine her brother buried somewhere beneath it. "So, it comes down to us then?" she asked.

"I don't want to use force, so just hand over your team's flag."

"How terribly noble of you," Tam said, from the ground.

"Hush you."

Harmony's small forehead creased, and then relaxed. Her fingers travelled towards the pouch clasped across her middle, and then froze. "I don't have it," she said.

"Alright then." Peace depressed the button on his weapon. He felt the buzz as it ignited, and held the weapon down, away from her for the moment. "Let's do this fairly. Fight me."

Harmony shook her head once, bottom lip trembling. "I couldn't..."

"Hold up your baton." Peace paused, glancing at Harmony's empty hands, and then around them. "You've lost it."

"She lost it," Tam confirmed.

"Then why are you lying there like that?"

"You want me to run off and risk life and limb? I'm quite content lying here until I'm needed."

"Give it here." Peace jumped forward, and pinned Harmony's foot with his own.

"I don't have it!" she yelled. In the scuffle, she managed to step on his foot, pinning them together.

Peace's free hand dug into the pouch, where he found nothing.

"Huh. Sorry." Peace switched his stun rod off. "I guess Wagner has it then?"

Tam reached up into the air, his fist at waist height. Harmony took something from his hand, and Peace instinctively tried to jump away.

Except Harmony pinned my foot.

He stopped, and pulled his leg free, just as Harmony's stun baton kissed the gap between two plates of combat armour. The pain was a white ball of fury in the centre of his chest, causing him to inhale sharply as he fell.

When he landed, Peace's shoulder buried into the black sand below. He watched as Tam passed Harmony her flag back, and then accepted her offered hand. She pulled Tam up, and then took a step towards her brother.

She crouched down, and opened Peace's pouch.

"Got it!" Harmony stood, and waved the blue fabric aloft in the wind.

15

A small group gathered in the palace gardens for Admiral Heydari's funeral. The late Admiral's two sons stood at the front of the gathering. One wore the dress uniform of a Lieutenant, and the other wore civilian clothing. They stood beside their mother, a lady who was hunched over from old age.

The gardeners had replaced the festival's bright and garish bunting with simple grey silks. At the foot of the palace steps, a small child softly played the harp across his lap.

Ju Tin had parked himself beside the refreshments. He closely examined a small biscuit topped with algae crab meat, and a lentil sauce.

"Where have you been all my life?" he asked, and popped the morsel into his mouth. His tongue licked the salty tang from his lips, and then the crowned prince reached for another.

Du Mon swatted his hand away. "I think you've had enough."

"Don't listen to him," Ju Tin whispered to the food on his plate. He turned to his brother. "You can't stop true love. The theatre circuits will soon receive my screenplay. It will be titled: *Forbidden Hors D'oeuvres*, or *Love at a Funeral*."

Du Mon sighed. He placed his untouched plate down at the serving table.

"You're nervous about something?" Ju Tin asked.

"Several members of the purple team are out of action." Du Mon scratched at his bad arm. "The red team caused fairly heavy injuries against the other groups."

"Well, you chose the teams."

"It wasn't really the teams that were the problem."

A small bell chimed, and the small group of mourners began to slowly make their way to the rear of the palace grounds.

Ju Tin gave a long glance at the serving table, and then followed Du Mon. "The real issue is Ivanov. If you want my opinion—"

"I don't."

"—You should kick Ivanov off the team. He's unstable."

"My hands are tied at the moment I'm afraid. Besides, Ivanov will help create a vibrant team."

"He'll create a dead team, Du. It's like someone stuffed a gorilla into a combat suit and taught it how to hunt."

The two brothers fell into stride as they meandered between the carefully trimmed hedges and flowerbeds. Tiny bees floated across the gardens like motes of dust.

"The other issue is Tam," Du Mon said. He'd started gnawing his lip.

"I thought he performed very well during the war exercise."

"He helped Kim win the game. Held her flag and baton, just so she could win."

Ju Tin smiled. "There's no rules against it. If anything, it just shows what a convincing negotiator she is. It could have gone the other way if Sunter had decided to just zap her and run."

Du Mon waved a bee away from his face in annoyance. "I think it shows that Tam Sunter wants to protect Kim at all costs."

"Is that a problem? Would you rather have been out there yourself?"

"Hush."

Their father stood at the mouth of the family mausoleum, as a procession of soldiers carried eight small ceramic jars across the manicured palace lawns. The family mausoleum was a large stone dome, recessed into the ground. As the eight jars of ashes descended into the mausoleum, the Martian national anthem played from the palace's speakers in a minor key.

Along the ramparts of the palace, a line of journalists recorded the ceremony, or spoke quietly into microphones. The people who bore the ashes returned from inside the mausoleum, and the Emperor closed the mausoleum's gate. He bowed once, and then turned to face the gathered group, and distant journalists.

"Admiral Abdul Heydari was dear colleague, and a dearer friend. Here now lies the man who taught me what it meant to love one's planet. What it meant to offer your life to protect those back home. I know there is little comfort when someone so loved dies so suddenly."

The Emperor paused, and looked up at the Palace's domed ceiling.

"All Martian life is sacred, but Heydari's life was indispensable. I wish I'd had the chance to tell him that. If you are listening, Heydari, I hope you will find rest here in the royal family's mausoleum. It is a small gesture, but I hoped it would ease your passing."

"Lyn, you and your sons are always welcome at the palace."

Ju Tin felt a tug at his elbow. He tried to ignore it, but whoever it was grabbed hold of his arm more forcefully.

"What is it?" he whispered.

An enormous, sweaty man filled the corner of Ju Tin's vision. "My apologies, Your Grace."

"Can't this wait, Captain Soona?"

"I'm afraid it can't, sir." The captain leaned in closely. "I have sealed documents on my person."

Ju Tin sighed, and walked away from the gathering. "Make it quick, please."

Soona waved his credentials across Ju Tin's wrist computer. Ju Tin waited, as the information appeared on the inside of his glasses.

"Have you read it?" Soona asked. He saluted. "High Command has voted to promote you to sub-Admiral."

Ju Tin rocked backwards. "That's *quite* the promotion."

Soona's head wobbled. "Yes. Pardon me for interrupting the funeral, but it is a war time promotion. Unfortunately, there won't be much ceremony."

Ju Tin nodded. "Is there anything else?"

"The late Admiral left standing orders for you. They've been ratified by Acting-Admiral Kang."

"I'm reading them," Ju Tin said, his eyes flicking up and down, "but go on."

"You are to oversee the prototype vessel *Black Tortoise* during its maiden voyage, in order to advise Prince Du Mon and ensure that the vessel is not recklessly endangered during its first engagement."

Ju Tin's eyes widened. "This is quite the honour."

I didn't want to pursue the Black Tortoise *command after I realised Du Mon wanted it. This* is *an order, however. And, technically, he'll still be in charge of the day-to-day operations of the ship.*

"Acting-Admiral Kang is awaiting acknowledgement. We don't have long before the prototype is launched."

Ju Tin looked over at his brother, who was watching the funeral. *It will be good to look after him. This isn't a selfish thing to do.*

"I'll report to Acting-Admiral Kang this afternoon."

Captain Soona saluted.

16

The Emperor farewelled each of his sons with a firm hug. Around them, officers loaded personal equipment and belongings onto a convoy of platforms. These platforms dutifully floated towards the immense cargo bays that rested in the shadow of the space elevator, which gently flexed and swayed. The wind whipped and buffeted the people gathered on the ground, screeching between the towering rock buttes in the distance. The Emperor's cloak and robes whipped about him impressively, a storm of gold and red fabric.

Du Mon avoided the gaze of his father as he received the embrace, and quickly separated from it.

"Are you mad at me?" the Emperor asked. His voice carried through the rebreather and echoed into Du Mon's ear via a small clip fastened to the prince's cartilage.

"I wanted command of the *Black Tortoise*, alone."

Ju Tin wisely made himself scarce, walking ahead to the elevator.

"Be good to your brother," their father said. "I happen to believe it will be good for the two of you to spend some time together. You can learn a lot from each other."

"I think you mean *I* can learn a lot from *him*."

Du Mon readjusted the straps on his rebreather, and tried to push past his father. Instead, the Emperor linked his arm through Du Mon's firmly, and walked with him. Officers stopped to bow respectfully to them both as they ran about their business.

"Ju Tin isn't the expert at fighting the outsiders. You are. Relish in the opportunity of working together, instead of trying to childishly compete with him. One day when Ju Tin is Emperor, he'll rely on you."

When the young prince exhaled over the channel, it sounded like the roaring wind around them. "I don't understand why you need both of your sons shipped off-planet."

"Things aren't safe at home. The Admiral's death is troubling, for one."

"What did the coroner's report say?"

"Heart failure, but it's more the timing. The Admiral wanted your brother to go along, and now he's dead. It could be coincidence, but I think it might be safer for both of you to be in space for the time being."

"Do you suspect anyone?"

The Emperor slowed his gait as they arrived at the wash station: a small foyer lined with air pressure hoses, so personnel could remove the caustic red dust before they boarded the elevator. Through the clear strips of plastic that hung like prison bars over the doorway, High Consul Maevin was shouting instructions to a squad of nervous-looking administrators.

"I have a hunch. I've asked Mith to look into the matter, covertly."

The prince nodded. "Good choice. Mith is a powerhouse. Plus it'll give her something to do while Tam is away with me."

His father grinned. "I thought so as well."

"Could you give a similar role to Plessis? She's been a bit...neglected during the special project."

The Emperor gave his son a firm pat on the back and sent him towards the wash stations.

"I already thought of that. Don't worry, she'll be plenty occupied."

The wash station was a blast of cold, pressurised air. Du Mon sprayed his hair liberally, then his dress uniform. The fine red dust peeled away, revealing the white uniform underneath, like a wound turning to scar tissue. As the wash covered him, Du Mon watched the rivulets of dirt as they were blown down and away from him, falling through the latticed floor and out onto the surface of Mars once again.

He stepped through the clear plastic strips into the holding bay where Consul Maevin was waiting for him.

"My apologies, Your Grace."

Du Mon looked around for his brother. Then he stepped close to the old man. "Consul Maevin, a delight. And here I was, confident that the wash stations *deterred* rodents from scurrying aboard the space elevator."

The High Consul's smile faltered slightly. "I've disappointed you."

"You promised me command of the mission."

"To be fair, Your Highness, I promised you would be *Captain* of the ship. A difficult proposition for me." The old man leaned in closely. "The late Admiral dearly wanted it to be your brother taking sole command of the mission."

Du Mon sniffed the Consul's pungent, bitter cologne. He leaned away again. "I'm dissatisfied with your efforts. As a member of the royal family, when I approach the consulate and negotiate a deal, I expect excellent results."

"You're disappointed," the High Consul bowed low. "You must believe me when I say I went to great personal risk ensuring that you'd remain Captain of the vessel. I only managed to secure the deal the night the Admiral died."

"How convenient."

"Not at all. Now I have some *unwanted* attention, regardless of the fact that Captain Soona was able to corroborate my story."

"Captain Soona isn't considered an upstanding officer."

Maevin scratched his chin, where wires of thick, grey hair were beginning to sprout.

"No, I suppose not. Enjoy your...excursion, Prince Du Mon."

* * *

The heavens darkened as the space elevator rose rapidly up through the Martian-made atmosphere. As the stars began to speckle the horizon, and the land curved sharply away into a sphere below them, the orbital platform rose into view.

If the space elevator was a human arm, the platform at its crest resembled an outstretched hand with curled fingers. From the hub and spoke system that spun slowly, five immense spires curled up and away from Mars. One of the spires was empty, with no vessel docked. Three of the spires were being used as service scaffolding to refuel mining frigates.

It was the largest spire of the orbital platform that caught the prince's attention.

Resting against it, the *Black Tortoise* waited. Long tentacles drifted behind the body of the starship. Each tentacle was armoured and segmented, like the legs of a crab. Wicked hooks and spikes grew along the spine of the ship. Its hull resembled a tangled yarn of red chitin, sinew, and cartilage.

A collective gasp escaped the senior officers, as they hurtled towards it. The prince wiped a tear that pooled in his eye. He felt a pressure lift from his shoulders now that he was seeing it in person.

There was a glint of silver and gold out amongst the stars. Du Mon squinted, and saw his father's flagship *Plato* slowly spinning in a wide orbit, guarding the orbital station. With a start, he realised the senior officers watching him. He scanned their expectant faces. Many were familiar to him, such as Jenna Whit, Sheree Wagner, and Tam Sunter. The new officers to his unit like Vishan Walsh, Kyuri Kim, and Tarigan, represented an exciting pool of fresh talent.

Tam gave a little wave, and subtly mimed a mouth flapping with his hand.

"Oh." The prince dug his tablet from his satchel and gestured above it. His notes for a speech floated a few millimetres above the screen. "We've worked hard to make it to this day. The *Black Tortoise* is not just the starship that will carry us into space over the next few weeks. It is the vessel that will carry Martian society to new heights. Little boys and girls will be able to sleep at night, knowing that the

Tortoise sits in the skies, protecting them from any new alien threats. The Earthen military, as well as the Earth-Lunar Mining Guild, will soon think twice before provoking us."

He looked up from his notes. Some polite nods. A lot of smiles. From the corner of his eye, Du Mon glanced at Kyuri Kim. Her face was deadpan, staring at a point behind him.

You're blowing it.

"Sorry. I guess what I'm getting at, is that we're pioneers here. All of us. Let's work hard and make sure the *Black Tortoise* is ready for whatever we find out there."

Tam was ready with the applause, and he started it off strong.

An amber light lit the interior of the space elevator. They quickly grabbed railings and crash seats as the elevator slowed. Du Mon felt his stomach plummet. The *Black Tortoise* grew, stretching across the horizon of the windows.

Beside the window, Ju Tin stood. His arm was crooked so that he could lean his body casually against the support rail. As the gravity shifted, he leaned back into the embrace of zero-g like a seasoned spacer. His feet were planted confidently rooted in the platform's foot stirrups. Ju Tin's red robes, attached to his dress uniform at the shoulders like a curtain, billowed gently under their weightlessness.

With a flash of annoyance, Du Mon realised the entire crew had formed a semi-circle around the new sub-Admiral.

"How strange to think, our enemy has become our shield." Ju Tin's voice carried easily over the other conversations. He caught a glimpse of the officers around him, reflected in the transparent steel of the elevator's window. "Pardon me." Ju Tin turned. On his face he wore an expression of awe and humility. Du Mon's heart sank.

"My brother is absolutely right. A young Martian girl will look up at the stars, and she will see the flash of our nuclear engines. She will make a wish, and that will be our gift to her." He twisted his body slightly, to face everyone gathered. Beneath the part of his fringe, Du Mon saw the intricate tattoo that encircled Ju Tin's forehead, declaring him to be the next Emperor.

The elevator was silent.

"Engineers, teachers, medical workers, and service people. All of them deserve our protection. These past five years have been uneasy for every proud Martian who stands upon the sacred red soil. We are a young and hardy people. Yet our enemies close in around us on all sides. Earth is jealous of our success. Now a new enemy, the Outsiders, looms at the outer edges of our solar system, invisible to our sensors." Ju Tin's voice echoed across the walls. "So what will we do? We, who have been chosen to command the shield of our people? Will we squander this opportunity?"

Instinctively, every officer gave the zero-g salute: pointing their chins to the ceiling. "No, sir!"

"What will we do, then?"

"Fight!" Sheree shouted, spittle drifting from her lips.

"Fight says you, Wagner?" Ju Tin asked. Du Mon's flesh crawled with goose bumps as his brother's voice slipped into the drilling lilt of a veteran navy officer.

"Aye sir." Sheree's chin raised even further, threatening to break her neck.

"What says all you? Shall we fight?"

"Aye, sir!" the officers shouted in unison.

"Then you best be listening to your Captain, fine crew. And you best be saluting him when he speaks."

As one, the crew spun on stirrups, or pushed themselves about on handrails and cargo to face the younger prince. They also offered their necks to Du Mon.

"Apologies, sir!"

"At ease," Du Mon said. Inside, he felt anything but.

17

Du Mon stepped aboard the Black Tortoise. He touched the bulkhead, grown from the very chitin that had repelled Martian lasers and missiles five years prior. He breathed in the scent of carbon lungs scrubbing the air. The smell of welding, glue and new paint still lingered in the air.

The *Tortoise* smelled cleaner than a ship usually did, because the air scrubbers weren't yet clogged with human skin, and the odours of a hundred people living in an enclosed space. The interior of the ship was modern: sleek white bulkheads and cabinets, with handles, signs, and handrails accented in yellow. Relief washed over him in waves. The touch of the chitin, the smell of the paint, the very fact that he was aboard: it all nearly overwhelmed him.

After countless simulations, months of mental conditioning, years of drills and war games...I'm not going to mess this up.

Teams of spacers ferried cargo through the starship's central spine. Officers floated towards cabins to stow their personal effects, and then to inspect their stations for the voyage. The captain's cabin was located behind the bridge, which was where he intended to stop first.

"You've been over the ship's personnel manifest?" Ju Tin asked, pushing off from a handrail and gliding ahead of Du Mon.

Du Mon paused, as a crate filled with rations floated past. "I've memorised the names of the entire crew."

"Good work."

As they floated, the people they passed each tilted their heads in salute. Du Mon felt his neck beginning to grow sore from the near-constant motion. "My only concern is that the Ship's Master was vacant on the manifest."

Ju Tin's laugh boomed throughout the spine.

"Why are you laughing?"

"You've worked with the Ship's Master before. In fact, she's waiting for you on the bridge."

Du Mon spun the name over in his mind. "Who is it? Someone from the academy?"

A young man saluted them both as he floated towards the junior officer's mess. His eyes were wide when they landed on Ju Tin, however, and he made a hasty retreat out of the spine.

"Excuse me, little brother. I just saw an Ensign who owes me alcohol rations."

"You beat him at mah-jong?"

"That's right. Probably a year ago now."

Du Mon raised an eyebrow as high as it would go. "You're going to shake down my officer before we even leave port? That's not very becoming of the future Emperor."

Ju Tin grabbed a handrail and swung his momentum away from the spine of the ship, floating towards the junior officer's mess hall head-first. He was grinning with his teeth, like a carnivore spotting a dumb, fat herbivore.

"You don't understand Du, he's *terrible* at mah-jong. I'm not going to demand payment. I want to rope him into another game."

Ju Tin vanished down the service tunnel, and Du Mon continued on towards the bridge.

As was standard on all Martian vessels, the bridge was blocked off from the rest of the ship by reinforced blast doors, guided on explosive maglev rails, so that central command could continue to operate, even while the rest of the ship underwent sudden decompression.

These blast doors were complimented by a secondary, thinner set of chitin doors that telescoped open. As Du Mon approached, a hidden terminal scanned his face, and the chitin doors apertured out towards him. It was an uncanny feeling: floating towards the doors as they opened like a mouth to swallow him. The 'doors' sealed shut centimetres behind him, and he floated through a green-lit vestibule, to another set of identical doors, three metres away, which opened to allow him onto the bridge. He hadn't even needed to slow his approach.

Above his head, the usual diagnostic summaries and images from the viewfinders sat. That was where the similarities to a typical Martian bridge ended.

Du Mon gasped. The bridge was alien.

Traditionally, the captain's chair was sat high and at the rear of the bridge, flanked by the operations and comms chiefs. From there, the captain had a good view of the viewfinders, summaries, as well as all the bridge officers sitting in recessed bays below him.

The *Tortoise* flipped that design onto its head.

Here, the Captain's chair was positioned at the centre of the bridge, and sat atop a rotating dais between the operations and comms chairs. Du Mon's eyes were drawn to the bays for junior officers, however. Instead of being recessed into the floor, rows upon rows of terminals were suspended in the air, like seating at a stadium, nearly encircling the Captain's chair. Each seat for the junior officers was built into the wall. If all the officers had been sitting at their stations, it would have been like walking into a courtroom with a jury.

Engineers scurried about, performing the final systems checks. They climbed over the walls or hung upside down as they tested circuitry. Du Mon allowed his momentum to carry him clear across the bridge, towards the Captain's chair. As he approached, he saw that the ground of the bridge was now covered in a dizzying array of Outsider biotechnology. Fleshy nerves, housed and protected by steel cables, crisscrossed beneath the transparent steel floor. They meandered beneath the Captain's chair, until they connected to a central stem, which terminated in an enormous, purple organ beneath the floor. As Du Mon approached, the organ gently pulsated.

The dais that the Captain's chair rested upon, rotated. As it spun, Du Mon realised that the chief of operations' chair was different. It was still a modified crash chair, but made from a fleshy cushion of nervous tissue, pincushioned with cathodes.

His wife was sitting atop the operations chair.

"Plessis?"

Kaya Plessis grabbed his hand as he approached. She pulled him down to harness, and planted a firm, full kiss on his lips. "Welcome aboard, Captain."

"What are you doing here Plessis? My father said he'd..."

Plessis beamed at him with adolescent excitement. It suddenly dawned on the prince.

My own father snuck my wife aboard, and Ju Tin probably knew about it too. Perhaps he even helped orchestrate it.

"When did you come aboard?"

"I've been here for a week, Du. You were just too busy to notice I was missing."

"I was supposed to meet the Ship's Master."

Plessis was dressed in the white uniform of an officer. She gestured at her lapel. It was polished, showing the four pips of a Commander, surrounded by a box. The words *Black Tortoise* were emblazoned underneath the box.

"You're the Ship's Master?"

"That's right." She gestured to the chair. "I've received all the relevant training, so I can connect to the ship's central nervous system.

Du Mon nodded. He'd seen schematics of the nervous system, but seeing the brainstem up close was something else. "It's so, *alien*."

Kaya Plessis patted the side of her chair. The fleshy tissue puckered, and then relaxed, releasing her from its embrace.

"This chair will be used by the Senior Operations Officer once the ship has concluded its maiden voyage. For now, I'll be holding it as the Ship's Master." As she spoke, Plessis' voice grew serious. She was switching to her professional self: the version of herself that Du Mon had fallen in love with.

"As Ship's Master, I'll provide the same services as the Senior Operations Officer, but with the added responsibility of tutoring you on the ship's capabilities and weaknesses."

Du Mon found himself smiling. "It sounds like I'll be in very capable hands."

Kaya launched herself towards the ceiling of the bridge, and Du Mon followed. They caught themselves on the handrails that jutted out from the roof. From up here, the prince could see the entire layout of the ship's central nervous system, exactly as it was portrayed in the diagrams.

"The most obvious difference is that this ship is partially alive," Plessis explained. "Or as close to Outsider life as we can synthesise."

She pointed to the corner of the bridge. Under the transparent floor, Du Mon could see the faint ripples of liquid.

"The central nervous system is suspended in a non-conductive biological plasma, similar to our blood. We've cultivated a type of artificial blood cell that can store carbon, and deliver it to the tissue. We deliver a bath of the cells from that pump." Plessis turned, and gestured to the other side of the transparent steel floor. "And we retrieve the spent cells by suctioning plasma from there."

Du Mon scratched his chin. "How do these artificial cells obtain new carbon?"

"The ship shares the same oxygen system as we do. We pump carbon dioxide from our breath into a set of mucus membranes, and then the depleted cells are forced through tiny, artificial capillaries, where they collect the gas by flowing across the membranes. The cells absorb the CO_2, and then they're pumped back into this chamber again. The breathing organ, which we had to grow ourselves, is located just underneath the brainstem there. It strips out the carbon, and delivers oxygen back to us."

"There's a hidden organ underneath the brain stem?"

Plessis nodded, eyes shining. "The Elder Seeker is in many ways the exact opposite of our own biology. We take in carbon, oxygen, and water, and then we produce carbon dioxide and heat. The Elder Seeker takes in carbon dioxide, as well as the heat from our engines, and produces oxygen. It's a similar equation, just flipped around."

"Wait, so this is our air scrubber? Are we breathing this system's oxygen right now? I didn't see that on the schematics."

"That's because it's classified. Now that you've got command, I'm allowed to share with you the specialist systems we've built. The air tastes good, doesn't it?"

Du Mon watched the soft beating of the organ. A cool breeze, delivered through vents in the roof, washed across his face. The air smelled clean, certainly, but there was something else. It like was the breath of a mother. A homey, lived-in smell, as opposed to a mechanical or chemical one.

"That's incredible."

"It's relatively simple too. Plants do it all the time. What was more difficult for the xenobiologists and engineers, was designing an organ that could do the same thing that a forest can do. I'll show you the diagram later, but the breathing organ looks like a radiator: a delicate weave of cell structures, paper-thin, that are folded over and over like linen, so that they fit into the smallest space possible. The organ is still ten metres tall."

"What happens if the system fails?"

Plessis laughed. "Why so morbid, Captain?"

"It could fail."

"Yes, it could." Her face became serious again. "Just like the chlorine scrubber in your helmet could fail, or the algae farms that service the palace dome and its surroundings could fail." She shrugged. "There are emergency systems installed. If we take damage to the central nervous system there's a minute chance that this system could arbitrarily fail. We are always moments away from death. That's true for all warships."

The relief Du Mon had felt upon boarding the *Tortoise* was slowly being eaten away. The familiar embrace of consciousness was returning. "Your command chair, it integrates with the heart-brain?"

"Yes, just like the Outsiders. The Senior Ops officer can send some simple commands to the brainstem that will give us an advantage in battle. We humans can't generate the same bioelectrical signals that the Outsiders do, so we've rigged up cathodes into the nervous tissue. As long as someone is sitting in the Ops chair, we can trick the brain stem into thinking it's receiving a genuine instruction from the Outsiders."

"This is all slightly fantastic, Plessis. You do realise that don't you? A ship that can sense what is happening."

"She can think too," Kaya added, pushing away from the ceiling, towards the bridge doors. "Not very well, mind you. Had to clone and grow the heart-brain from tissue samples, you know, and what a mess that was. Cloned brains never really have the same capabilities as natural ones. We still have a capital-grade quantum computer installed behind the bridge. It's something, though."

Du Mon swam through zero-g after her. "It's incredible, Plessis."

"Wait until you see the tentacles. We can get the ship to practically eat an Earthen frigate, like a great squid latching onto a pirate ship. Did you ever see images of those things in History class? They looked awesome."

"Plessis, wait."

Du Mon caught up to her, just as the bridge's first door opened to accept them. He caught the edge of the doorway and grabbed hold of her, slowing their momentum to a standstill. They floated in the vestibule between doors. Plessis crossed her arms lightly, and allowed herself to slowly spin upside down in the small space.

"What's wrong, Captain?"

"I just wanted to apologise, Plessis. I've been overworked. I guess...I thought everyone else was slacking off in comparison. Seeing all this, though. You've obviously been working hard, but you managed to somehow still have time for me."

A single teardrop left the corner of Kaya's eye. It drifted through the air for a moment before she reached out and caught it with the skin on the back of her hand.

"You never even made an effort."

"I didn't, and I'm sorry. To be honest, I was a bit shocked when I saw you aboard."

"No kidding. You looked like someone had stolen your pickled Outsider head."

"Don't even joke about that," Du Mon said with a smile. "I really like that head."

"So how do you want to play this, husband? All professional and no fun like when we met? Like an old married couple bickering and stuttering apologies? Or somewhere in-between?

"The last one, I think."

"Good choice. For our next stop on the ship's tour, I should show you our bedroom."

Du Mon floated after his wife, as she expertly glided towards the Captain's quarters, located a short distance from the bridge.

"We're going to be okay," Du Mon said. "It's all coming together."

With her usual intuition, Kaya Plessis saw the look on her husband's face, and understood what he wanted to say. "That's right. There's no way the resistance can get to you here."

18

Harmony Xu sat exactly five metres from Du Mon as the *Black Tortoise* separated from its docking clamps. The Martian national anthem blared from the speakers as the bridge sang proudly, chests puffed, and chins pointed.

She seethed as the anthem concluded. *All these people, willing to spill their blood for him.*

As Du Mon commanded the helmsman to direct their course for the asteroid belt, the prince wore a particularly punchable expression on his face. His smile was pulled as thin as a piece of string, and his eyelids were hooded with self-satisfaction.

"Crew, brace for standard Martian gravity. Helm, begin four revolutions a minute."

The *Black Tortoise* began to rotate, and Harmony felt herself settling deeper into her chair.

Her console lit up with green acknowledgements from both the standard network system onboard, as well as the quantum computer, both of which were routed through traditional silicon and graphene to her screen.

Harmony pinched her thumb and forefingers together on both hands, and the quantum computer began running its potential impact simulations, and then feeding those calculations to the silicon system so that they could be interpreted.

As the gravity increased, Harmony was finally able to unstrap her feet and sit properly in her terminal's saddle.

"Ensign Kim," Prince Du Mon said from Captain's chair. "Run continual impact simulations along our trajectory. Feel free to factor in micro-debris as well. We might as well put the computer through its paces."

Harmony entertained the thought of replying with a snarky answer. *Of course I'm running simulations.* When she responded, however, Harmony kept her face deadpan and professional. "Running simulations now, Captain."

"You're doing great," Du Mon said with a smile. "Eventually, you'll learn to anticipate what the Captain needs before he even asks for it."

Harmony imagined delivering a fly kick directly into the prince's smug face. *Sorry Captain,* she'd say. *That was an impact the computer didn't see coming.*

Senior Ensign Walsh leaned across from his station. "You got singled out there, didn't you?"

"Very observant, Vishan."

"I saw we're on the graveyard shift together. You have a favourite game?"

"I like crew bingo."

"Classic. I've been working on one where you bring up the ship's schematics, and pretend you're stuck on a derelict and have to escape."

Her eyes lit up. "Oh, let's try that one then!"

Vishan gave her a playful nudge, and then returned to his instruments. She allowed herself a small smile and a sideways glance. *Thank Deimos for Vishan! I probably would've gone crazy sitting on bridge duty in silence.*

The hairs on the nape of her neck bristled.

Someone is watching me.

When Harmony looked up, Du Mon quickly glanced away to speak with the comms officer.

What a creep.

She turned back to her terminal, and flicked through the simulation results it was running. The fact that Harmony had chosen to specialise in network systems at the academy had surprised her instructors, as well as herself.

Are you certain? Her cryptology teacher had pressed. *You're far too good at specialised programming. You'd get an excellent job planetside. You could work your way into a habitat dome easily.*

It was partially a practical decision. If the resistance needed her on a starship, having systems knowledge would be a more employable skill. There was more to it than that, though. There was something about systems that spoke deeply to her.

It's nice to find out why things break. There's a reason for why computers or pipes stop working. Maybe if I could learn about backflows, overloading, and stress points, I could somehow understand myself better. Five years ago, I was set to take Du Mon away from Mars. I could have served my purpose to the resistance, without killing the man I loved.

The butterflies she'd felt for him, once upon a time, had now turned to bile in her gut. It was nauseating sitting so close to the man who'd handed her over for treason.

Harmony made the gesture for 'bathroom' above her console. The terminal retracted slightly, allowing her to swing one leg away from her saddle, and onto the wall railings. Harmony descended the steps, and nodded at the Captain as she left. Du Mon nodded an acknowledgement, and returned to talking with his wife Plessis.

Poor woman.

The bridge doors swallowed Harmony, and then spat her out on the other side. She took a moment to gaze up at the ship's central artery as people milled about. Only a few days ago, officers and cargo had floated between the hub-and-spoke beams that held the ship's internal structure together.

Out of curiosity, she cracked open a hatch beside the bridge doors, labelled *ventilation maintenance*. Inside there was a web of pulsating veins. A pressure gauge peeked from underneath a strand of flesh. Harmony closed the hatch again with a wet cough.

A group of engineers were laughing as they patrolled along the 'ceiling', stuck fast by the force of the ship's rotation. *Like spiders.* Two spacers were hauling crates of rations along the left of the ship's internal cylinder, appearing to Harmony as though they were walking along the wall. One of them disappeared down a hatch, climbing down a ladder into the kitchen.

She made her way towards the marine barracks, located between the docking clamps and starfighter launch bays. Harmony calculated her path, relative to where she was standing. From the perspective of anyone standing at the bridge door, Kyuri Kim took a casual stroll up along the interior walls of the *Black Tortoise*, up to the ceiling, before gripping a service ladder and 'falling' upwards feet first. Harmony's vision swam slightly as her weight increased, but she landed firmly on the outer ring of the ship's hull. She held herself against the ladder for a second, catching her breath.

Don't ascend or descend too quickly. Got it.

The marines were in good spirits. The main lighting had been switched off, with only a single halogen rod illuminating a fighting mat in the centre of the common area. Ivanov had a burly arm around the neck of Lieutenant Shiwa, and was trying to trip him back over his outstretched leg.

Harmony scanned the faces in the darkness. From across the makeshift ring, Sheree Wagner gave her a small wave.

"Nice hair," Harmony said, searching the crowd for Peace.

"You like it?" Sheree asked, running a hand through her close-cropped hair, which was now dyed a neon green. "I wanted to commemorate our little team. Ivanov doesn't approve of the colour either, so that's a win in my book."

Harmony smiled up at the larger woman. "You've got some history, judging by what he said out on the dunes."

Sheree scratched a spot underneath her nose and then inspected her finger. "I was his superior officer in the *6th* Division. That was before I was demoted. It's a long story."

Ivanov successfully tripped up Lieutenant Shiwa, slamming the man's shoulders into the practice mat with a soft crunch. He shouted a victory cry that could have been heard over in engineering.

"Ivanov has something to prove." Sheree crossed her arms, and rested her head against the cool bulkhead. Her face vanished into the shadows of the chamber, until just the whites of her eyes glistened from the darkness. "It's probably my fault, though."

Harmony kept the corner of her eye on the burly Ivanov as he challenged the next marine to the mat. "Why would it be your fault, Sheree?"

"When you have your own command, everything is your fault. That's the rough part of leadership."

"Would you want your old position back?"

"I used to. At one point it wound me up so much I stopped sleeping and eating."

"You were ashamed?"

Sheree leaned forward. The faint light caught the soft scar flesh that criss-crossed her skull, and trailed down between her eyes. "I was ashamed."

Harmony gently touched her own scars, a V-shape beneath her neck, where the beauty clinic had finished attaching her face transplant. Her other vitals had been altered too. Her irises had been dyed a chestnut brown. Her fingerprints had been melted off, and then new ones had been etched into the flesh with lasers. For three years, nano-machines had tweaked her DNA away from the markers of Harmony Xu, and then dissolved in her blood, leaving her as Kyuri Kim instead.

Someone had even hacked into the Martian citizen database, and created a background for the newly-created Kyuri Kim, complete with medical record, a fake employment history, and an invitation to join the Military Academy. All told, the package should have cost Harmony all the loyalty she was capable of earning in her lifetime. Peace had somehow found the money though, through his "contact" in the resistance.

Sheree mistook Harmony's silence as a discomfort. "My scars are pretty hideous."

"I wasn't thinking that. I really wasn't. Why were you demoted? Were you on a mission that went sour?"

"We were lasermen for the mining frigate called *Rand*."

Harmony inhaled sharply, and felt her skin beginning to pucker. "You were at the Kuiper Incident?"

There was a flash of pearl from the shadows, and Sheree leaned forward. Her smile was weak. "I was responsible for that disaster. That's what the Captain's report said, at least."

"Every officer at the academy studies the Kuiper Incident now. It's a touchstone conflict."

"How comforting."

Harmony backpedalled. "My teacher was very even-handed. You weren't ever mentioned."

Sheree began to nod, but she gave up before letting her head fall. Her shoulders sagged instead.

"That's probably because I'm still serving. Once I retire from the navy, the details will be declassified, and then children will be cautioned about the infamous Sheree Wagner: shame of the Martian navy."

"Don't say that."

"That's what they call me, Kim. A sanitised version, anyway. You should hear what Lieutenant Shiwa, *Lord of the Service Medals* calls me when he's had a few drinks. If you were a marine, you'd have to do the same to fit in."

"You were outgunned."

Sheree pursed her lips. "Did you know the name of the incident is misleading?"

Harmony shook her head.

"The long-distance probes had brought back a solid-methane asteroid from the Kuiper belt." Sheree made a ball with her fist, and then sent a little finger-ship towards it. "We rendezvoused with the stupid rock just past Jupiter. There was no warning. One moment we were playing cards in the break room, the next an enemy missile had ignited the asteroid's solid methane surface, and vapourised most of our spacers. It nearly cracked the *Rand*'s portside."

Harmony shook her head. "In our class we studied how the comms officer wasn't being vigilant enough. I've seen the sections of *Rand's* logs that are available to cadets, and there wasn't any indication of the Eco-Terrorists approaching. They killed their engines from eight thousand kilometres away, and coasted in cold. You can't blame yourself for your superior officer's mistakes."

"I don't," Sheree replied coldly. "The bridge crew were lazy, but they were eventually court-martialled for that. I was left in command of a few marines aboard a mining frigate, pinned by missile impact against the flammable asteroid we were mining. The twin bay next to mine was struck, and I saw my marines sucked into the vacuum. They were shredded by debris. Their suits were venting air in all directions, like balloons released too soon."

Harmony reached out and grabbed Sheree's calloused hand in her own. "That must have been frightening, thinking it was the end."

"You know, I don't think I've ever been so frightened." Sheree laughed. She wiped her eyes. "I left my post, and I shouldn't have."

"Why?"

"I assumed the bridge was dead. The ship was struggling to pressurise, and we hadn't heard any orders or requests from the Captain after twenty minutes of combat."

"So you left your station and went to the bridge?"

Sheree gave a wry smile. "I don't know what I thought I'd be able to do."

"You wanted to save your soldiers. It's admirable, Wagner. All Martian life is sacred."

Sheree sniffed. "You know, when I arrived at the bridge, I found the Captain drunk at the helm. He'd plugged his alcohol rations into the water intake on his spacesuit. Figured we were all doomed to die. I negotiated the surrender of the frigate while missile after missile ablated our starboard armour. Ivanov's cousin was manning the laser turret I'd abandoned, while I was begging for my life on the intercom. They took out his station as well, the last line of defence. Then the missiles stopped, and I watched the enemy's lasers boil and pop the bodies of my marines as they floated through space."

"That's—"

"—and I've looked over the logs myself. I appreciate that you did a little study on it, Kyuri. You weren't there. I broke the chain of command when the enemy only had a few dozen warheads left. If I'd helped blow the missiles up, we might have been left with some functioning defences. If I'd stayed at my post, or even been counting the missile impacts, we could've parted ways, shaking our fists, and then waited for rescue. Instead, we were picked up by the *Montessori*, and I was court-martialled."

"What happened to the Captain?"

"He was also demoted, but he resented me for playing the hero while he sat waiting to die. So, at my court-martial, he used his final defence to testify about how I had ultimately left his ship defenceless and at the mercy of the Eco-Terrorists. Jeopardised all our lives. I don't blame myself for breaking rank. I blame myself for thinking I was somehow protecting everyone by running off. I was just—"

Sheree broke off in a choking sound.

Harmony wrapped her arm around Sheree's middle awkwardly. They watched Ivanov as he brought another opponent to the ground. He gestured at Snyder, daring him into the ring. Gum Snyder shook his head. His arm was fastened into an exo-sling to protect the healing bone.

Ivanov spotted Peace in the audience and waved him into the ring. "Come on Tarigan! Let's see your stuff."

"I think I understand," Harmony said.

"No. I'm sorry, but you don't."

"Hear me out." Harmony took a deep breath. "A long time ago, I risked my life aboard a battleship. I broke the rules to protect someone I cared about. I was so stiffened with fear that I made a stupid mistake. When people found out about what I'd tried to do, I nearly ended up in court."

Sheree blew a low whistle. "By Deimos' bulge… I guess that is pretty similar. Wait, a battleship? What were you doing on a battleship before joining the military?"

Ivanov threw Peace onto the mat, hard. The younger man jumped up again, laughing despite the bone-crunching impact. He ran at the goliath of a marine, and collected a fist in his gut for the trouble.

From the edge of the wrestling mat, Snyder booed Ivanov. Peace kept on grinning.

He clambered to his feet and tried to climb atop the other man's shoulders to reach his neck. Ivanov spun around, swinging loose punches into Peace's kidneys as he tried to dislodge the lean man. The whole time, Peace cackled like an infant.

Harmony smiled as innocently as she could. "I'll tell you all about it one day. Just believe me: I understand. I don't want to leave you like this, but I need to speak to Lieutenant Junior Tarigan about something."

Sheree Wagner wiped her nose on her forearm. She watched Peace, as Ivanov finally bucked the smaller man off his shoulders. "Him? Bit of a strange one."

Harmony patted Sheree on the shoulder, and made her way deeper into the barracks. Peace landed on his back, and saw Harmony waiting at the edge of the crowd. Peace stood, brushed himself off, and bowed respectfully. All while grinning ear-to-ear.

Ivanov didn't return the bow. His face was red, and he was panting.

"Why are you smiling? You lost."

Peace limped his way through the gathered onlookers. "Yes, Ivanov. You certainly beat me in a fair fight."

The marines murmured to themselves. Ivanov wandered away from the mat, grumbling.

"You shouldn't play with him like that," Harmony said, under her breath.

Peace slicked his hair back from the handsome face he'd chosen for Mav Tarigan.

"He's such a delightful man to terrorise. So much strength, and very little of it is up here." Peace tapped his temple.

Harmony nodded. They both stood looking at each other. Peace's smile was growing broader by the second.

"He hurt you pretty badly, didn't he?"

"I'm in so much pain, you wouldn't believe it. Thank goodness that my face doesn't twitch anymore."

"Just be careful. You might accidentally let your eyeball slip a few centimetres in the heat of battle."

Mav Tarigan's face became serious. Peace wanted to talk business.

"I've read over the new instructions from the resistance cell above us. You're not going to like them."

Harmony rubbed her eyes, which now felt a little too small inside her face. "I'll still do it, even if I don't like it. If I had any qualms about this sort of work, I would've just gone and started an apprenticeship with our mother instead."

Peace grinned. "That's the stuff. We've been told to commandeer the ship before we arrive at the Lunar Shipyards."

For a moment, Harmony felt the ship's spin. "Are you serious?"

"Shh. Yes."

"You and me? Ivanov almost killed you with his bare hands."

"You're still going on about that? We'll have some help. I've been told there are other operatives aboard."

"And you don't know who they are?"

"Not yet. There are further instructions, time-coded for once we're outside the range of a simple rescue from Mars. The resistance doesn't ever reveal its hand too early."

"I thought we were just going to cripple the ship. You know, prevent it from being used against our people?"

"Looks like they have bigger plans."

"So what are we supposed to do until then?"

"We're going to work out the weak points here. Places where we can apply pressure, and force the giant to fall."

"You're still thinking about Ivanov beating you."

Peace broke out in a loud, raucous laugh that turned the heads of the other marines.

"You should lie down."

Peace rubbed his kidneys. "In addition to my psychological warfare, I probably should have tried a bit more actual warfare."

"I'm going back now. The bridge is going to think I have a UTI if my bathroom break goes on for much longer."

Peace nodded, began a slow and deliberate hobble towards his bunk at the rear of the marine's mess. "On your way back, could you do me a favour, and fetch the ship's surgeon?"

19

The Lunar Shipyards loomed, filling the view screens on Tam's fighter. As he continued a wide orbit, Tam settled back into his crash chair and checked his controls. If he got sucked too far into the moon's gravitational well, he'd be forced to burn his emergency fuel just to finish the slingshot manoeuvre. It might leave him drifting out in space.

Then they'd have to send out a rescue party, just like when you had to go find your brother adrift near Jupiter. Tam rolled his shoulders back, one after the other, and tried to loosen the tension that was eating at him.

"Instruments are detecting new mass signatures near the surface of the Lunar Shipyards."

"Yes, I saw that." He hadn't, actually. Tam waved a hand across the controls, and his heads-up display shifted to detect mass as well as heat. He quickly skimmed the information that trickled down the side of his viewport. Jenna had found their target quickly.

A green triangle that represented Jenna flew resolutely to the starboard of his fighter, occasionally bobbing to avoid micro debris hurtling towards them. He studied the area inside the triangle, and could just spot the twinkle of Jenna's thrusters, almost too distant and too fast to see.

In the weeks since the *Black Tortoise* had launched, he'd tried and failed to speak to Jenna. Tam checked the distance between himself and the green triangle that represented Jenna. The kilometres between them were slowly ticking up. Jenna was accelerating.

Even when separated by the vacuum of space, she's avoiding me.

"I didn't realise it was a race," Tam said lightly. "If I'd known ahead of time, I would've put more power to the engines."

The kilometres between their fighters slowed, and then remained constant.

"I'm not racing you." Jenna's voice betrayed less emotion than the ship's computer.

"But you want to beat me?"

The radio was silent.

Tam tried to keep his emotions even, but a chill entered his tone, despite his best efforts. "Are we going to talk through whatever is bothering you? Or are you just going to ignore me for the entire mission?"

Jenna sighed, and it sounded like the Martian wind howling over a habitat dome.

"Luna is approaching."

Tam fired his reverse thrusters, slowing his descent as a dazzling orb raced to meet him. The computer helpfully threw a telescopic feed of Luna onto his viewfinders. Earth's moon looked like it was poisoned. Clouds of yellow sulphur drifted across its surface, pockmarked by the black rings of factories. Silicate lava bubbled across its surface in circular vats.

"Are you picking that up?" Jenna asked. "Luna's spin has shifted. It's no longer tidally locked to face the Earth."

The moon spun almost imperceptibly on its axis as they approached.

"Something big has impacted it."

"Or changed its internal mass."

Silently, Tam and Jenna both armed their missiles, and began keying targeting data into the computer.

"Where is the *Black Tortoise*?" Tam asked.

In response, a small icon appeared at the top of his viewfinder, with the simplified telemetry data glowing beneath it. The *Black Tortoise* was only beginning its slingshot manoeuvre now.

"Enemy activity," Jenna called.

A tremor shook the surface of Luna before a cloud of dust and rock erupted from its surface. The plume of cloud was jettisoned into space, like a short tail sprouting from the moon.

Tam waited.

From the hole grew a churning mouth, grinding rock to dust. As it emerged further, its shape became clearer: the mouth of a blind worm, eating its way through the very crust of the moon.

"*Tortoise* this is flight lead," Tam called. "Be advised, we will be engaging the enemy shortly. Check your approach vector, we have identified an Elder Seeker emerging from the Lunar Shipyards."

He goosed the throttle of his fighter forward, increasing speed. Jenna fell in behind as his flight wing.

"Nothing fancy Whit," Tam instructed. "We're doing the classic spine approach."

Jenna made a clicked her microphone in acknowledgement.

As the Elder Seeker slipped into the emptiness of space, it began to billow and buck like a paper dragon, generating momentum through a means that still baffled Martian scientists. His fighter rocked slightly, and Tam reached over to switch on the automated debris lasers. They'd eat away at his fuel cells, but it was better than being skewered on a pebble, or some other innocuous object that was orbiting the moon faster than he could anticipate.

As the Elder Seeker approached, he pulled the flight stick back, zipping up and over its head as the churning jaws spun through the vacuum where he'd been seconds before. He killed his momentum, travelling along the length of the Elder Seeker as it soared through space towards the *Black Tortoise*.

Once again, Tam felt his stomach churn at the immense size of the creature. This one was even larger than the creature that had attacked the Ceres mining facility five years ago. It was at least 45 kilometres long, with layers upon layers of red chitin along its head and back, protecting the creature better than any blast steel ever could. Tam found what he was looking for as he slipped along the underside of the creature. An Outsider village.

One of the strangest features of the Elder Seeker creature, was that its flesh was home to a tribe-like race who carved their dwellings into its very carapace. Tam kicked his fighter into a roll, and kept the corner of his eye trained on Jenna's signature, to make sure she was following. She was, until suddenly Jenna cut the roll short, and dove away from the underside of the worm.

"What—" He didn't have time to complete the reprimand, however. From the same corner of his eye, where he'd been watching Jenna complete her roll, Tam spotted the impact collision a fraction of a second before his ears registered the electronic scream that told him he was about to become pulp on the worm's underside.

It was experience that helped him avoid the second, smaller Elder Seeker as it swam beneath the first, guarding the larger one's weak underbelly.

"It's got a kid?" Tam shouted. He wanted to follow it up with a pithy joke, but the jaws of the smaller Elder Seeker clamped shut, wrenching free the rear fuselage of his fighter, and grinding it into a fine grit before Tam had a chance to get his bearings.

"You're hit," Jenna called out. Her voice sounded calm, as though she was pointing out a distant constellation.

Tam twitched instinctively, and narrowly avoided a flick of the larger Elder Seeker's tail. His stick wasn't responding properly. He pulled on the stick, hard. With a portion of his rear fuselage missing, however, Tam's fighter was beginning a slow spiral that would end with him crashing into the Elder Seeker's underbelly.

"Take the lead," Tam shouted, and tried to lock onto the creature's underbelly with his missiles.

"Aye sir."

Tam gave up on a proper missile lock, and squeezed the trigger on his flight stick. The first missile fired hot from his fighter: all exhaust engines igniting from within his fighter's missile tubes. Tam winced, hoping the other missiles wouldn't detonate prematurely, as he held the trigger. Missile after missile erupted from the recessed tubes at the side of his fighter, kicked out sideways while ignited, before being released against the underside of the creature.

Once the missiles were within range of striking, they'd drop the main rocket stage, and instead deliver a payload of mining droids, which would begin drilling their way down into the central nervous system of the Elder Seeker.

With the missiles away, Tam let go of his steering stick, and his fighter collided with the underbelly of the larger Elder Seeker.

A cloud of shrapnel erupted from the nose of his fighter as he collided with the red chitin of the creature. The impact easily tore through the metre of transparent steel that stood between him and the void of space. Tam let out a small yelp, before the darkness enveloped him.

Tam was dead. His body floated in the darkness for a time as he struggled to comprehend what had just happened. Tam looked down, and the controls of the starfighter slowly appeared through a dark fog. He slapped at the controls of his starfighter in frustration, sending the steering stick careening from side to side. He watched the grip bounce twice, before reaching out and grabbing it again.

"Tech?" he called, peering out from underneath his simulator goggles.

The technician was on the other side of the engineering bay, hunched over and making quick welds to the steel chassis of a half-assembled drone.

"What is it now?"

Tam pointed at his *Mk-III* flight stick that was, in reality, a prop attached to the floor by strong magnets. "Any chance you have a *Mk-I* flight stick tucked away back there?"

The technician tapped his temple, and his face shield turned transparent. He was red-faced and covered in a film of sweat as he surveyed the mountains of cargo and equipment that hadn't been unpacked yet.

"You want me to find an ancient flight stick, amongst all this?"

"That's a pretty generous offer. Yes please."

"After I nearly killed myself pulling that sim gear from a box strapped on the third pylon, you want me to scurry up again and find a flight stick that's a slightly different shape, so that you can immerse yourself in your little game better?"

Tam dug his toe into the floor of the engineering bay. He wrapped his arms around himself like a damsel on the theatre circuit. "You're not going to make me beg, are you dear? You know..." the pilot dropped his voice into a sultry baritone. "I could just...order you to do it. That would make it okay then, wouldn't it? That way, we won't be so ashamed of our forbidden love."

The technician threw his welding gear to the floor and waved over a spacer who was biting her lip in an effort to hold in her laughter.

"Come here, I need a hand. I placed the Lieutenant Commander's things in a crate labelled *clown equipment*."

Tam gave a wink to the spacer before he realised Jenna Whit was watching him from beneath her own sim goggles. Three metres separated them. Before they'd begun the simulation, she'd pulled her crash chair as far away as the cables between them would stretch.

Tam expected her to begin her usual gloating, but Jenna sat studying her own control stick instead. "I've always felt sorry for Renn," she said.

"Who?"

"That technician. He always ends up being assigned to you."

Tam pulled his head sharply to the right, cracking it. "Don't tell anyone, but it's because I always request him."

"You're kidding."

"Not at all. It's how I entertain myself between flight missions." Tam waggled his eyebrows at Jenna, but the distance between them was no longer just physical. "You're upset."

"It's a pretty cruel thing to do. I heard Renn asking the spacers for a good luck charm. He thinks he's cursed because you've been paired with him on four separate assignments." Jenna picked up the foil ration of juice she'd left beside her crash chair, dropped her sim goggles onto her chair, and made good speed towards the exit.

"Hold it there, sprout." Tam vaulted over his own crash chair, and felt something pull sharply inside his thigh. *Noted, don't do that again.* He regained his composure, and followed Jenna out through the automatic doors and to the left. The hallway curled slightly as he chased after her.

"Hold it," Tam grabbed her elbow. "Care to explain what happened back there?"

Jenna pulled herself free, and blew a strand of hair from her face. "You died, Ace."

"You changed the simulator, without warning me."

She stepped to the side, allowing an engineer to skirt past. "I was growing bored with it."

Tam rubbed his eyes with the heels of his palms. "You were bored of killing a living alien ship?" He wiped his hands down his face, letting the skin sag. "I'm up for a challenge just as much as the next pilot Jenna, but you just programmed a suicide run. We're barely able to halt one Elder Seeker, let alone two."

Jenna shrugged. "I'm not the one who collided with an object in space. Are you sure you're not just mad because you made a rookie mistake?"

"Is that what this is about? Proving that you're more talented than me?" Tam shook his head. He addressed the empty hallway loudly. "I have an announcement! Jenna is a better pilot than me! While I was caring for my wife and child, she was running the simulator. I'm a failure!"

She rolled her eyes. "Now you're just being childish."

"*I'm* being childish? Jenna, you've been avoiding me. You run away from every conversation I've started. You only want to be in the same room if your job requires it. What's gotten into you? We were best friends..." Tam cut himself off. He'd nearly said, *before Mith.*

"This has nothing to do with avoiding you." Jenna pulled her hair from its clasp, and refastened it again. "We have nothing in common anymore. I used to marvel at the way you handled your *Invigilator* through space. Your brother was the only one who could beat you on the simulator."

A wound in Tam's heart tore slightly. It was the wound he often forgot about, until someone mentioned his brother.

Jenna saw him pause, and so she pressed on. "You were this ball of character, even after your brother died. I can't remember how many nights I spent listening to you. You'd have the entire flight crew howling in laughter into the early hours. All the pilots wanted to be you, myself included."

Tam nodded, and pursed his lips thoughtfully. "You don't feel that way anymore."

"I don't know how I feel."

A spacer, who was pushing a cart of wires and sensor arrays, coughed politely. Jenna and Tam parted for a moment to let him past. They stood silently. Jenna sipped on her juice ration, squeezing the packet between her thumb and forefinger. Tam remembered when his brother had died, it was Jenna who had chased him through a hallway. Back then, she'd refused to give up on him.

This version of Jenna gave up on me a long time ago.

Jenna sighed and crossed her arms. "That way you talk, where you make everything a joke? I don't find it charming anymore. It just bothers me. I feel like you're more interested in bouncing a baby on your lap, than flying a fighter."

"Don't bring my kid into this, Jenna. That's low."

"I know, I just..." She ran her hands through her hair violently, pulling out the clip and raking her scalp in frustration. Jenna gave a throaty scream, before she sagged against the wall. "Forget it. I can't be bothered trying to explain it to you."

Tam nodded absently. An ensign poked her head into the hallway from a service ladder above, checking on the source of the screaming. She saw Jenna, hair tousled, and Tam facing her across the hallway.

"Everything okay down there, ma'am?"

Jenna pushed herself away from the wall and began scaling the ladder up into the main artery of the ship. "Everything is just fine."

Tam stood in the hallway for a long time after Jenna had left. He ran the conversation over in his mind, trying to piece together what Jenna was struggling to say.

She wants things to be like they were back then. Is it just the years between then and now? Have we changed so much that our friendship can't be salvaged? Maybe she's just upset because she's better than me on the simulator now. I could always put in a few extra practice rounds. Tam brightened when he saw Renn the technician leaving the engineering bay.

"How'd you go?"

"Found the *Mk-I* stick."

"I know you could do it, tech. That's why every night, before bed, I prostrate myself before a map of the Martian sky and pray to Rigel, my lucky star."

The technician rolled his eyes. "That's ridiculous—hang on, what do you ask it to do?"

"I whisper to Rigel, and beg it to let me always have you as my technician."

Renn muttered to himself as he brushed past. "Now I have to invent a missile that can extinguish a supergiant star."

The other technicians and spacers wore huge grins as Tam wandered back towards his simulation chair.

What's Jenna talking about? I've still got the gift for comedy. They're still jazzed about my earlier comment.

The crew's smiles remained fixed. Every head rotating smoothly, following him. Someone broke out into laughter. The technician beside them gave a sharp elbow to the ribs.

"Shh, not yet."

Tam's smile faltered. "Hey, are you going to share the big joke with me or not?"

He stopped when he saw his crash chair. Renn had miraculously found a *Mk-I* control stick. Unfortunately, he'd chosen to weld it to the middle of the crash chair, right where Tam was supposed to sit.

20

Harmony kicked the yellow ball with her inside left foot, and it curved along the sloped walls, up towards the goalposts that had been screwed into the roof above. Walsh was ready. He hung from the ceiling by his feet, and his head whipped around, following the ball's trajectory. With a small squat, he lowered his shin along the far end of the goal posts, and the ball ricocheted. It spun, landing on the right-hand sloping wall.

The gymnasium was located at the bow of the *Black Tortoise*, which meant it was perfect for three-dimension futsal. Sheree and Jenna both chased after the dead ball, running up the walls like two martial-arts masters on the theatre circuits. Jenna, from Walsh's team, was there first.

"Too slow!" Jenna shouted. She kicked the ball further ahead of her, and it arced across the domed roof, spiralling over Harmony's head, and approaching the goal posts from behind.

"I'm still healing from a broken rib," Sheree complained.

Harmony judged the ball as it skipped along the polished gymnasium walls towards her. Her head was aching with the mental strain of judging where the ball would end up. Harmony leaned out wide, stretching her hands towards the incoming ball. She felt her fingertips brush with the ball, but it wasn't enough. It bounced off her hands, and threw the goal posts. There was a moment's pause, and the goal posts lit up yellow. A buzzer sounded, announcing the goal.

"Switch," Sheree called out breathlessly. She trundled down the walls towards Harmony, who dashed out, trying to reach the ball. Unfortunately, Vishan Walsh was a natural in zero-g. He ran in the opposite direction as Harmony, and managed to reach the ball on the circular gymnasium's walls before Harmony did.

"Try to keep up Kim," Walsh yelled. He checked her approach, hooked his foot under the ball, and launched it overhead.

"I'm fit enough to keep up with you," Harmony yelled back. From her perspective, the ball sailed overhead and didn't come back down. It bounced once on the surface above them, then hung in the air, perfectly suspended in the middle of the room.

"Again, Walsh?" Jenna called.

He fell to his knees, panting, and examined the yellow ball as it slowly spun above them. "Huh. I thought I'd judged it right that time."

"I'll fetch the stick," Harmony said. She ran over to the concave doorway and stomped on the switch twice. It opened, and she stepped out into the main artery of the ship. She paused at the lockers outside, and wiped her face with a towel.

The last few weeks she'd settled into a rhythm aboard the *Black Tortoise*. Round after round of flight tests, simulations, computations. Then down-time. *The down time makes the long shifts worth it. Almost like I belong here with Sheree and the others.*

With a hiss, the gym door opened again, and Jenna stepped outside, followed by Walsh and Sheree.

"Walsh," Sheree said. "I swear by Deimos, if I hear you mention the difficulties, you're having with aligning the laser turrets one more time..."

"But we've never faced this problem with our older, symmetrical models of battleship."

"I was just about to get the stick," Harmony said, draping her towel around her neck.

Sheree reached into the common lockers and pulled out a foil ration of water. She took a greedy slurp, and smacked her lips. "Leave it there for a minute, we all needed a break."

"I'm going cross-eyed," Jenna complained.

"It's good to see you getting along," Harmony said. "I was worried you might start a brawl when you realised you were bunking together."

Sheree took another sip from her foil packet. "As long as Jenna doesn't break any more ribs, I don't mind bunking."

"Seems a bit unfair that a pilot needs to bunk with the marines," Walsh chimed in. "On other battleships you usually have your own mess."

Jenna shrugged, and pulled a stool out from the bulkhead so she could pull off her shoes. "Space is at more of premium on the *Black Tortoise*. We've got a *lot* of mass stored in the ship's armour. It'll be worth it when we see a fire fight, but it means we're all packed in here together."

"So no more special treatment for pilots anymore?" Sheree asked. She patted Jenna on the back.

Jenna made a face of disgust. "Unless you're Sunter."

"Well," Sheree scratched a spot underneath her nose. "He is a Commander. Makes sense he'd have his own room."

Harmony felt a chill go down her spine. The others threw smart salutes, and Harmony spun around to also salute.

Too close.

"At ease," Du Mon said. He sheepishly handed the long rod of aluminium to Sheree. "I was watching you all playing through the gym's camera, and figured you might need this."

"Thank you, sir," Sheree replied. "But you needn't have gone to the trouble for us."

"Nonsense," Du Mon's smile wrinkled his nose. "It never hurts a captain to help out the crew once in a while."

"Yessir," Jenna said. She cast a sideways glance at Sheree. "Will that be all, sir?"

"Actually, I was just hoping to have a quick talk with Ensign Kim here."

"Of course, sir." At this distance, Harmony could smell the prince's cologne. *He hasn't changed it after all these years.* "How can I assist?"

"This way, if you don't mind?" the prince gestured away from the others, back towards the bridge. Harmony looked at the others over her shoulder reluctantly as she left.

Huh? Walsh mouthed.

Harmony winced, and then turned a radiant smile towards Du Mon. "Is she a good ship Captain?"

"Very good," the prince replied. "Kim, I just wanted to speak to you briefly about the...*attention* you're receiving aboard this vessel."

"Oh. What attention would that be, Your Grace?"

The crossed through the ship's main artery, as the shifts changed. Bleary-eyed officers left their sleeping quarters. They passed laughing spacers on their leisure shift, and exhausted technicians with blotchy, tanned skin from welding.

Du Mon chewed his lip, choosing his words. "Well, from Ensign Walsh for one."

She chuckled. "He's a good friend."

"Perhaps. Mav Tarigan seems awfully familiar with you as well. Did you meet before this mission?"

Harmony's blood ran cold. "No, we just seem to get along."

The prince wobbled his head from side to side. "I've been going over the logs from the war game. He was pretty friendly if you've never met before."

Harmony was certain the prince would be able to hear her heartbeat as it hammered in her ears. *Play it off. If he suspects you and Peace are someone else...*

"He grew up in the same habitat dome as me. We hadn't met before the war game though. You know how it is. You hear a familiar accent. It's like meeting family."

She nearly choked on the last word, but managed to keep her voice even.

"You're a good-hearted person," Du Mon said. "The problem with good-hearted people is that many people can misinterpret how you talk and act."

Harmony paused. She crossed her arms closely in front of her, and leaned forward with a look of naïve incredulity. It was a practiced move. "You're saying some of the men aboard are interested in me."

It had a visible effect on the prince. He stopped dead in his tracks too. *Pupils dilated, a hitch in his breathing. Still in love with the innocent girl routine. He hasn't changed a bit.*

"I'm afraid so," the prince said. He ran a thumb and forefinger along his uniform's tight collar as he tried to separate the fabric from his skin.

"I just thought it would be important to let you know. I don't want anyone onboard…"

"You don't need to worry about me sir, I can handle myself."

The smile was beginning to hurt. *How come I can grin like an idiot for hours around Sheree, but it's agony to force it with the prince?*

"There's something else," Du Mon said. He brought up the ship's roster on his wrist computer, and it floated in the air between them, then twisted his arm around so they could both read it. "I can see here you're rostered on with the other junior officers for your next few bridge shifts."

"Yessir."

"If you don't mind, I'm going to make a slight alteration to the schedule, and place you on the same shift as me."

Harmony felt her stomach lurch. *The shuttle bay isn't too far from here. Maybe you can quietly jettison him into space?*

"You seem stunned."

"Oh," Harmony plastered the smile back onto her face. "I was just worried that it might inconvenience you."

The prince smoothed back his hair. "Not at all. It's important from you to learn from senior officers as well. It's how I got started, learning from Captain Dav'i. Shall I put you on the next late shift? It'll be much quieter, so we can spend the time talking. It'll be pretty informal."

Harmony's mind reeled. *Can you refuse the offer now? Perhaps…* She grabbed the prince's shoulder and beamed. "That's perfect. Walsh and I desperately need to recalibrate the laser turrets. We have to rewrite a subroutine for close-quarters targeting so we can hit some of the blind spots that were found during the last laserman simulation."

"Well…" the prince said, his brow furrowing.

"If you're there, we'll be able to discuss Outsider tactics as well, to help improve the subroutine. It'll be perfect."

Du Mon chewed it over in his mind for a moment, and then nodded. "How could I refuse such an earnest request. I'll make sure Walsh is on the shift as well."

"Perfect sir. Was that all?"

The prince looked about them. *Searching for something to talk about.*

Harmony held her breath.

Du Mon's smile weakened as he shook his head. "I suppose not. Thank you for your time, Ensign Kim."

Harmony saluted, and spun on the ball of her heel. After ten paces, she allowed herself to breathe again. *The orders from the resistance will come any day now*, she told herself. *Then we can stop this charade. Any day now.*

Walsh was talking animatedly to the other two. Judging by his finger-laser gestures, he was regaling them with the important issue of laser curvature around dense objects and gravitational wells.

"All sorted?" Sheree asked.

Harmony smiled, and was surprised to find that it felt genuine this time. "All sorted. Since we've got double leisure shift, are we swapping teams?"

As she stepped back inside the gym, Harmony tried not to think about the camera hidden somewhere inside the room, watching them through one-way steel.

Any day now.

As Sheree fumed at Walsh, who was struggling to prod the ball out of its suspension, a small pain began inside Harmony's chest. *These people are the closest thing I've had to friends, and they don't even know who I am.*

For so long, it had just been Peace and her. *That won't ever change, but there's something...nice, about all this.* A tiny voice inside her tried to point out something terrible.

If you want to free your mother, the voice said, *you'll have to fight these people you've befriended.*

21

The Emperor Liu Wei left his retinue of advisors, as well as his security detail, at the entrance to the royal mausoleum. The chambers had been designed by his father. From the inside, the mausoleum resembled a geode with the top caved in.

Above his head, the sun peered through a hole that the architects had constructed into the ceiling. A beam of sunlight streamed through it, landing on a gold plaque, almost blinding him. As the Emperor approached the centre of the chamber, the noises from outside ebbed away. It was replaced by the quiet roar of his own eardrums.

Liu Wei took three careful steps, each one lower than the last, so that he arrived in a kneel before the golden plate. It was two metres tall, and two metres wide. He examined the full etching of Admiral Heydari.

"Abdul," he breathed. The word hung in the air for a moment, before vanishing through the hole in the roof. The Emperor allowed himself a moment of weakness. Large, salty tears fell from his eyes and trailed through his beard. "I let my position get in the way of our friendship."

He lightly kissed the image of Heydari on its forehead. He wiped his eyes on the sleeve of his robe.

"What a charming tomb," said a quiet voice.

The Emperor froze. The intruder must be standing behind him, which meant they didn't care about the restricted parts of the royal palace, and thus they didn't care about *his* authority. They were standing behind him, which meant they had either silently incapacitated every member of his retinue, or his retinue had allowed someone to approach him.

In either case, I can't rely on them anymore.

When he turned around to confront the intruder, the Emperor was confronted by two marines at the mausoleum's entrance, automatic gauss rifles at the ready. Consul Maevin was with them. It was a projection of him, sitting comfortably in an upright marine's palm, like a tiny goblin hitching a ride on a giant.

Behind the two Martians who flanked the exit, were the toppled bodies of three attendants. The rest of his retinue was nowhere to be seen. *They've either fled, or they helped orchestrate this.* The Emperor strained his eyes, and they magnified so he could see out into the distance. A sweating Captain Soona stood in the palace gardens, peeking into the mausoleum from a distance. Soona was surrounded by a squad of soldiers. They all had their guns drawn.

"Maevin? What's the meaning of this?" the Emperor kept his voice low and steady.

"We can cut the theatrics, Your Grace. I've discovered four of your spies poking their noses around in consulate this week alone. We both suspected it would come to this."

The Emperor slowly rose to his feet. He examined the steely gaze of the marines who prevented his escape. "It seems you've been preparing for some time, if you've managed to sink your talons into the navy."

From the marine's wrist computer, the tiny projection of Maevin brushed something off his trousers. "I've done what I had to do, to prevent you from taking control of the entire government."

The Emperor spread his arms wide, hoping to persuade the marines, more than Maevin. "I've made no bid to take control of the Martian government. If there *were* anyone were gunning for total control, it would be you, High Consul."

The projection of Maevin grinned. "No bid for control? Your youngest son is now in control of the largest weapon in the Martian arsenal. Your eldest has obtained the rank of sub-Admiral. You might have the local population fooled, Emperor, but those of us who know the facts are terrified for what this might mean for the future of the planet."

"I've made no bids to dissolve the parliament. The consulate and the navy still hold majority power."

Maevin grinned without mirth. "Even a third of the government's power, residing inside one man, is too great a sceptre. I love my planet, and I can't stand by letting the royal family and its chosen few hold our great culture back any longer. The royal family must be purged, to make way for a proper government, controlled by the people alone."

"Controlled by you, I think you mean."

The marines tensed, awaiting the command to kill, so Liu Wei made sure to hold his gaze upright, to communicate a sense of authority for as long as possible. "Why not take me to the courthouses and simply remove my authority? Why must there be bloodshed?"

"I wish it were that easy, Emperor. The spacers would riot if it came to an open trial. You'd give some manipulative speech to sway public opinion. I'd be quietly executed, and

Mars would never see her true potential. No, Emperor. If you went to trial, you'd have to be gagged, for the safety of Mars and her citizens."

"You're talking a lot about how killing me will be a noble act, Maevin. Are you still trying to convince yourself of that, while you hold the trigger?"

"This execution will be recorded, and then celebrated in the streets. You are not a god, Emperor. You are just a man."

Liu Wei nodded. "My family then?"

"Some will be spared. They'll only be imprisoned. Your sons will have to join you. An hour ago, I sent instructions to the *Black Tortoise*. That battleship is now too far away to threaten the planet. Not only that, but if the mutiny aboard succeeds, the navy and consulate will control the greatest weapon Mars has ever built. We'll be able to launch a glorious victory against Earth, effectively ending the cold war, and ushering in a new era of prosperity for Martian society."

"My sons will stop your mutiny."

The projection of Maevin shook his head. "The message to revolt reached my people aboard the *Black Tortoise* about forty minutes ago. Your sons are already dead."

Liu Wei's stomach wound itself into a coil of sickening anxiety. He gently tugged on the knuckle of his thumb and his hearing dimmed itself. He raised his hands in surrender, and chose his next words carefully. "I think you're just attempting to brainwash these two fine marines."

Maevin would no doubt have given the order to shoot in his next breath. Even through the goblin-sized hologram, the Emperor could see the command well up inside him: the words to *execute* were trying to spill out of the lips of a bureaucrat.

Two pinpricks of light erupted from the Emperor's palms, caused by twin explosions deep inside his prosthetic elbows. Each palm released a hundred tiny ball bearings of shot in a perfect cone.

He'd chosen the words *these two fine marines*, for two reasons. Firstly, it confirmed to his prosthetic limbs that he wanted to attack the Marines. Secondly, it called into question the moral character of the two men who had decided to kill him. For a tenth of a second, they'd both lowered their eyes.

The marine on the left was dead before he hit the ground, his face suddenly more misshapen and cratered than the surface of Phobos. The other marine took the shot across his neck and torso. His body armour absorbed a lot of the impact.

The Emperor photographed his surroundings in his mind's eye, and then shut off his sight and vision. He lifted the hem of his robes, and his kneecaps dropped onto the floor. They bounced and skittered towards the entrance of the family mausoleum.

He felt the noise as the first kneecap, a stun grenade, exploded in a phosphorescent ball of light and sound. The floor trembled from the 300-decibel noise. If the other marines outside weren't wearing hearing inhibitors yet, they'd be vomiting or unconscious. The second grenade spat a thick, noxious fog of yellow sulphur straight up into the air.

The world around the Emperor was fuzzy as his brain drew it from memory. Next to the plate where the Admiral's ashes lay, there was a plate for his great-great-grandfather.

It was a well-kept family secret that his great-great-grandfather's ashes were actually kept in a regular ash museum.

Liu Wei pulled his great-great-grandfather's golden plate towards him, and slipped inside the concealed tunnel. He closed the panel behind him, and switched his senses back on. For a moment, there was silence as he turned the secret locking mechanism to secure the golden plate and its lead backing.

Then the air was filled with the distant chattering of automatic rifles, as the marines outside the mausoleum, who were still standing, fired blindly through the smoke of the stun grenade, trying to hit the spot where they thought he was. The Emperor felt his way down the tunnel, following its twists and turns with the augmented map that spun in front of his mind.

"Maevin, if you've touched my family..."

He stopped, and crouched down atop the concrete floor of the tunnel. The Emperor sent the emergency signal to all his living relatives. Then he brushed himself off, and continued down the twisting corridors below the royal habitat dome. Maevin had wanted to execute him quietly, in his home, and then celebrate it afterwards. The High Consul wouldn't want to provoke an all-out civil war.

As he limped without kneecaps towards his personal safe house, the Emperor began mentally composing his next speech: a speech that he hoped would send Mars spiralling into a civil war.

22

Du Mon sat facing Harmony on the ship's bridge. It was the late shift, and Ju Tin invited himself along. The crowned prince had managed to find an engineer's foldout table for their card game. Tonight, Walsh was teaching an ancient card game called Hanafuda. The goal was to create complex sets, using cards that featured alien plants and animals.

"What's this thing with a long beak?" Du Mon asked, drawing the January bright card from the deck, and matching it with another pine card.

"That's called a crane, but you can't do that." Walsh returned the drawn card to the pile, and pointed at Du Mon's hand of cards. "You need to play from your hand first and then go for a blind draw."

Du Mon scratched his temple. "I don't have any matching cards though." He threw a smile towards Harmony. "I wish I had the Ensign's luck at cards."

"You need to do it in the right order, Captain." Walsh was trying to stay cheerful, but it was clear Du Mon's skill at cards was beginning to irk him.

Du Mon shrugged it off. "My brother now knows what card is on top of the deck."

"That's easy, then." Harmony put the January bright card at the bottom of the deck. "Problem solved."

Ju Tin studied the cards in his hand, and placed one into the field without creating a match. "There's a lot of luck involved in this game, Walsh."

"It's not for everyone."

"No, no," Ju Tin grinned. "I like that aspect of it."

Walsh gestured to Harmony so she could take her turn. "I love how beautiful the cards are. Kim, during our next downtime shift, I can teach you how to play Mah-jong."

"Hey, now you're talking," Ju Tin leaned in and put his arm around Walsh. "Are you much of a betting man, Senior Ensign?"

Walsh gave a sly smile. "I could be persuaded, Your Grace."

"If that's the case, count me in. I can bring some alcohol rations, courtesy of an Ensign."

"I wouldn't mind," Harmony's smile was as bright as the ship's exhausts. "These night shifts are nice and quiet, and I get to have such good company." The tablet beside her blinked to life. She lost a card to the field, and then matched it with a draw from the deck. "Hey, that's lucky."

The tablet blinked again, signalling an urgent message.

"Sorry everyone, I just need to check on the quantum computer." Harmony stood and yawned. "Pardon me." She collected her tablet, and saluted. Du Mon watched her leave.

Walsh played his turn and then stood as well. "If you don't mind Captain, I'm going to run a deep sweep with the sensor array while we wait."

"Need a hand with it?" Du Mon asked.

"Oh, um. You don't need to trouble yourself Captain. I'm perfectly qualified to run it by myself."

Ju Tin gave Walsh a friendly push out of the room. "Of course you are, Senior Ensign. You see to your duties. It'll allow my brother and I to have some time together."

Walsh exited hastily, in the same direction that Harmony went in. There was nothing particularly unusual about that. Both the quantum computer and the sensors array were installed side-by-side behind the bridge. Du Mon still looked like he might stand up and join them, until his brother spoke up.

"Jealousy doesn't look good on you, Du."

The younger prince spluttered. "I need to oversee my ship, Admiral."

"And it's my duty to oversee you."

Du Mon leaned back in his chair. His bad arm was beginning to throb. "Is there something formal you'd like to say?"

"It's nothing formal just yet, but that doesn't mean it won't end up on the record if you keep up your behaviour, little brother."

"Out with it, then."

"You need to back away from your junior officers. Give them room to breathe. Stop spending so much time with them."

Du Mon blinked. "You're lecturing me about spending too much time with junior officers? Father praised you for bunking in the petty officers' barracks during your first tour of duty."

The crowned prince cast a thoughtful look upwards, before crashing his gaze back onto Du Mon. "Yes, I made many comrades in that barracks. If I had my time again, I'd still probably do it. However, my time in the barracks never

jeopardised either my ability command, or my personal life."
Ju Tin leaned in towards his brother, so that his lips tickled
Du Mon's ear. "You see, I was never in love with any of the
junior officers."

"I'm not in love with her."

The bridge door spiralled open with a hiss. Kaya Plessis
marched onto the bridge with her arms crossed. "I don't
believe you."

Du Mon stared daggers at his brother.

"You see, I've been broadcasting your 'behaviour' to
Kaya." Ju Tin said, with a sniff. "I think it's time the three of
us have a good, old-fashioned, family chat."

23

Sheree awoke with a start. It had become routine for her: the small cry as she sat up in bed, narrowly avoiding the bunk above. The nightmares were becoming more frequent while she slept in space. A lingering image of someone bubbling in space returned to her. Sheree balled her pressure sheets up in her fists.

I stopped having these nightmares long ago, didn't I? Maybe my conversation with Kim reignited them.

In the dim light of the women's barracks, Sheree traced the numb scar tissue across her face, trying to remember what her face had felt like before the Kuiper incident. She slipped her knees out from the pressure blankets, and rolled into position to begin her morning push-ups.

It's never too early for exercise, and it might take my mind off things.

Reaching underneath her bunk, Sheree found the back weights. With a snap, she attached the weights to a magnetic clip between the shoulders of her coveralls.

Sheree closed her eyes, focusing on the feeling of her palms pressed against the chilly floor of the starship. A familiar feeling. She widened her palms slightly, shoulder-width apart, and began. *Up, hold, down, hold.* The burning sensation in her biceps was comforting.

As she exercised, Sheree kept an ear trained on Jenna Whit's breathing. The last thing she needed was to be berated. She worked until her arms began to complain, and then stretched herself a little further, huffing slightly.

With a final push, Sheree let herself drop quietly to the floor. She felt its cool panels as they pressed against her cheek, and listened to the sounds of the ship. Somewhere in the distance, a machine hummed almost musically. Occasionally, footsteps in heavy boots thudded along the hallway outside, or the roof of the main artery above her. If she listened even more carefully, Sheree could hear the faintest, irregular thumping in the distance, like an ancient heartbeat, followed by the swish of coolants, plasmas, and other liquids.

Something heavy rang out against the wall outside, not too far from where she lay. Jenna Whit sat up groggily from the top bunk.

Was that you? Jenna mouthed.

Sheree waved her hand ahead of her, palm horizontal. *Negative.* She got to her feet carefully. Sheree stepped with bare feet towards the door, and pressed the manual release on the door panel. Silently, the door relaxed its grip on the magnetic railing that it hugged. Sheree pushed her fingertips into the door jamb, and cracked it open wide enough to peer through.

It took a moment for her brain to register what she was seeing.

A pool of liquid lapped against the edge of the doorway, dark and viscous. A figure was hunched over in the marine's mess, with their back to her. Sitting against the wall, a few metres away from where she watched, Sheree saw Gum

Snyder's prosthetic leg outstretched, bent away from him at an odd angle.

"Shh," the hunched figure said to the person against the wall. They drew backwards, which was when Sheree realised the hunched figure had been holding their hand across the other's mouth. "You've had a rough month, haven't you?"

When the figure stood, Sheree saw the expression of shock frozen on Snyder's face. Across his neck was a deep gash that geysered blood away from the dead man's body.

The murderer turned suddenly. *It's Mav Tarigan.*

"You done?" a voice hissed.

Tarigan was joined by Ivanov and Shiwa. The three marines from the 6th division watched Snyder die with disinterest.

"Almost," Tarigan whispered back. "Just Whit and Wagner left."

"Contact," Sheree hissed, and hit the door's emergency lock. The door froze in place on its mag rails.

Ivanov cocked his head, listening. He approached the slit in the door, which was when Sheree saw that he was covered in blood.

"Oh, you're awake?" Ivanov asked.

"You didn't...?"

Ivanov grinned. "There's not too many marines left on His Majesty's ship."

Jenna leapt out of her bed. With trembling fingers, she punched her wrist computer's radio channel, and dialled the bridge. There was a pause, and then a testing error illuminated the darkness of their cabin.

"I'm afraid we've cut off your communications," Shiwa called out. "Why not just open the door, and we'll make this quick?"

Ivanov licked his lips. "I can't promise I'll be quick. I have half a mind to jettison Wagner into space, so she can feel what my cousin felt. Can you jimmy the door's controls, Peace?"

Tarigan stood at the controls on the other side of the door. "I'll see if I can manage it."

Jenna shook with rage as she pointed at Ivanov. "So it's mutiny then?"

"It's much more than that. This is a revolution, and you're on the wrong side of it." Ivanov turned to Mav Tarigan. "Peace, you guard the door. Shiwa and I will take care of the quartermaster and fetch the guns."

Sheree backpedalled from the door when Peace, stepped closer.

Have these three always known they'd overthrow the ship? Have they been sparring with me, waiting for the signal to slit my throat in the night?

"The door will be opened sooner or later once Harmony gets into the system," Peace said. His face twisted. With teeth bared, the corners of Peace's mouth pulled upwards, rising higher, contorting his face. His eyes recessed into his head, as his teeth and lips stretched up past the bridge of his nose.

Sheree recoiled, and Jenna gagged at the sight.

Peace tapped a bloodied blade against the side of the metal doorframe. "Any moment now."

"Barricade the door," Jenna called.

Together, they pushed a footlocker out from underneath the bunk, and rested it against frame at knee-height.

"What's that going to do?" Sheree asked.

"Push it upright."

They did. The locker leaned against the doorway, blocking the slit that Peace's contorted face was peering through.

"Mutiny," Jenna whispered, rubbing her upper arms. "I can't believe it."

"It must have been planned before they even boarded," Sheree replied. "We need to warn the Captain."

Jenna's face blanched. "If they take the bridge, we're all as good as dead."

Sheree searched the room for a decent weapon. *I should have slept with a combat knife under my pillow.*

"Back here," Jenna hissed. She was examining the emergency access panel that sat on the far end of their room. As quietly as possible, Jenna pulled the handle to open it. Inside, the entrails of the ship pulsed and hummed. Thick veins, the size of a person's forearm, were woven together with cabling.

Jenna stuck her head inside the space, and looked around. "There's enough room to squeeze inside," she said.

"For you, maybe."

With a tentative first step, Jenna swung her leg inside the tight space between the ship's hidden nervous system, and the bulkhead wall. For a moment, she thought about how there was alien chitin brushing her back, and how close the vacuum of space was. "Come on. We need to find the bridge, or get close to it."

"Are you still there?" Peace called out from behind the upright shoe locker.

"We need guns," Sheree hissed.

"The bridge has a mutiny cache. We can try to cut off Ivanov before he manages to break into the armoury."

Jenna grabbed a firm handhold around a metal bracket that was holding pipework in place. She tried not to think about how hot and claustrophobic the air was. With a heave, she managed to climb half a metre, her back scraping against the wall.

"I'm not going to fit," Sheree whispered through the hole.

Jenna looked down between her knees, and saw Sheree's broad shoulders were bruising one of the ship's arteries, as it squashed the delicate tissue against the chitin behind her. The muscular woman stepped back inside the sleeping quarters.

"I'm going to stay here," Sheree whispered, "so those monsters outside won't know anything is wrong."

"You want me to leave you here?" Jenna hissed. "Are you crazy?"

"I'll be fine," Sheree laced her fingers together, and gave Jenna a leg up.

24

Walsh swallowed when he stepped into the chilly sensor bay. Rows upon rows of instruments and screens lined the walls of the station. A few magnetised crash chairs sat idly. During a day shift, there would normally be three junior officers running a slew of simulations against the data streaming into the *Black Tortoise*'s data banks: testing and probing the information they were receiving to try and spot hidden enemy ships, bursts of solar radiation, or to record flybys of distant celestial objects for the scientists back at home to chew over.

He waved his credentials over the door access to the quantum computer, and the steel door that guarded the ship's brain slid open. This was the part of the ship where Walsh felt the most at home. The machines and circuits were capable of running thousands of simulations per second. Walsh respected simulations.

There's satisfaction in seeing data transform into a tactical victory. It's just a shame the computer can't tell me how this conversation will end.

The quantum computer hung from the ceiling like an immense chandelier. Walsh smiled. He'd watched too many theatre circuits: the old, two-dimensional ones that portrayed human life before Mars.

Harmony was now a pair of legs that disappeared into a crawl space beneath the console gateway: the link between the quantum computer and the silicon system.

"Kim?" he called.

The foot closest to him recoiled for a moment. "Who's that?"

"It's Walsh." He crouched down and gave a little wave. Harmony was trembling as she turned a torque wrench in the confined space, trying to pry an access panel free from the underside of the gateway. She turned and her foot relaxed, stretching it out once more.

"Is something wrong?"

"Well, I just wanted to talk."

"Can you find me a length of graphene cable in the supply cache?"

Walsh stood, and opened the orange cache that was mounted on the wall. "How long?"

"Just a metre would do it."

Inside the engineer's cache, someone had left a pair of wire cutters sitting loose on the bottom lip of the box. *Some people.* He picked them up, and cut slightly more than a metre's worth of superconductive cabling, stripped both ends of it, and then secured the tool in its proper bracket. *Leaving tools lying around near the quantum computer. How irresponsible can you be?* He locked the cache, and fed the cabling slowly through the crawlspace to Harmony.

"Thanks Vishan," Harmony said with a sigh. "What do you want to talk about?"

"I want to talk about us," he said, feeling his blood run cold as soon as he'd said it.

"I can't hear you very well. Can you come down here?"

Walsh lowered himself onto his haunches and watched Harmony as she freed the panel. She fished a soldering gun from her uniform's trouser pocket. There was a brief flash of light, and Walsh smelled the sharp scent of melting tin. Harmony stuck her face up into the space where she'd soldered the cable onto the machine, and then gave a little nod of approval to herself. She then pulled the other end of the cable towards her, which is when she remembered Walsh was still crouching and watching her.

"Sorry Walsh, what did you need to talk about?"

"Well—" it was even harder to say it the second time.

"Actually, Walsh," Harmony called out, "I'm not going to be able to hear a single thing over the noise of the cooling system." She pressed her body to the side of the crawlspace. "You're going to have to come closer for me to hear you."

Walsh cast a wary glance back to the outside door. He half-expected someone to enter right then and throw a concerned look at two Ensigns lying in a crawlspace together.

Be a man, Vishan.

He got down on his hands and knees, pressing himself against the freezing metal of the crawlspace wall so that he didn't touch Harmony. He stopped with his head at her stomach, unable to continue any further without brushing against her.

"We've been on a lot of the same shifts for a few weeks now."

"Yes." There was another flash of light. Harmony blew on the spot she had just soldered, and angled her head around to try and check that the tin had properly adhered the cable to the soldering pads. "I've had such a great time on this mission. At the academy you hear horror stories about your first post. It can be really isolating if you don't have people aboard who you can connect with." Her eyes crinkled when she looked down at him, crushed in the corner of the crawlspace. "The fact that you've been doing extra night shifts, for my sake, really means a lot."

She reached down and squeezed his shoulder, before raising her soldering gun up to fire another burst of molten tin at the cabling.

"I was hoping we could continue to spend time together after the mission."

Harmony nodded absently, examining the soldering spot closely. "I'd really like that too."

"No, I meant, I'd like to see you after the mission is done, Kim." Vishan took a deep breath. His hands were trembling. "I didn't just align our shifts because I was afraid you were lonely. Maybe it started that way. The truth is that I wanted to spend time with you because I'm interested in you."

Harmony lowered her soldering gun and laid it on the floor of the crawlspace. She studied his eyes for a long time, looking for something.

Walsh drew his lips into a thin, flat line. "I'm about to die of anticipation here."

She snapped out of it, and gave him a devilish smile. "Sorry, it's just so unusual to see you flustered. I was enjoying myself."

Harmony pulled herself down and towards the exit of the crawlspace. She had no qualms about brushing up against him as she slid down to his eye level. Vishan pressed his back further against the cold metal. A muscle in his shoulder was starting to seize.

"I'm sorry the prince invited himself along to our shifts."

Vishan remained very still as Harmony's lips moved, centimetres from his own. Her chestnut eyes seemed infinite. "I don't really mind. The sub-Admiral is good company."

"We both know I'm not talking about the Crowned Prince. I think if Du Mon hadn't invited himself along, we would have both been much happier these past few weeks."

Vishan blushed slightly. "I suppose so."

"You know, you've been a perfect gentleman on this mission. I appreciate that about you Walsh. Lesser men might've assumed I was interested in them just by the proximity of our jobs."

"I didn't want to assume."

Harmony leaned across and kissed him on the cheek. Walsh's brain hiccupped, and then rebooted.

"Let's just see how this all pans out. There's something you should know. I've been burned before, Vishan. I once had someone promise me the stars, but once they got to know me, they abandoned me really quick."

"I can't fathom what was wrong with that person."

Harmony slid past him, and out into the sensor bay. "They're probably waiting for us. Let's go finish that game, shall we?"

Walsh was about to follow when he spied the soldering gun lying on the floor. It bothered him, so he reached out and grabbed it. "This might seem insensitive after what we just talked about Kim, but you should really—"

His brain was beginning to operate through the haze created by Harmony's kiss. Walsh looked up at where the cable had been soldered. It was firmly fastened onto the test plate, used for checking systems or interrupting operations while the quantum computer was being factory tested. He followed the cable with his fingertips, hoping the coarse rubber casing would tell his brain what was wrong. He peered into the access hatch that Harmony had pried open, and saw it had been soldered onto the circuitry that linked the gateway directly to one of the bridge consoles.

Walsh squinted, and craned his neck into the tight space. His cheek brushed against the frigid lip of the service panel. He studied the technician number stencilled onto the spot where the cable had been fused.

Kim's connected the gateway directly to her personal system. He dredged up what he remembered from the academy. *Test privileges. The system is bio coded to the Captain unless it's being serviced by a factory technician back on Mars.*

Harmony's face was deadpan when he looked at her for an explanation.

"Why have you wired into the gateway like this?" Walsh asked. He tried to crawl out of the space, but Harmony was crouched in the exit and he couldn't get out. "Wouldn't this stop the computer from operating properly? Kim?"

"Walsh, if I asked you to stay here, and barricade the door until I returned, would you do it?"

"I—"

"Be honest with me, Walsh?"

"What are you asking me to do?"

Harmony sighed. "I'm running a systems-failure drill during the next shift. I need someone to stay here and make sure the drill isn't tampered with."

Walsh frowned. "That doesn't make sense. During a drill, the system engineers would need to access this room to fix the problem."

Harmony laughed lightly, but she didn't move. Walsh stared deep into the eyes of the woman he'd fallen for, and realised that he didn't recognise this side of her. For a moment, she was no longer the tiny, bubbly Ensign that he had spent weeks obsessing over. For a moment, she looked as cold as a computer.

"Walsh?"

"Yes, Kim?"

She dug around in a different pocket of her trousers. "You're too smart for your own good."

Walsh followed the motions of Harmony's hand as she pulled something from her pocket.

"I'm sorry, things got complicated."

She launched herself into the crawlspace, right at him. Instinctively, Walsh lashed out with a leg. His far knee caught Harmony in her side, but then he felt a blinding pain in the side of his thigh.

"Oh—" he gasped, and tried to pull himself deeper into the crawlspace, away from her. He saw the combat knife as Harmony withdrew it from his thigh.

"Help!" his voice was deafening in such a small space.

Harmony grabbed a fistful of his uniform shirt, and her other hand sank the knife into his gut, just above his hip bone. Walsh grabbed her face with one hand, pushing her away from him. With his other hand he tried to grab her wrist that held the blade. From this angle, reaching across his body with his non-dominant hand, his grip was too awkward and weak.

She pressed the knife deeper, splitting the soft skin as his arms feebly tried to swat her away. Walsh could feel the warmth in his body leaving through the gash. He tried not to think about which organs were now ruptured.

"Why?" Walsh felt his head swimming as he tried to concentrate on his combat training. Grab the blade, hold it in place. He remembered the soldering gun. He let go of Harmony's face. She was trying to bite it anyway. His fingers scurried blindly over the crawlspace's floor.

Has it always been so cold in here?

Walsh felt the handle, and cursed as it spun away from his fumbling grasp. He stretched, feeling the skin in his stomach split and tear even more as he reached behind him.

"Stop moving," Harmony panted. "If I don't do this...it's my mother. You understand? Stop it. Just stop squirming."

He spat at her. It was a spray of hot, red blood that she took full in the face. Harmony gagged, blinking through the spray. Walsh opened his mouth wide to scream as loudly as he could before his body gave up. Something metallic slipped between his lips, pinning his tongue in place. The soldering gun flashed bright white.

Walsh saw the light shine from behind his eyeballs. Harmony melted her way through the roof of his mouth, towards the brain stem.

Harmony vomited quietly across Walsh, then she tucked his legs inside the crawlspace. Her hands were trembling as she placed the cover back across the crawlspace, hiding the body.

"It isn't your fault. He forced you to kill him."

She studied the door that led out from the sensors bay. She had a spare electromagnetic fryer, a similar model to the one she'd used to disrupt the temple's holographic system. It was too close to the sensors and computer hardware, however. If she cooked those systems, they might end up stranded out here.

Harmony checked her wrist computer. Three hours remained until the main work shift began. She pulled a new length of cable from the engineer's cache, cut it into two short pieces, and stripped the ends of the cabling. After pulling the casing from the door's interior panel, and resoldering two contact points, Harmony dug a microboard from her pocket and plugged it into her tablet.

She stopped. Outside, two muffled voices seeped underneath the door. Harmony's heart pounded painfully inside her chest. Her fingers curling around Peace's bloodied combat knife.

The voices faded as they passed. Harmony's fingers relaxed, and she turned back to the access panel. She dragged a program from her tablet onto the microboard, and then pulled the board free. After snapping a bridging pin, the microboard was ready. Four flashes of light lit up the interior of the sensor bay as she soldered everything in place.

* * *

Harmony stepped into the low-lit corridors of the *Black Tortoise* and the door slid shut behind her. She took a step forward, but was suddenly overcome by another wave of nausea. She leant back against the door to steady herself.

It's for your mother, Harmony.

The interior spine of the *Black Tortoise* was a quiet chamber as she crept back towards her quarters. Suddenly, an amber glow cascaded across the ship: the colour of danger.

"Battle stations," came Du Mon's voice, as it echoed throughout the ship.

Harmony froze. *The prince knows.* Perhaps he'd realised who she was, or maybe Peace and the others had failed to kill the other marines. Officers and spacers spilled from their sleeping quarters. Harmony forced her legs to move.

People brushed past Harmony, knocking her about in the frantic dash to stations. She felt herself being crushed down towards the floor in the throng of bodies. *Or maybe you just forgot how to walk.*

"Are you okay ma'am?" a young, broad-shouldered spacer had stopped. He bent down and held his hand out. "Do you need me to carry you to the ship's surgeon?"

Harmony managed pulled herself up. "I'm fine, thank you."

"But your head is bleeding."

With shaking hands, she wiped Walsh's blood and spittle away from her forehead. "I'm fine." With shaking legs, she took three steps towards her quarters and then paused, before steering herself towards the armoury.

25

Kaya's eyes were wet.

"How could you? You're cosying up to a junior officer, while I'm desperately trying to make things work between us?"

"Work between us?" Du Mon found himself standing instinctively. He began to move towards her, but stopped when she held up her hand. "What are you talking about? Our relationship has never been better."

Ju Tin sat patiently, his eyes darting between them both.

Jenna shook her head. "I've kept my distance. This week I even stopped myself from reaching out to touch you. Is that what you want? A commander instead of a wife?"

"No," said Du Mon. However, as soon as he'd said it, he realised that describing was exactly what he wanted. "I want to talk with you, and discuss battle strategies. I want us to work seamlessly as a team, each doing our bit. I don't need you to reach out and hold my lifeless hand. I can't even feel it, Plessis. I don't want you berating me when I come home, telling me that I shouldn't work so much, when my work is the only thing holding me together."

Her mouth drooped at the corners in frustration. "You want to be Dav'i, don't you? You want to be married to the job, with a commander beside you who stays loyal no matter what."

"Your sister never questioned her Captain," Du Mon said. "I don't want you looking at me with those sad eyes every time I come home, pointing out all of my shortcomings. I don't even want you to touch me, because it reminds me of how broken my body is. How stupid I was at Ceres. When we met, I was trying to be so noble and dignified, all out of some misplaced sense of sacrifice. Maybe I am showing more attention to Ensign Kyuri Kim."

Kaya's hands clenched into fists. "How dare you."

"Kim's a junior officer, but so what? She listens to my instructions and does them. She doesn't list my faults. She doesn't interrupt my stories. I've a wealth of experience that she can draw upon."

"So you're admitting that you've fallen in love with her?" Ju Tin probed.

Du Mon felt the anger inside himself rising. A blistering pain that travelled up his throat and boiled like poison on the back of his tongue. "It's none of your business, brother, because I haven't done anything wrong. Just for the record, I hate you for coming here and throwing your weight around. First you tamper with my command, and now you're trying to control my relationships as well."

Ju Tin gestured around himself. "What piece of your command have I taken? I've given you the bridge, I haven't asked for any special treatment."

"Every glance of admiration you've stolen away from me, is a slap in the face. Every encouraging word to a junior officer that I should've given. Every game. They're *my* crew. *I* chose them, they should be adoring me—"

"—don't take your insecurities out on your brother," Plessis interrupted. "The only reason High Command let you come along was because he'd be watching you."

Du Mon froze. "What did you say?"

"Ju Tin is here so that you can have this command. Even though the theatre circuits portray you as a hero, my dear husband, it doesn't change the fact that you're a green Captain. You're unproven."

"I proved myself at Ceres."

"You took charge, but that doesn't mean High Command deserves to give you the most powerful ship in the fleet. It should be someone with decades of experience sitting in that Captain's chair. The only reason Heydari signed your name before he died, was because he knew you'd be closely supervised."

Du Mon felt something bubbling beneath his rage: a terrible jealousy. The two mixed together, forming an even more potent bile in his gut. "It seems once again I'm overshadowed by my older brother."

"I don't want you to compare yourself to me," Ju Tin said. "You're a capable officer, but you are also the youngest. Be content with the path that is laid out before you. One day when I'm Emperor, I'll need an Admiral to serve beside me. Given time and experience, that person could be you."

"I don't want to be your Admiral," Du Mon hissed through clenched teeth. "I want you to be back on Mars, so I can have one small piece of the solar system that belongs to me."

The viewscreens around the bridge screamed an alarm. In glorious detail, the three members of the royal family saw what was heading towards them.

The object was slipping sideways through space ahead of them: an immense ship, bathed in the crisp, unfiltered white light of the sun. As Du Mon watched, more of the ship appeared. It was growing out of a point in space ahead of them, spilling out of nothingness and ballooning out into reality, like a theatre trick. It was triple the size of their ship, and growing.

"Collision detected," the computer said.

"Battle stations!" Du Mon shouted.

The bridge lit up in a brilliant amber, as all three scrambled towards their stations. Admiral Ju Tin sat in the comms saddle, and Du Mon climbed into his Captain's chair. He cinched the elastic webbing across his body, and began shouting orders to the officers who stumbled onto the bridge.

26

Nuk'kikik allowed the fine, cooling mists of the ecosphere to wash across his mandibles. He ran a rake of bony filaments through his jaws, drinking the dew as he waited. The planetship where he'd spent the last four years of his life was modelled on the gargantuan forests of a distant sphere. The towering trees upset him, he realised. He longed for the cold embrace of the void, the clack of his barbed feet against the welcoming chitin of an Elder Seeker.

That's no longer a life you can afford, he reminded himself. *If you keep dreaming about the void and its view of the spheres, you'll go mad.*

He'd seen it happen before. His broodsister had climbed to the highest tree of the ecosphere and refused to leave it until hunger claimed her. Sitting there in the branches, almost in the centre of the ecosphere, had been the closest feeling to the void.

Nuk applied a salve of saliva to his hand, and cleaned his eyes with it. The mists always felt a little too alkaline for his lidless, white saucer-eyes.

He realised, with a pang of concern, that the ecosphere's leader was watching his fidgeting. He couldn't communicate Savannah's name through skin signals because it meant 'flat plains' and Nuk's language had no words for it. He'd taken to calling her *broodmother*. It fit her role.

"You wish to go?" Savannah asked, sitting with folded limbs, her back straight against the tree. Her body was covered in a mottled brown fur, which often made it difficult to see her against the tree bark. Nuk'kikik suspected that the ecosphere had been designed by her species because she seemed completely calm in the mists and the foliage.

The light that streamed down between the foliage was a mottled, sickening green. He much preferred the stark white light in the void.

I wish to go, his skin said. *I wish to die for my brood.* He meant his new brood, the odd assortment of creatures that he now lived with in the ecosphere.

Savannah's eyes were a similar shape to the tree leaves, and the same shade of rich green.

"We all wish for that, Nuk."

She'd always seemed to understand him, even without a translation device. It was possible she was one of the few species who could see the kaleidoscope of skin pigments that he used to communicate. Perhaps she'd learned the language of the flesh just like he'd learned to read the shape of her mouth.

What amazed him was that other creatures could understand Savannah when they weren't looking at her. It was almost as if the shape of her mouth could communicate with them invisibly.

"Do you crave the hunt? Or just the death?" With each option, she held a palm out, as though each paw balanced a heft that she could actually feel. Then she clasped them together. Nuk felt the soft reverberation through his feet. "You must crave both to be a hunter. They are the same."

I wish for both, broodmother. The skin across Nuk's torso was green and ultraviolet, the two mixed together in the centre of his chest.

When Savannah's mouth opened wide, he saw the rows upon rows of jagged teeth between her lips. A long claw protruded from the middle of her forearm, and she used it to dig at something in her gums.

"An Elder Seeker is nearby, through the spacefold."

Here? Why?

"Perhaps this brood is lost. Are you ready to hunt your own kind? To bring them peace?"

He thought about his broodsister again, scratching herself against the ecosphere's trees until her barbed feet were blunted. Every instinct in her body screaming at her to return to a life of servitude, harvesting the spheres.

I wish to free them. I wish to hunt, or die hunting.

Savannah pulled a leaf from a low-hanging branch, studying the small imperfections along its body. "We will exit the spacefold soon. This Elder Seeker we've detected is strange. It is too light, too small. It flies too straight."

Nuk felt his skin flush with nervous energy. *I wish to go.*

She gestured through the trees, towards the great waterfall that misted the entire ecosphere. "Hunt or die. Both are acceptable."

It is only unacceptable to wait, Nuk's skin replied. He allowed his body to fall forward as he began to run. On hands and feet he scurried, his limbs felt certain as he climbed a shale rockface, made slippery with the mists of the ecosphere. The forest surrounded him on all sides as he ran.

Above him, the artificial sun shone in the ecosphere's centre. If he stared up and past the carefully-contained explosion of light and heat, Nuk could see the forest as it curled over and above the sun, disappearing in all directions.

The waterfall was the clearest landmark among the forest. It towered above, spraying a deluge of torrential water every minute, coating the inside of the ecosphere in a mist that flowed along the land, descending upon leaves and creatures alike, before evaporating or being recycled by the water table beneath the tree roots.

Nuk continued to climb towards the waterfall. Someone waved and their beak moved. Another creature further up was moving their tiny arms and legs in a dance of celebration. Enormous larvae that hugged the trees shot pink clouds of gasses, which Nuk decided was meant as an encouragement.

They've come to wish you well on the hunt.

He studied the faces of the other species, many of whom no longer looked strange or alien to him. They now looked like a family. A brood that had been forged through a common enemy. As he approached the waterfall, his feet and hands felt blinded by the intensity of the reverberations.

He broke out from the trees, and faced the immensity of the ecosphere's water source. It towered above him, disappearing behind the sun above. The water pummelled an artificial lake, which stretched out arms of twisting rivers amongst the great forest. If he explored the ecosphere every day for the rest of his life, he'd never be able to explore its entirety.

Nuk picked his way across the enormous boulders that broke up the surface of the lake. As he approached the mountainous cliff face that the waterfall fell from, Nuk finally spotted his broodbrother waiting underneath the curtain of water.

You came to see me off? Nuk thought.

Of course, his broodbrother replied, his skin flashed brilliant blues and purples. *I wouldn't miss your first hunt.*

I won't fail the brood, Nuk looked back at the bright assortment of creatures who waited on the ground or in the trees, watching him leave the ecosphere.

His broodbrother sent a soothing green that reminded him of their true broodmother's underbelly. *You and I were destined to save our people, ever since we were hatchlings.* His broodbrother reached over his own back with a triple-jointed limb, three metres long. He plucked one of the larvae that he'd been growing on the flesh there. *Eat well.*

Nuk'kikik bit into the side of the larvae, and let the juice run down his mandibles.

You are too generous.

Nuk swallowed the larvae's head last, and enjoyed the tickling sensation as it made the long journey down into his gut. He retched slightly, and brought up a glowing mucus to paint his eyes and mandibles.

His broodbrother walked him to the ecosphere's exit. He pulled the metal hatch free from the cliff face, and Nuk climbed into the darkness. His eyes relaxed, adjusting to the comfortable darkness, instead of the piercing, green-tinted light that seeped out beneath the tree leaves.

As he climbed away from the ecosphere, Nuk felt his weight grow heavier. By the time he'd emerged into the exterior systems of the starship, Nuk was feeling crushed by the weight of the ecosphere's spin. The rest of the starship outside of the ecosphere did not spin. He leapt from crushing gravity into the weightlessness of the void, and immediately he felt the tension in his limbs relax.

Nuk allowed himself to drift through the ship. He looked back, and saw the ecosphere. It was the size of a small moon, spun by enormous electromagnetic engines that he would never understand. The rest of the ship was an armoured cocoon around the ecosphere. In the dim light, Nuk pushed off from the edge of a support beam, and enjoyed the short ride.

He arrived at a jellied doorway and pressed himself against it.

A small vibration through the jelly told him that the broodmother was saying something to him, from far away inside the ecosphere. Nuk couldn't understand the vibrations, so he simply waited, burying his head into the barrier like a larvae suckling. Another vibration of communication, and then a pause. He felt the barrier relax into something slightly softer, and he moved through it.

Nuk poked his head into the void, and nearly shed his skin in delight. The planetship bent away from him in every direction, slipping through the spacefold as easily as he had slid through the jellied doorway. Ahead, he could see the dark red creature that the ecosphere had detected. Nuk reached over and grabbed the freezing metal doorway, and calculated his trajectory. The Elder Seeker was slowing, and slowly turning about. He shuddered at its movement. No doubt, this was a terribly sick creature. It was hardly writhing. Instead, its body listed about like a tree branch, floating atop the ecosphere's lake.

He gave himself a practice push, but held on, imagining how his body would move. He tried it again, and then on the third try he launched himself towards the sickly Elder Seeker. Nuk's mandibles chattered with excitement. He reached out in all four directions with his limbs, embracing the emptiness, the utter lack of anything.

I've missed this.

His body began to slowly spin as he floated through the void. He allowed it to do so, watching the celestial lights spin around him in the only dance his species knew. The Elder Seeker approached far too quickly, and Nuk was almost disappointed when the tiny claws on his feet hooked onto the creature's rough armour.

Strange.

He studied the shape of the Elder Seeker. It was short, like a youngling. Its body didn't snake like it should have. Instead, it was bulbous: a grotesque tangle of chitin, tendon, and muscle. Trailing behind the Elder Seeker were tendrils that flapped in the void. Beneath his feet, he couldn't feel the steady heartbeat. He felt the rumble of machines. This Elder Seeker felt more like the ecosphere, than the home of a brood.

Nuk scurried across its surface, searching for the characteristic homes that should have been burrowed into its armour. *Wrong, wrong, wrong.* Occasionally he felt something below that might have been organic, but it was swallowed by the deafening shakes of machines. There were no nerve endings out here for him to communicate with the Elder Seeker. Below, he felt currents of electricity, but they were barbaric imitations of a creature's nervous system.

Nuk grew worried. He scurried towards the tail end of the creature, avoiding the strange metal objects that stuck out through the Seeker's skin. The creature was spinning cleanly, just like the ecosphere. At the tail end, Nuk saw the glow of fusion.

An abomination, he realised. *A fusion of Seeker and machine.*

From deep within himself, Nuk felt a rage that he hadn't felt since most of his brood was killed by the Administration.

Is the Administration responsible for this? he thought. The rear of the abomination crackled with a radiation that felt like theirs. Nuk wondered whether any of his people were cowered inside, hidden somewhere, still slaving away for their distant, ever-disappointed masters.

One of the metal objects sticking from the skin was spinning. Nuk turned and watched as a long, thin tube faced him. A light grew from deep within the tube. Luckily, Nuk had seen other species on the ecosphere training with similar weapons.

He dashed along the body of the Seeker on all fours, forcing the tube to spin again. A line of distortion crackled towards him, and Nuk felt the skin on his upper arm blister before it was frozen again by the void. His mandibles twitched in pain, but he carried forward.

Hunt or die. Hunt or die.

He reached the tube and pulled at it. His arms rippled with the effort as he pried the reinforced metal loose from its housing. There was a flash of electricity, and then he felt the weapon break free. Nuk let it float away through the void. Then, he heaved a heavy dollop of acid from his mucus sac. A luminescent ball of mucus landed in his palm. Nuk carefully applied it to the red armour under his feet, following the fault lines of the sickly carapace.

The chitin broke away far too easily. This Seeker's armour was growing in a way that was strangely uniform. The natural curves and waves of the armour had been replaced by regimented lines. Nuk pulled a toothy shard of the armour away.

He used the shard to pry a larger chunk free, cracking the armour open.

Sorry old girl, he said to the Seeker. *It'll be over soon.*

Nuk's fears were confirmed when he broke through the chitin, far too early. Underneath, he saw the steel shell of a starship. He stood, staring at the incomprehensible sight. The creature his people lived in harmony with, in unity with, now reduced to a skin that was being worn by starship.

A shadow fell across him, and Nuk looked up. He saw them: small little shapes of death that flitted along the body of the Seeker, searching for prey. Nuk judged the distance, and then hurled a long splinter of chitin through the void.

27

Tam twitched, as the Outsider that was crawling across their hull threw a piece of chitin with the grace of an athlete. The Outsider's tri-jointed limbs tossed the splinter of the ship's own hull almost as fast as the eye could track.

"Computer, replay that."

In the corner of his vision, Tam saw the lowest two portions of the Outsider's shoulder act like a human's arm in the midst of a throw. The final segment of its arm remained locked at a right angle from the Outsider's upper elbow. The handheld the splinter against the length of its forearm until the point of release.

Even with the replay, Tam couldn't even track the splinter before it skewered his drone. His view shifted, as the computer allocated a new lead drone for him to fly.

"Watch out for its throw." He couldn't see Jenna because his sim gear filled his vision. He half-expected a click of acknowledgement, but he was only answered by silence. Tam sighed. "And you lectured *me* about shirking my duty."

He brought the swarm of drones back around.

"Computer, launch Lieutenant Whit's drones and slave them to my controls." The computer beeped an acknowledgement.

"I can't use missiles," Tam said to Renn. "I might accidentally hit the *Tortoise.*

"Switch to anti-capital ship lasers," came the technician's gruff voice.

The Outsider pried a longer piece of the ship's carapace from its hull, a spear of about two metres in length.

Tam's swarm hemmed the Outsider in from behind, as his lead drone fired its laser, followed by the others in his swarm. The Outsider jumped, taking the concentrated burst from the drones along its side. He watched the Outsider as it soared away from the ship.

"It jumped?" Tam shouted. As soon as he'd said the words, however, Tam realised the Outsider had measured how it needed to escape. It grabbed hold of one of Tam's drones mid-jump, and in a sweeping motion, lanced two more drones with its incredible reach.

The Outsider swept its spear away, out towards space. The two drones that were skewered on its blade flew away from the ship, sailing into space. At the same time, the Outsider flew in the opposite direction, landing safely back on the hull of the *Black Tortoise.*

"Huh," Tam said. "It's got some moves."

"Its species have probably spent centuries in zero-gravity," Renn said.

Tam's drones spat alternating bursts of lasers, dancing backwards as the Outsider feinted back and forward. From his perspective through the sim gear, he was floating in space, dodging the wicked tip of the Outsider's spear while trying to line up a new burst.

Jenna was right. I've gotten rusty. Tam took a deep breath, and then he sent his drones back into the fray, belching invisible bursts of laser.

28

Plessis glanced across the bridge and cursed quietly. Two officers were missing from their stations, in the middle of a battle. Above her, the view screens continued to relay an endless and staggering amount of detail about the enemy vessel.

"Ship measures over sixty kilometres from bow to stern," she called.

"Any other signs of hostility?" Du Mon asked.

"Only the Outsider that's attempting to breach the hull. Running sensor sweeps."

On the view screens, the Outsider was in a deadly dance with the ship's drones as it pulled armour away from the *Tortoise*.

"Sunter, fight defensively," Du Mon commanded into his console. "If we lose the drones, we're defenceless. Try luring it towards a quadrant of the ship where the laser turrets are still operating."

"Got it," Tam's voice replied over the bridge's speakers. It was thick with concentration. "I'll keep it busy as long as I can."

Du Mon steepled his fingers as he concentrated, examining the hostile ship. "It looks like different technology to what we encountered at Ceres."

"Agreed," Plessis replied. "You wouldn't believe they were made by the same species."

"It's got to be alien," a young woman's voice shouted.

For a moment, Plessis considered reprimanding the officer for the interruption. Under the amber glow of the bridge's alarm, she saw a pair of wide eyes belonging to a young ensign. An ensign who would have been her age when Plessis first saw combat.

"Captain, I'm afraid we're missing officers Kim and Walsh from bridge duty. Pilot Jenna Whit is missing from her station. Two bays of marines aren't manning the laser turrets. The tactical officer is having to aim them remotely instead."

Du Mon licked his lips. "We can't afford to be missing any officers." He hit the all-hail on his console. "Officers missing, move to your stations immediately. This is not a drill."

"I'll investigate," Ju Tin said, rising from the saddle he'd been occupying.

A metallic clanging resounded across the bridge.

"Are we hit?" Plessis shouted, her eyes scanning the console in front of her.

"Negative," the senior tactician replied.

The metal clanging grew in its urgency. Ju Tin backed away from the command dais in the centre of the bridge, listening intently. At last, he bent down and cracked open a maintenance hatch. The crowned prince of Mars stepped back, and Jenna Whit tumbled from the wall, gasping for air. Her hair was covered in a mucus from the ship's oxygen veins.

The Admiral held out a hand, and helped her up. "There's a perfectly good door, you know."

"Mutiny," she managed to gasp. "Ivanov, Tarigan and Shiwa are staging a mutiny."

Ju Tin froze. He turned, opening a panel beside the bridge's doors, and retrieved a service rifle. He tossed the next one to Jenna. "Are you able to still fight?"

Jenna snatched the weapon from the air. She weighed the bulk of the weapon in her hands, and measured her eyes along the scope. Then she gave a nod. "Just give me a second to catch my breath."

Du Mon bit at the fingernail on his index finger, and pulled it free. He glanced at the viewscreen. The enemy ship hung solemnly over them. The Outsider danced along their spine, systematically pulling chitin free, and whittling away their drones. His brother and a pilot were equipping themselves to face a group of rogue marines.

"Message from Mars," Kaya Plessis said.

"It can wait," Du Mon hissed. He opened up the camera logs, searching for where Kim and Walsh went.

"I'm afraid it's marked as urgent. It's from your father." Plessis waved the message from her console in his direction. It landed atop the camera logs. The message was simple, sent via radio waves in a wide burst.

Revolution at home. Stay safe.

Plessis watched her husband retreat inside himself. Du Mon reread the message several times, chewing the words over in his head.

"Delete," he said. The message vanished. "Scrub it from our system. We can't let word get around."

"Yessir."

Du Mon heaved a ragged breath as he looked off into the distance, staring at nothing in particular. "I've failed us."

"The fight isn't over yet."

The young prince cocked a half smile. He raised his voice a little. "I knew it would come to this. Even with the perfect team, I'm the weak link."

"That's not the case, Du. Stop talking like that."

The prince unfastened his crash netting. "Can you take things from here, Kaya? I'm going to go fight the mutiny."

"Nonsense." Plessis unfastened her own netting, and stood. With a firm hand, she refastened his own netting. "The bridge relies on its Captain, and a ship relies on the bridge. You delay the Outsider, and prevent any more of them from landing on us. I'll go handle things, just like my sister would."

Du Mon brightened slightly. "She did always fix things for Dav'i. Do you think he ever doubted himself?"

Plessis smiled. "My sister wouldn't stop complaining about how insecure Captain Dav'i sometimes was."

Du Mon smiled. "Does this mean we're okay now?"

She shook her head. "After today, I'm going to need some time to re-evaluate things. Our relationship. Everything. Excuse me, Captain."

* * *

Plessis leaned against the wall as she peered through the door gap into the marine's mess. Her rifle slipped into the darkness, like a serpent sneaking creeping into the night, tasting the air.

"Any movement?" Ju Tin mouthed.

Plessis leaned on the barrel of her rifle, prying the door open slightly. Her eyes peered into the darkness.

"I'm going in."

Plessis kicked the door wide, rifle welded to her cheek. Jenna was behind her, crouching.

Their eyes slowly adjusted to the darkness. She took another step forward, gun scanning left to right. The soles of her boots stuck to the bloody floor.

Ju Tin produced his tablet, and held it above his head. His chambered pistol brought up the right-hand flank. They found the first body crumpled, head between its knees. The second belonged to a female marine. She lay on her back, staring at the ceiling with a look of confusion etched onto her cold features.

"How abhorrent," Ju Tin said. "To take Martian life so casually."

The light from his tablet illuminated another man's face. His prosthetic leg was bent oddly, and a waterfall of dried blood cascaded from his throat, down the sleeve of his uniform. Plessis looked away from the expression on Snyder's face, searching instead for any movement. There was a soft gagging sound as Jenna quietly vomited.

"Some of the marines fought well, despite being surprised," Jenna said. "Looks like several of Ivanov's colleagues were killed as well."

"No sign of the rogues," Plessis said. Her gun was trained on the darkness of the men's quarters further back. "Whit, go check on Wagner."

Jenna scurried across the room, treading gingerly. At the doorway to the women's quarters, she paused. Ju Tin remained at the door, checking the sloping hallways for signs of movement. There was a gasp, and Jenna backed away from the door to the quarters. A dull moan of scraping metal filled the mess hall, as the door pried itself open manually.

"Sorry," Sheree Wagner said. Her voice trembled slightly. She stepped further into the mess, which was when Plessis saw the glint of silver pressed against the large woman's throat. "They've got Kim. If I didn't surrender, he'd…"

Peace stepped into the room after her. His arm was curled around Sheree's neck, so that the knife pinned her against his bicep. Peace looked in bad shape. His jaw hung to one side, and a bright blue bruise was already forming along his chin.

Sheree was in much worse shape. She was deflated as she stepped into the light. The skin under one of her eyes was split. Blood trailed from both nostrils. Between her eyes was a bruise that matched Peace's.

"I'm sorry," she said. Her eyes had lost their defiance. Sheree was broken. "He said they were going to go kill Kim. I opened the door for him."

"Now, my assoc–, my asso–, my colleagues will be here soon with guns they've obtained from the armoury," Peace said. His voice lisped as he tried to speak. He licked his lips, glancing between the three of them. "So, I figure you'll all be dead in a few minutes. If you don't mind, I'm going to ask you to lower those guns you've got. Otherwise Sheree here will start breathing through a new hole."

Ju Tin was gauging whether he thought he could shoot Peace without hitting Sheree.

"Come on Tarigan," he began. "We've played cards together. I know when you're bluffing."

"First, my name isn't Tarigan. It's Peace." He tried his best to smile with a broken jaw. His body was firmly wedged behind the door of the women's quarters, ensuring the thick sheet of metal was shielding most of his body. "So I doubt you understand what I'm capable of."

Ju Tin took a slow, almost leisurely step to the right, to get a clearer angle of Peace.

"Well then, Mr Peace," Ju Tin said. "Most people in your situation would have some demands, I assume. Don't you want us to hear your demands?" He cocked his head in the direction of the hallways, and Jenna crouched behind him, ensuring that the other mutineers didn't surprise them.

"I have plenty of demands," Peace said. "But you won't be able to help me with them."

"Hey now," Ju Tin sounded like he was genuinely wounded. "I'm a pretty important guy. Perhaps I can bend a few ears your way. In fact," he took another lazy step towards Sheree. "I bet I would make an even better hostage than Wagner here. If you took the crowned prince captive, people would have to listen to you, wouldn't they?"

Peace chuckled, and Sheree gasped as a thin trickle of blood traced the contours of her collarbone. Ju Tin took a step backwards.

"I'm not some madman you need to talk down from a building," Peace said. "The only thing I want is for your family to die. All of them. You understand? By now the Emperor will be dead, and good riddance to bad news."

"Do you really want an entire family killed?" Ju Tin asked.

Plessis felt her eyes droop slightly. The crowned prince's voice sounded heavy in the air. Jenna's forehead began to perspire as she tried to keep her gun held in a straight line. Sheree's head nodded once, sharply, as she struggled to stand underneath the pressure of the prince's voice. Ju Tin started creeping forward again. He was now three metres from Sheree and Peace.

"To kill someone is a terrible thing Peace. All Martian life is sacred, all of it. In Martian society we don't shed blood. We rehabilitate. We heal. We till the poisoned ground until something beautiful flourishes. Don't you want to be part of that?"

Even Peace looked like he would fall asleep at any minute. The tip of his knife was doing an erratic tap dance through the air as he struggled to hold onto it.

"Wouldn't you rather hand the weapon over, and be part of my father's dream? We need you Peace. We don't want to harm you."

The moment was shattered as a gunshot reverberated through the hallways of the *Black Tortoise*. It was so sudden and unexpected that Peace very nearly dropped his knife. Plessis looked down at Ju Tin's mag pistol, expecting to see the tell-tale metallic embers drifting from its nozzle. Ju Tin, however, looked just as shocked as Plessis felt. He spun around.

Jenna's gauss rifle ejected another round. The projectile left her weapon so quickly that it left metal splinters in the air, which fell to the floor of the mess hall like glitter.

"Contact!" Jenna's voice sounded like a whisper compared to the explosive shots from her weapon. Plessis kicked over a metal table and aimed over the top of it, hoping the top of it was made from steel.

The doorway above Jenna was suddenly turned to molten slag as a shot from the enemy went straight through it. The metal of the doorway melted, and then solidified a moment later, faintly etching a spiralled tunnel where the projectile had barely missed Jenna's head.

Jenna was rolling. Her rifle was tucked against her stomach as her shoulder caught the floor. She crawled to the lockers in the corner of the room as Plessis kept her weapon aimed straight into the hallway.

Ju Tin had fallen back against the bulkhead of the mess. He was out of cover, and caught between the knife-wielding Peace on one side, and the doorway where enemy fire had just come from.

Joe Shiwa's head appeared through the hallway door for a split second, and then it was gone. Plessis kicked herself for not being quicker on the trigger.

You might hit an innocent on the other side of the hallway if you miss, she reminded herself. *Plus, if you miss, these rifles need time to cool.*

She backed away from the table, making her way further into the darkness, and away from the spot where Shiwa had spotted her. It was a risky move. If he came through now, she'd be completely exposed.

"Three of them!" Peace shouted over the ringing in their ears. "Contact on your r—"

Ju Tin fired at Peace, silencing any more information from him. The mag pistol glowed orange for a brief second as the shot exploded from the barrel. When Plessis' hearing returned, she could hear Sheree screaming.

Plessis crouched at the rear of the room, concealed behind the doorway to the marine's bathroom. She chanced a glance to the left, and saw that Ju Tin's shot had taken Sheree's ear clean off. Blood gushed from the wound. Peace's knife remained firmly at her throat, however.

He must have missed.

Ju Tin's face was pale as he lined up another shot, which was when Shiwa stepped into the doorway and fired a round directly through the table where Plessis had been crouched a moment ago.

Plessis felt her heart stop as the table she'd been using as cover crumpled like paper. The force of the shot picked it up, throwing the table across the room and smashing it against the far side of the mess.

Jenna was ready. She fired from her spot at the lockers, and gave Shiwa a hole straight through the centre of his chest. The blast picked him off his feet, and threw him back at the wall. He took a step forward, which was when he must have realised his spine was severed between his lungs. He fell forward instead, crashing to the ground.

Peace chose that moment to push Sheree straight into Ju Tin. The crowned prince coughed as Sheree collided with him. His hands instinctively went to catch her, gun reaching up to blow Peace away.

The younger man was underneath the prince's aim. His blade traced Ju Tin's hand that held the gun. Then it flicked across his wrist. Ju Tin dropped the gun with a shout. Sheree pushed herself away from the crowned prince, trying to get at Peace's legs. Peace ran the blade of his knife across Ju Tin's belly, opening him from hip to hip. He allowed himself to fall, grabbed Sheree as he crashed to the ground, and placed the blade back across her throat. Then he was up again, pulling her by the jumpsuit to her knees.

Plessis looked at Sheree, and realised all the fight had left the fierce marine. She stared at the long gash that ran across Ju Tin's belly. She was crying, Plessis realised. Peace was whispering something to her. Sheree hauled herself to her feet, allowing Peace to use her as a shield as he backed away towards the doorway.

"I'm so sorry," Sheree mouthed. "It's all my fault."

Then she was gone, pulled into the stark whiteness of the ship's corridors. Plessis stood. Her head was pounding. She touched her ear, and found a liquid was pooling from it. Jenna was across the room, and pulling the prince into the women's quarters.

Plessis staggered towards them. Her gun refused to remain still as she pointed it towards the mess hall's exit. Suddenly, Plessis felt the collar of her jumpsuit get tugged. She was pulled roughly into the women's quarters by a pale-faced Jenna, who pushed the door shut as far as it would go.

"What are you doing?" Plessis asked. Her rifle felt heavy. Ju Tin had left a slick of blood as Jenna had dragged him. *It must be my turn to throw up.*

"Shh," Jenna said. She took Ju Tin's pistol, opened the doorway a crack, and tossed it through. She closed the door again.

The mag pistol clattered across the metal floor. There was a pause, and then Plessis heard something metal bounce inside the mess. It skipped twice and then stopped. Jenna was on top of her, pulling them both down to the ground.

"What—"

Plessis felt the heatwave and suddenly couldn't breathe. The floor below them grew warm. Blue flames licked beneath the close metal door. Plessis curled up in a ball as the shock of the explosion picked her up and shook her. Her shoulders slammed against the floor again and again as the secondary shockwaves threatened to pull the ship down around them.

Jenna staggered to her feet, dropping her gun to the floor as she tried to stand.

"Stupid, crab-headed—" she climbed into her combat suit. Her voice was muffled through the visor. "— Underdeveloped, lobotomised, spineless gorilla. Ivanov always loves the spectacle of a grenade. Get a helmet from under the bunk, Commander."

Plessis dug Sheree's helmet out of a footlocker. She looked up at Jenna the pilot picked up her discarded rifle.

"Are there any other helmets?" Kaya Plessis asked.

Jenna shook her head.

"That means either the prince or I are going to breath in the smoke."

Jenna looked at Ju Tin's wound, and nodded. She placed a firm hand on Plessis' shoulder, and then crossed to the exit.

Plessis looked back at Ju Tin. His eyes were clenched tightly as he tried to apply pressure to his stomach. Plessis could smell something foul coming from the wound. It smelled like a vac toilet.

"The wound is septic," Plessis said. A new alarm sounded, and suddenly a powdered spray seeped through the walls and floors. The heat from outside slowly began to dissipate. "The fire is going out."

Ju Tin took a bloody hand, and weakly pushed the helmet towards Plessis. "Take the helmet, Kaya."

She almost resisted, but there was something in the prince's face that gave her pause. She fastened it over her face. The neck inflated, locking her breath inside the chamber.

Jenna cracked the door an inch, hissing through her teeth as the metal burned her fingers. A wall of grey chemical smoke and white flame ballooned in the centre of the room. Jenna hunched over, and closed the door behind her.

Plessis realised her small hands had reached out and grabbed Ju Tin's giant ones. She helped him push a little harder, trying to keep the life in him. "We're in a pretty bad spot. I can't believe Jenna left you here like this."

"She did the right thing. Go help Lieutenant Whit. She needs backup."

"You'll die."

The crowned prince nodded painfully. "I died two minutes ago when Tarigan cut me open."

Plessis steeled herself, as her brother-in-law coughed wetly. A few red bubbles formed on his lips. His chest heaved.

"I'll stay until you die."

Ju Tin tried to crack a smile, but he didn't have the energy. He took a deep breath, and it seemed to take all of his energy to do so. The crowned prince inhaled again, but his eyes lost their focus.

Plessis pulled her hands free and wiped them on her jumpsuit. She picked up her rifle from the floor, and cracked the door open. A fine powder fell like snow, smothering the fire as she picked her way towards the exit. The metallic floor creaked, and she shifted just as part of the flooring collapsed into the maintenance tunnel below. Plessis picked her way carefully forward, and out into the bright white hallways. Blood was speckled on the floor, a trail that disappeared around the curve of the hallway.

People were arriving now. Spacers in suits were brandishing breach equipment, poking their helmeted heads into the mess, and assessing the damage.

"Phosphorous grenade," Plessis shouted to the eldest spacer.

"Well, shoot." The old man cracked open his helmet's visor to scratch his nose. "She wasn't designed to take that. It's amazing we aren't venting air right now."

"The chitin behind the bulkhead is the only thing keeping us safe. Seal this entire area quickly. If the Outsider breaches us in this section of the ship, we'll be exposed to the vacuum." Plessis took a shuddering breath and pointed down the hall. "I need every person you can spare. We've got mutineers aboard who are trying to scuttle us. They've taken a prisoner."

The oldest spacer looked a bit uncertain. "I can't seal this section quickly with fewer people."

"They've taken Wagner."

He swallowed. "The one who grew up in the spacer district?"

"That's right."

The old man sent three hulking spacers with her.

The blood trail was beginning to thin out along the ground as they went. They followed the hallway as it bent left and then right. Plessis read the maintenance numbers painted along the floor.

"They're probably heading towards the engines or docking bay."

"You reckon they're gonna blow us all up?" one of the spacers asked.

"They need a ship to get back home, stupid," the other one said. Judging by their similar appearance, they might have been brothers.

They do need a ship, Plessis thought. *Ivanov must have a smoother brain than I thought he did.* Her calves were beginning to ache. She'd been crouching, shooting, and running without a break for the past ten minutes, and the exhaustion was beginning to catch up with her. *Not far to go*, she thought. *You've just got to get to this next junction and then you can rest.* When they arrived at the junction, and Sheree's blood trailed down the next corridor, Plessis negotiated with herself again. *Okay, until the corner and then you can stop. Last stop is at the floor marking. Alright, just until the next junction.*

She coughed loudly. Her lungs felt like cement, weighing her down. One of the spacers offered an arm around her shoulder to help. *I must have swallowed smoke. I need water, and a lot of it.*

They ran on. Ahead, a rifle shot rang out. *Please be okay Jenna.*

Plessis and her soldiers turned the final corner and nearly ran straight through the middle of a firefight. Jenna was tucked in behind two cargo containers, trying to find a clear shot at the marines, who were piling aboard one of the many escape craft stored in the launch bay of the *Black Tortoise*.

The escape craft were shaped like broad, flat beetles. Plessis had once heard them described as *glorified coffins*. Ships that were capable of simple flight, and sustaining a small complement of people for a month until they were rescued.

Peace was pulling Sheree up the ramp towards the rescue craft, shouting and complaining the entire time. Even from a distance, Plessis felt sick when she saw what Ju Tin's mag-pistol had done to the young man's face.

It was now difficult to discern where Peace's flesh began, and where the machinery underneath it ended. The ballistic from Ju Tin had hit Peace in the right cheek, and now the bottom-right quarter of his face was a tangle of wires and metal scrap.

They'll have to return to the ship, she realised, *unless they're allied with the aliens. No, that seems too far-fetched, even for the Martian resistance.*

Harmony was helping pull the limp Sheree into the escape craft. She was shouting at Peace while they both hauled the green-haired, muscular woman. Ivanov was brandishing his gauss rifle to cover them. The grenade attachment under the barrel glinted in the bright chemical lights.

He had already sent four or five bursts in Jenna's direction, judging by the molten globs of metal that were dripping from the shipping containers, and the bulkhead behind her.

"Why are you worrying about her?" Ivanov shouted. "Drop the coward. We've got company."

"We're taking Sheree with us!" Kim shouted. "What the Deimos did you do to her, Peace? She fainted the moment she saw me."

"You told me to bring her, and here she is!" Peace was hunched over, trying to pull Sheree's limp body up the ramp by her forearm.

"You let someone blow her ear off! If you were a delivery boy, I'd demand my money back."

"I can remove the other ear too. Then she'll be symmetrical."

Plessis crouched low, judging her aim at Ivanov. She gestured to the spacers to get back.

"Should I use the other grenade?" Ivanov called, crouching behind his own supply crates. "I can probably get her from here."

"Enough with the grenades Ivanov!" Peace yelled. "It's a miracle you didn't kill us all the last time."

Ivanov cast a glance back at Peace. "I just thought—"

"—yes, Ivanov, I know. A big grenade makes a pretty boom boom. I can't believe you even understand what a revolution is."

Ivanov fired another round as Jenna poked her head out. It slammed into the crate she was taking cover behind. Jenna must have been worried that her crate was going to collapse soon, because she slipped ahead towards Ivanov, keeping behind metal crates as she did so.

Ivanov was difficult for Plessis to hit. He'd chosen a good spot: difficult to flank, without the enemy having to run through his periphery. She lined up the shot. Ivanov was a faint blur above the container crate as he lay prone for cover. She waited.

Sheree was up the ramp and inside. Peace returned with his own gun that he must have picked up from Shiwa.

"Move it, monkey. I'll cover you."

Ivanov scooted back, breaking Plessis' line of sight. Jenna was up and aiming. Peace saw Jenna take aim, and almost called out a warning. Instead, he took cover behind the escape craft's entry hatch.

Ivanov was running with his back exposed when Jenna fired. Her shot bore a hole right through his back. Ivanov stumbled, tripped, and hit the launch bay floor.

Plessis charged out into the launch bay. "Close the blast doors," she shouted over her shoulder at the spacers behind her.

Peace saw them spill into the bay. It was impossible to read his face because a quarter of it was missing. Plessis could see that his right eye was spinning uncontrollably, like a planet on its axis. He lifted his gun up, and a shot rang out in the launch bay.

Plessis stopped dead and looked down. She waited for the pain to arrive, but it didn't. Peace disappeared into the escape craft.

I'm not dead? Plessis thought. Jenna also popped her head up from behind cover, her face scrunched up in confusion.

In unison, they both looked at Ivanov. He'd stopped crawling. A ballistic though his skull had made sure he stayed behind. The interior shuttle bay doors screeched open, just as the escape craft's engines ignited.

"Lock the blast doors!" Plessis shouted again. She crouched low, and fired a shot that slammed into the side of the escape craft's engines.

The three spacers were scratching their heads at the bay's console station. "Commander? The ship keeps throwing up error messages."

"Contact the bridge."

"Yes ma'am," one of the spacers said.

The launch bay engineer's body was slumped over the controls. Judging by the smoking hole burrowed through his torso, he'd met a similar fate to the other people who'd gotten in Ivanov's way. The spacer pulled the body away from the controls, and carefully laid the corpse fall on the ground at the circular station. He spacer tapped at the screen. "No one is responding."

Plessis sighed, and slid into the console booth instead. "No other option then. Leave the bay, and lock the pressure doors."

The spacer glanced at the escape craft, and then back at Plessis. Then he quickly grabbed Jenna by the elbow, and marched her towards the exit.

"What are you going to do?" Jenna shouted.

Plessis didn't respond. She hit the emergency pressure controls, and a dome of reinforced transparent steel rolled out from behind the controls and closed over her head, sealing her into the command station. An orange light lit the interior of the chamber as it began to pressurise the internal space.

Her fingers darted across the console as she threw the emergency lock on the blast doors. Ordinarily they'd open once the interior doors were closed. Plessis found the subroutine, buried in the code, that halted all door commands ship-wide. It was a process that wasn't documented in the ship's systems manual because Plessis had built a backdoor.

She filtered the logs down to calls for door access. Her instructions were at the top, written as an error code. She scrolled down to find the other calls. Someone aboard the escape craft was remotely trying to crack the door open using a tablet. Plessis pulled up the ID of the tablet, but whoever was tampering with their systems came back as a simple 'test device'.

How frustrating. Is that the 'Peace' person who was pretending to be Mav Tarigan? Or is Kyuri Kim the mastermind of this whole operation? Then there's Sheree, who complicates things even more.

Faintly, Plessis heard the sound of the pressure doors sealing behind Jenna and the spacers. She counted to five, in order to give the spacers enough time to arm the safety features built into the exterior hallway. A bright spot of glowing orange lit up on her sealed dome. She looked at it, trying to comprehend what it was. The spot was so strange, like a star painted on a tiny planetarium.

Looking out into the launch bay, Plessis saw that the escape craft was sitting at the blast doors. Its ramp was partially lowered, and Peace was leaning out of the door, his rifle glowing after the first shot he'd just sunk into her pressurised dome. The console screen jumped as whoever was trying to hack into the ship's system desperately tried to recover the control they'd had of the system.

Why are you hesitating? Plessis asked herself. *Are you afraid of what Du Mon will say?* Her thumb hesitated for another heartbeat. *It's because of Sheree. You'll be sending her to certain death.*

Another shot sank into the transparent steel dome. The molten metal dripped like honey away from her. Peace jumped from the ramp and landed heavily on the floor of the shuttle bay. He scooped up the rifle from Ivanov's dead body, and aimed the grenade attachment at her protective dome.

They've figured it out then, Plessis thought. *If they don't kill me here, at the launch engineer's station, they won't escape.*

Peace fired. The grenade was a shining ball of silver as it flew across the room. Plessis stamped her thumb onto the controls, and watched in fascination as the explosive slammed into the transparent steel dome above her, denting it inwards. She felt almost tranquil now that the command had been sent. There was nothing left for her to do. There was a brief second as the grenade bounced, preparing its white-hot flames inside its body.

The blast doors opened to the vacuum of space.

Peace's hands went to his ears, and he dropped the rifle as the pressure dropped in half a second. The explosive rails built into the blast doors were designed to allow a ship to exit as rapidly as possible. Two bodies inside the shuttle, belonging to Sheree and Kim, were tossed out into space like ragdolls. Peace pulled out towards the vacuum as well. His body curled involuntarily into a ball. He bounced once against the underside of the escape craft, then against the edge of the exterior doors, then he flew out into space. The grenade followed him. No oxygen, no flames.

The escape shuttle was pulled forward slightly by the escaping air, and the *Black Tortoise* lurched as its spin was thrown off by the explosion of oxygen and pressure escaping.

Plessis was thrown from her chair. She tried to reach up to close the blast doors, but couldn't find the energy to touch the controls. Now that the adrenaline had left her system, relief and exhaustion flooded in. She reached down and pulled her jumpsuit towards her face.

In a small bubble that protected her from death in outer space, Kaya Plessis buried her face in the red stain that her brother-in-law's blood had left on her uniform.

29

Nuk'kikik was growing tired as he leapt and dashed, back and forth, weaving along the exterior of the abomination. The tiny flying ships stung at him, burning away his flesh layer by layer whenever he stood within their line of sight for too long.

I could kill the abomination and its makers in minutes if left alone.

Another one of the flying creatures strayed within his reach, and he swatted it with a brutal downwards slash. He felt himself slipping. The slash forced him to anchor against the abomination to complete the movement properly. One of the creatures came in low and close, suddenly smarter than the others. It tucked in under his arm and discharged a burst of heat under his armpit, severing the limb from his body at the joint, leaving behind a stubby third of his arm.

Nuk grabbed the limb before it floated away, and pried the splinter of Elder Seeker chitin from its grasp. His mandibles chattered with the pain. He held onto the limb for a moment, wondering how good his new brood's healers were. The abomination rocked suddenly, and Nuk caught sight of three objects as they spilled out of the side of the creature, out into the void.

He watched the three objects, and saw the limbs as they curled up.

Poor little creatures.

His wrist vibrated, and he glanced at it as he ran, spinning and weaving to avoid the invisible spears of light that the small machines threw at him. A kaleidoscope of colour appeared on the screen, repeating. The instruction was simple, relayed from the ecosphere that hung above him.

Return, it said. *With haste.*

Nuk licked his hand and applied the salve onto his eyes. He felt a pure rage inside him. Rage at being unable to kill the poor creature that had been enslaved here. Rage at the machines who had just burned through his arm. Through the viscous fluid smeared across his white saucer eyes, Nuk studied the floating creatures. They were drifting in the direction of the ecosphere.

His two sets of knees retracted in opposite directions. Then his feet disengaged, and he launched himself away from the spinning abomination, out into the cold embrace of the void. The smallest creature was nearest to him. This one was flailing and spinning. It had a hard head, and an exoskeleton. Nuk caught that one around its middle. His good arm took the impact roughly, and then they were both spinning around and around.

He reached out a foot to collect the next one. This one had no exoskeleton. It was swollen, probably female, with pink wounds across its face. His foot brought the body up towards his hand, and the three of them continued to spin.

Nuk's head whipped around and around, trying to gauge distance despite the confusing motion. The many white lights in the void were like onlookers. Studying them from afar as they continued their strange dance.

My broodmother, my real one, told me a story about the onlookers. Nuk reached out and took the final creature with his foot. This one had a damaged head. Nuk's arm was struggling to hold onto the two others, so he just let his barbed foot dig into the leg of this one, holding it fast.

The onlookers eagerly await to approach, his broodmother had told him as a hatchling. *Amongst all the lights in the void, there lies a few who watch us in return.*

What are they watching us for? He'd asked back then.

They look for imbalance, she'd replied. *They lend aid when someone seeks to correct an imbalance.*

Nuk saw the ecosphere approaching quickly. He began a controlled swing of his limbs, adding a slight counter-motion to his spin. Then, gradually, the spin began to slow as he changed it to another direction. He reached out with his free leg, waiting for the impact against the ecosphere's shell.

I always loved those stories about the onlookers, he thought. *Perhaps that's why I joined the ecosphere. I wanted to restore an imbalance against my tribe, even though I'm now dead to them. I wanted to correct the evils of the Administration.*

His foot felt the scratchy shell of the ecosphere, and Nuk allowed his leg to absorb the impact as he connected.

How long can these ones stay in the void? Nuk wondered. He'd heard, with astonishment, that many creatures died when exposed to it. With a careful push, Nuk launched himself towards the jellied doorway that led inside.

Swimming through it was much more difficult now, as he was weighed down with several of the smaller creatures.

Through the foggy liquid, he could see a gathering on the other side as he swam.

Then he was through, collapsing onto the ground of the ecosphere's outer shell. As he lay there, looking up at the odd assortment of faces staring back at him, the pain in his arm began. Nuk hissed, clutching at the stump.

The ecosphere's broodmother was moving her jaw again. He could feel the vibrations through his feet.

"He's brought new recruits," Savannah said. "Take them to the healing trees. Take Nuk as well. We need to leave immediately."

Why are we leaving? Nuk said through his skin. *I could have destroyed the thing they rode inside of.*

"They are here."

Who are?

"The Administration. They've followed us."

Then it is too late. We are all dead.

"Nonsense. We have the advantage: they'll want to investigate the sick Elder Seeker out there."

30

In unison, the bridge cheered as the outsider leapt away from the *Tortoise*, and back towards the alien vessel. Du Mon sagged into his chair, breathing raggedly. He'd been awake for at least twenty hours.

He glanced at the empty chairs where his wife and brother should have been sitting. The prince staggered to his feet. He needed someone to take charge in his absence.

"Commander Plessis?" he asked. The computer gave the audio cue for an error.

A senior ensign was reading through the ship logs, trying to identify why the ship's systems were damaged. "We're still being jammed, sir. It reads like a testing bug."

The prince pointed at the senior tactician. "Tactical, you have the bridge until you're relieved. Standing orders are to evade any further attacks from the enemy."

Du Mon exited through the puckered door of the bridge and out into the main artery. There was a commotion of spacers running. A marine was hauled past in front of the prince, her body slung like a hammock between the arms of the two spacers as they hurried towards the doctor's station. The prince halted an engineer who was running towards the launch bay with a hastily-assembled drone.

"What's happened out here?"

The engineer turned to him, sweating as he tried to keep the bulky drone steady. "Traitors aboard sir. There was a firefight in the marines' mess. I hear there's at least ten dead. A team is trying to crack into the systems room."

Du Mon consciously slowed his breathing as he staggered towards the ship's surgeon, located at the mid-portion of the *Black Tortoise*. The prince braced himself for the groans and cries of injured and dying Martians. As he approached, however, Du Mon heard an even more terrifying sound. The doctor's station was nearly silent.

He stepped inside, just as the surgeon was inspecting the body of the marine who had been hauled past him. The surgeon placed a device against the base of the marine's skull, and consulted his tablet while the two spacers stood awkwardly, the body slung between them.

"She's long dead," the physician said. "Lie her over there with the others."

Du Mon walked past the beds. Most of them were draped in crisp, white sheets. A few were dusted with black stains from soldiers who had been placed down in a haste, and then removed. The prince saw his reflection in the mirrored storage units. Purple bags hung below his eyes, aging him. His wiry hair looked dishevelled and uneven, sticking out at strange angles. His skin was waxy.

At the far end of the surgeon's station, Du Mon saw four people lying on beds. He picked up his pace. Jenna was the closest. She was sitting up in her bed, and talking to the attending nurse.

"Lieutenant Whit," he said, clasping her hands. "You made it. I heard that people had died, and I thought..." Du

Mon saw something in Jenna's face that stopped him. She looked like she had aged ten years since leaving the bridge.

"I'm sorry Your Grace," she said. "We were outgunned."

Du Mon spun around. He checked the bed behind him, but it was one of the marines. His forehead was wrapped up with so many bandages that he almost looked comical. The prince looked at the digital chart above the bed and watched the brain monitor flicker.

Du Mon forced himself to look away. The next bed had a person lying in it, but their face was covered by a sheet. Du Mon choked back the tears, until he realised the body was far too big for Plessis. Something in the back of his mind bothered him, but he forced himself to move to the next bed.

Plessis lay motionless, her hair pooling around her head like a blonde halo. Her hands were tucked in beside her sides, sitting atop the thin sheet,

"Kaya," Du Mon said. He grabbed her closest hand and held it tightly, bringing it to his lips and kissing it furiously. "Kaya, wake up."

With her free hand, Plessis wiped the drool from her mouth and cracked an eyelid open.

"I need to sleep, Your Grace."

Du Mon felt the relief wash over him. "Are you hurt?" He glanced up at the monitor. "Where's the surgeon?"

"Don't bother the physician," Plessis whispered. "It's just exhaustion, and a few burns." Then she smiled. "You called me Kaya just then."

"I did."

"You haven't called me by my first name in a long, long time."

The prince planted a kiss higher, on her wrist, and pressed the back of her hand into his cheek. He felt hot tears as they tipped over the edge of his eye lids, and trickled across his waxy skin towards her fingers.

"I put you in danger," he said. "I should have gone instead."

"Then we might have lost two princes." She winced, and opened her eyes.

"Two princes?"

"You understand me, don't you, Du? Don't make me say it."

Now it was her turn to cry: faint little tears, only slightly larger than a grain of sand, that merely painted her cheeks a tone darker.

The prince realised why the body under the sheet had bothered him so much. He turned around slowly. Plessis squeezed his hand faintly as Du Mon left her bedside and stepped towards Ju Tin's bed.

The young prince clenched his fists tightly, and relaxed them. Then he reached up, and gently pulled the fabric down. The sheet was a coarse cotton blend. *My brother. Laid to rest in rough sheets. Surely silk would've been more appropriate.*

For some reason, the small detail offended him. Fifteen minutes ago he'd entertained the thought of bludgeoning his brother, but now that Ju Tin was actually dead, he was surprised at the intense pain it brought.

Du Mon paused when the blanket had travelled past his brother's eyes, which were now forever welded shut. The fabric was stuck to his brother's lips slightly. A few spots of blood and saliva had fused the sheets to the soft skin. With a tug, it was free. A small portion of the lip skin broke free, but there was no blood that trickled from the wound.

Ju Tin looked peaceful. He looked like he was napping, with folded hands in the palace gardens. There was an absolute stillness to him, however. A stone-like texture to his flesh.

"Who did this?" Du Mon asked.

"Mav Tarigan," Jenna said. "But at the end he called himself Peace."

"Peace," the prince tasted the word. The name stirred at his memory. It was important, but he couldn't put his finger on why.

"It sounded like Ivanov was the leader," Jenna said. She propped herself up further, ignoring the machines around her as they whispered to her, begging her to recline again. "But then Tarigan shot him. It doesn't make sense."

Du Mon's thoughts drifted back to the message from his father. *Revolution at home. Stay safe.* He placed the sheets back over the face of his brother.

"Maybe they weren't working together."

Jenna shook her head. Her hair swung about her face like the strands of a mop.

"They definitely were."

"What I mean is, just because they were both fighting against us, doesn't necessarily make them allies. Ivanov was only invited aboard this mission because High Consul Maevin requested it. Shiwa was recruited for the same reason."

Plessis cracked an eye open. "So you had two officers come aboard at the request of Maevin, and they both took part in an operation to overthrow the ship. I'd bet the uprising at home is connected."

Jenna finally succumbed to the pleading of the medical computer, and collapsed into her bed. "So what happens now? By the time we get home, we mightn't be welcomed back with a parade. In fact, we might find ourselves welcomed with a quick march down to the courthouses."

Du Mon nodded slowly. "The alien ship withdrew suddenly just now. I'm not sure what the purpose of attacking us was. Are they connected?"

Plessis frowned. "I can see the mutiny being the work of the consulate. I can't imagine them having access to an Outsider, or a ship that size."

"An unfortunate coincidence?" Du Mon rubbed at his temples.

"You'd have to ask them," Jenna said.

"Captain?" asked a tentative voice from the air.

"Yes?"

"This is Ensign Yu. We've broken into the systems room and disabled the tampering that was affecting our systems. I just thought you should know sir, there's a body here. It belongs to Senior Ensign Walsh."

Du Mon felt his stomach churn. "Another casualty? How was he killed?"

"We checked the security footage once we were inside the system sir. It...it looks as though he was stabbed by Ensign Kim."

"That can't be right," Du Mon said. "Can you check again?"

"Um, I'll go over the footage again more thoroughly sir."

"Du?" Kaya Plessis called.

He stepped beside her cot, and took her hand again. "Yes, Kaya?"

"Kim was one of the traitors. You said earlier that perhaps Peace wasn't really working alongside Ivanov, and I think you're right. I think he was teamed up with Kim."

Du Mon chuckled. "I'm sure you're mistaken. If he had threatened her or someone close to her, she might have appeared to be helping him."

"They were squabbling like best friends, Du. They knew each other well. It almost sounded like she was the one giving the orders."

The prince patted Kaya's hand. "You've had a long day."

"Not long enough that I'd make a mistake about this, Your Grace."

Please, rest now, the computer cooed. Commander Plessis ignored it.

"I know what I saw. They were working together. I don't know why they wanted to take Sheree, but they were both hauling her into the escape craft."

"Don't worry," Du Mon said. "I'll question her myself and get to the bottom of this."

"Sir?" Jenna smiled apologetically. "They were jettisoned into space."

The prince waggled a finger inside his ear, pulled it out, and studied it. "You jettisoned Kim and Wagner out of an air lock?"

Jenna scooted backwards in her bed slightly. "It was self-defence."

"I see." Du Mon patted his wife's hand firmly. From where she sat, Jenna could see the tendon in his neck straining against the skin, threatening to burst through.

"Captain?" came another voice from the air. "Tactical to Captain, this is urgent."

"I need good news, Helm."

"The enemy ship is leaving."

Du Mon cracked a hysterical grin. He directed it towards Jenna, who saw the whites glinting in his eyes. "Look at that. They've decided we're too tough a target."

"Sir, I'm afraid there's bad news as well."

"Yes?"

"They're disappearing through that...rip in space, because something is coming."

"I need more information, Tactical."

"It's the sun."

"I beg your pardon?"

"The sun is coming towards us, sir. Travelling at light speed. It'll be here in—"

Du Mon opened his mouth to give the command for evasive manoeuvres, but he was no longer aboard the *Black Tortoise*. He flinched, but held in the need to scream. His eyes weren't working properly. All he could see was white. He scrunched his eyes tightly. The air was on fire, as though he was trying to breathe through a battleship's exhaust flames.

He hunched over involuntarily, with his elbows braced against his thighs. The thunderous sound of an explosion erupted again and again in a far-off distant place. The air cooled down rapidly, becoming breathable again.

He cracked one eye open slightly. Even the light was becoming more manageable. Before there had been no detail, just a white-hot impression flooding his vision, a picture of the back of his eyeballs being irradiated. Now, he could glimpse a highway constructed from light.

The light was still painful, but he could now see other highways that stretched above him. Far off in the distance, between the stretches of brilliant energy, he could see the grey abyss of space, filtered through a hundred thin coronas of light.

"What's happening?" Du Mon asked, and was relieved that he could faintly hear himself over the din of distant explosions.

The prince caught a movement through his eye lashes. There was something ahead of him. He took a tentative step forward on the highway, and found that while the energy below him did give way slightly, it was able to support him. He looked down. He was naked.

"How…"

He took another step forward. Two objects were suspended ahead, one above the other. Tears streamed from his eyes as Du Mon tried to make out what they were.

"I can't see," Du Mon shouted. "It's too bright."

The highway dimmed, until it was as bright as the reflection of white concrete in direct sunlight. Du Mon wiped his eyes. Suspended above the walkway was an eyeball with a milky-white iris. Below it, a mouth was also floating. There was nothing else.

From the highway, a hot spiral of energy spun itself free. It snaked up towards him. Du Mon flinched away, but the energy unspooled into a net of crackling energy that settled across his skull. There was a warm tingling sensation across his body.

The lips puckered, assessing him. "Du Mon of Mars."

"Yes?"

"Your species has been found in possession of the Administration's technology."

The prince felt a pain begin in his low abdomen. "The Administration? That's you?"

"That is us." The eyeball and mouth swung on some invisible point, like that hand of an ancient analogue clock revolving. From the space that they vacated, a second eyeball and mouth appeared. Du Mon felt pinpricks across his skull from the net of energy. The eyes rolled upwards for a brief second, and then fell back in focus on him. "You have crafted a war machine." The mouths spoke in unison. "It is impressive that you have fused Administration gifts with your own primitive technology."

Du Mon ground his teeth. "I take it that you're referring to the *Black Tortoise*. Many good people gave years of their lives to create that ship."

The eyes and mouths made another partial revolution. A third eyeball materialised, with a brassy iris. A pair of dark lips appeared below it. "Giving time?" The two other mouths said something else, but their sound was swallowed by the booming voice of the third pair of lips. "What a delightful concept. To you, time is something given and taken away? How frustrating it must be, knowing that you will one day run out of a thing that you have no control over."

Du Mon swatted at the tendril of energy that was tethered between his skull and the highway of light. The energy stung as he broke it apart for a split second, but then it joined back together with a flash.

"The Administration controls this plain of existence. You are in possession of our technology. In fact, your existence in this portion of the galaxy wasn't authorised."

"Wasn't authorised?" Du Mon rubbed at his forehead in frustration. It felt like his thoughts were struggling to find their way out of a dark chamber. "You believe Martians shouldn't exist? No one has that sort of authority."

The eyes and mouths revolved once more. Now four of them watched him, forming a half-circle above the growing pile of mouths. "We *are* authority. Your species was caught, just now, boarding an ecosphere: a detestable symbol of rebellion, used by the handful of creatures who seek to defy us. Now your species is a threat."

Du Mon shook his head. "I don't understand."

The mouths were silent as the eyes watched him. "We will show you."

From the highway, Du Mon saw images reflected. A bright, perfect image of the Outsider crawling along their ship, swatting away the drones. Du Mon sucked in a breath. He could see the saliva bubble and sway as it clung to the creature's eyeballs. He could imagine how the texture of the Outsider's skin would feel.

"It was clever of you to enlist the help of a defected *Outsider*, as you call them. See here?" The image changed, and the Outsider leapt away from the ship.

Du Mon watched Kim as her skin began to bloat and blotch. The Outsider caught her roughly around the middle, and pulled her towards the giant alien ship.

"See here? Your people are taken aboard the ecosphere by one of the defectives. If we hadn't been watching closely, we might have missed the transaction taking place. Your species has broken our laws by existing without permission. One of our Elder Seekers was killed in this sector, and now you wish to join forces with the defectives who are in rebellion against us."

Du Mon squinted as he processed the information. "What's your relationship with these Outsiders and Elder Seekers?"

The eyeballs and mouths revolved again. Now there were five.

"The Outsiders were one of the first species we brought into order. We gave them the gift of Elder Seekers after the destruction of their home world. Now, they harvest planets for us, and scout new species who require order."

"Order? It sounds more like slavery. A bunch of eyeballs and mouths, enslaving another species."

The bundle of mouths smiles. "Perhaps I've been too slow to reveal myself."

The eyeballs rotated, new ones filling in the gaps at a blur, and then spinning as well. In a few seconds, there were more than a hundred eyeballs, spinning in concentric circles like the rings of Saturn. Each ring orbited in a different direction to its neighbour in a dizzying blur of colours. The size of the Administrator continued to grow, as the eyeballs spread out wider and wider. The mouths in the centre were now crushed together, compacted into a ball of lips, teeth, and tongues at its centre.

The eyes stretched out into the distance in all directions. Everywhere Du Mon looked, at least a hundred eyeballs were watching him. From every angle, a great cloud of pupils studied his naked form.

31

News travelled quickly on Martian ships. By the time the Outsider had scurried back aboard the enormous star vessel, one of the spacers had leaned in close to Tam, their breath smelling like cheap alcohol.

"Are you fighting still?"

"No." Tam peeled the visor away from his eyes, and saw the look on the other man's face. "What's wrong?"

"There's been a mutiny." Several other spacers crowded around his chair, looking about nervously. "Someone detonated a grenade."

"Was that the explosion I felt earlier? Are we all safe in here?"

"Yes sir. We barricaded engineering while you were fighting."

Tam slapped the closest spacer on the shoulder. "Good move. Can we get a message to the bridge?"

"We were jammed earlier. I can try again if you'd like?"

Tam pulled himself up from his chair and stretched. His forearms were sore from the tension of flying. It felt like steel hooks had been inserted into his shoulder muscles. "I'll go check it out."

"What about us, sir?"

Tam felt the nervous energy that buzzed around the engineering bay.

I could command them to come, but they aren't soldiers. In fact, if I unlocked a weapons cache for them, they might accidentally shoot each other in all the excitement.

"I need you to hold this position."

They all nodded in relief. "Can do boss."

In the corner of the engineering bay was the officers' locker. There were others scattered throughout the ship in key locations. He keyed his code into the cache, and pulled the lid open. There was a faint hiss, and then Tam checked his shoulder. The spacers were curious, trying to peer into the box, but they stayed well back.

Don't want to risk a mutiny here as well.

Tam pulled out one of the officer's gauss revolvers that had been charging inside, as well as two clips of ammunition. He ignored the spare dress uniform, several pairs of boots, and the bottles of simple medicine. Tam shut the lid, and it sealed automatically.

"Can someone fetch the door?"

One of the technicians was at the ready. Tam released the safety on the pistol, and gave him the nod. The door slid open easily, and Tam stepped through. A slight breeze wafted across his neck as it closed behind him. It felt chilly.

The corridor outside was in low-power mode. The sirens had been lowered from contact, to battle stations. A series of yellow lights blinked along the roof. Far away, he heard the sound of boots running.

Tam hugged the wall as he went forward, head tilted against the cold metal walls so that he could see up and around the corners. The scurrying of footsteps grew in urgency as he approached.

Tam saw the spacers as they frantically sealed the doorway to the marine's mess. Welding torches and scrap metal were being ferried from the other direction. Beams of steel were being quickly laid across the places where the door had come free from its hinges. Tam saw the blackened floors and the blood stains.

"You heard the Commander, quick!" the lead spacer was shouting.

Tam lowered the pistol, holding it behind his back as he approached the crew. "You're sealing off the marine's mess?"

"Aye sir," the spacer threw a quick salute, and then leaned back to push another person up to the door. "Ship's hull is damaged all because of that alien. Then this happened. We're making sure if it breaks through the won't lose atmosphere."

Tam nodded. He thought about telling the spacers to stand down from welding the door. The Outsider was gone, after all. *Better keep them busy, until you're certain that we're safe.*

Tam's mind went to Jenna. "Anyone left inside?"

"No sir. The Commander and the other pilot went to the surgeon's station not long ago. Didn't look well."

"Right you are," Tam said. He pushed through the throng of people, ducked underneath a steel beam that was being carried, and nearly slipped on the blood slick across the floor. He caught himself against the floor, and went forward more carefully.

That could be Jenna's blood. Tam steadied himself again, but the wall was no longer there.

He fell sideways, and landed in a pool of light.

In fact, everything was hot and bright. He pulled himself up, and felt around for his gun. Squinting, he dug around in a stream of the energy underneath him, but couldn't find the weapon anywhere. He managed stood. The light flowed in either direction, as far as the eye could see.

"Tam?" Jenna called. She was further down the stream, her body lying half-submerged in energy. He saw the curve of her side, and looked down, to see that he was naked as well.

Tam waded forwards, struggling to see, struggling to breathe, as a terrible heat radiated up from the surface of the light. As he approached Jenna, the light lessened a little, as though someone had thrown a switch.

Tam crouched down beside her. "Are you okay?"

Jenna was trembling. "Where are we? What happened to the ship?"

He looked up at the beams of light all around them. "I don't know."

She nodded, and tried to sit up. "There was a mutiny, you know."

"Did they shoot you?"

She shook her head. "Almost. They killed Ju Tin. Kaya Plessis was beside me..." Jenna looked around, trying to spot the Commander. "She's not here."

Tam peered across the blinding horizon as well. "She could be further ahead. I could try and explore a little."

Jenna's hand grabbed tightly onto his knee. "Don't worry about it then. I'd rather not be left alone in this place."

A sound of explosions washed over them from somewhere far away. Tam felt his heart skip with each gentle shockwave that reached him. "I'll stay then."

Jenna took a deep breath, and released it with a smile. "Thank goodness."

Tam pulled his legs underneath him to sit. He scrunched his eyes closed. "You should close your eyes too, so you don't go blind. It'll be the end of your flying career."

Jenna made a snorting noise. "That's if we get out of here, Sunter."

"I'm sure we'll get out of here. Once you're ready to walk, we'll give it a shot."

"That's just like you, isn't it?" Tam heard her sigh.

"Jenna, I've been trying to get a lock on what happened between us. What's *going* to happen if we get back? What do you even think of me?"

"Well," there was a pause as she thought about it. "I think you're a fungus."

Tam rocked backwards slightly, as if he'd been punched. Then he leaned in again. "Um, since your family are fungi farmers, I'm not really sure if that's a compliment or—"

"—Are you familiar with the mushroom called ash cap?"

Tam dredged up an ancient memory from his academic studies. His biology instructor had been very attractive. He remembered a flash of long, red hair.

"I know they're important for terraforming." He cracked an eye open to watch her response.

Jenna's face lit up. "They are. Extremely important."

"So, I'm important? Great. Good chat."

"Hold up." Jenna put on her serious face, although a faint smile tugged at the corners of her mouth. "Important yes, but filled with poison."

Tam tried his best to avoid visibly deflating. "I see."

"We use the ash caps to seed the soil across Mars. They thrive on the toxins there, and absorb it all into themselves. They make everything better around them."

Tam pointed at himself. "And that's me?"

"People gravitate towards you, Sunter, because you make life easier. At least, that's why I wanted to be with you. Maybe it's a combination of your positive outlook, and your sense of humour. You can make yourself a vital part of any team."

"But?"

"But when I wanted to get really close to you, to become more than your friend, that's when I found the poison."

"Wait, you wanted—"

"—I saw it when your brother Jace died. I saw it when Mith knocked back your proposal the first time, and I spent a week dragging you out of every underground bar on Mars. You're so good at uplifting others Tam, when it's your turn to be helped, those closest to you find themselves facing all the poison you've extracted."

Tam was about to object, but then he caught himself. He tried to remember back. There had been long glances. Smiles. Words of encouragement that had sounded too intimate, which had balanced on the line between compliment and flirtation. He closed his eyes and nodded.

"I hurt you. When Mith rejected me, I used your friendship to get back up again, and then went straight back to her."

"I would have been your friend Tam, but you only wanted to speak to me when it was convenient. I was a disposable friend."

"Do you think you were in love with me back then?"

"I don't think I was in love *with* you. I think I was in love with the *idea* of you. I'd built an edifice in my mind about who you were, and what it would be like to be married to you. Neither were correct."

He knew it was a trick of the mind, but Tam could imagine a poison bubbling like sulphur in his own gut. Throughout his life he'd been good at knowing how others were really feeling, and how to fix things. This time he was the cause of the damage, and he had no idea how to repair things.

"I guess we have to start over," Jenna said.

Tam felt the pressure inside him subside a little. "What's in the middle of acquaintance and friend?"

Jenna's hand rested on his knee again. They locked eyes for a long time, the longest since he'd married Mith.

"Let's go with close colleagues. That seems about right."

Tam pursed his lips thoughtfully and looked up. "Only if you go back to fetching me coffee packets before our shift begins. I've been getting my technician Renn to do it, but I think he's secretly adding something to it. Actually, I get this weird rash way down here every time I drink it."

Jenna held up her hands in disgust. "Fine, I'll fetch the stupid coffee."

32

Du Mon felt crushed beneath the weight of the eyes that watched him. He could no longer see how far they stretched, and yet he was certain that even the pupils at the very fringes of his vision could see him with perfect clarity.

"Do you see your people down there?" the bundle of a thousand lips asked.

The highway of light magnified what was below it. From his vantage point, Du Mon could see a dozen or so other beams of light. Suspended atop each were various members of his crew.

"I see them."

"Like you, they are guilty of taking the Administration's technology, and consorting with defectives."

"Are you planning on killing us?" Du Mon asked. As soon as he'd said it, he felt a sense of peace wash over him. The complete powerlessness he felt gave way to an emptiness. *Perhaps this is what was supposed to happen all along. All these years I've slaved away, just to end up here. How cruel.*

"We try not to kill, that would be a waste of energy."

"Your energy?"

"No, a waste of potential energy. However, your species will be removed from its star system..." The eyeballs rolled upwards for a second, and then locked back onto Du Mon again. He felt the crushing weight of the infinite gaze once again. It took everything within the prince's willpower not to turn and run from it. "We suspect that the defectives who we are hunting will join forces with another civilisation in your solar system."

"You mean the Earth-Lunar alliance?" Du Mon thought for a second, and then nodded. "That would make sense. They have to know about the *Black Tortoise* by now. Earth would be willing to sign away their own moon if it meant destroying Martian civilisation."

"We're so glad you see things our way," the mouths said in unison. "We could take your entire civilisation away, and intermarry you with the Earthen population..."

Du Mon held back his vomit.

"...Alternatively, we are willing to support your civilisation in the arms race that is no doubt about to take place once we leave this sector."

"Hang on," Du Mon said with a frown. "How does that follow? Slavery, or you give us weaponry?"

The eyes rolled upwards again, but this time it might have been out of irritation. "We aren't giving you a choice. That's the point. We want you to fight the defectives, and whoever they ally themselves with in this system."

"Why don't you do it, if you're so big and powerful?"

The collection of mouths orbiting at the centre of the Administrator smiled as one. "Why waste energy? We're offering you the chance to become the dominant force in this star system. Your culture will outlast that of your enemies for centuries."

"So, all I have to do is betray the majority of humanity?"

"Correct."

Du Mon looked again at the faces of his crew, isolated on slivers of light below him. His eyes lingered on the face of Tam and Jenna. Tam was talking animatedly, and Jenna was giggling. Further along the same beam, he could see Plessis as she sat on the ground. It looked like she had tried to find others, but had collapsed.

"I know you probably don't care about this," Du Mon said, "but for the longest time now I've felt like my life really had no particular purpose."

The eyes watched him.

"Perhaps I've been kidding myself. I've spent the past five years building the perfect team, or as close to it as I could manage. I made sure I was on the cutting edge of everything. And yet, here I am. I can't help but think that if I do get back to Mars, I'll have to do the same thing all over again. A new batch of soldiers to train. Then they'll go to battle and die, and I'll do it again, until one day I'm the one who won't return. I just thought if the people around me were good soldiers, no, perfect soldiers, then it would cover my own lack of experience. It'd protect me from myself."

"Are you willing to take our offer? Destroy the defectives, in exchange for our technology and protection?"

"I'm willing to do that."

"Then we arrive at the conditions of the agreement. You will take leadership of your nation, as our selected ruler."

Du Mon nodded sadly. "A puppet ruler."

The mouths all curled around at the corner. "Yes, something like that."

"It's not what I wanted, but then again, I never really knew what I wanted. Fine. I'll take control from my father and rule instead."

"We'll also require a token of your loyalty."

"What does that mean?"

"So that you don't betray us, we'll keep some of your associates here as insurance. They'll be treated well. If we are happy with your work, they will remain protected."

Du Mon nodded. "There's some good spacers down there."

The eyes looked down at the light highway. "No. It has to be someone important to you." The highway zoomed onto the faces of Tam, Jenna, and Plessis. "Judging by your brainwaves, you are most attached to these three. We want you to choose one for us to keep."

Du Mon's eyes widened, and shook his head slowly. "Between those three? No, I can't."

"If you don't choose, we'll keep all three instead. You need to choose someone to wait with us for the next year, while you establish yourself as the ruler of Mars."

Du Mon swallowed. He looked between his wife Plessis, his best friend Tam, and his most trusted soldier Jenna.

"I need to talk it over with them. To discuss what needs to be done. Tam has a family. Jenna is young, so she shouldn't stay trapped here as a political prisoner. Plus, I'll need her abilities as a fighter to help me take the throne of Mars."

"So then, it's your wife you're choosing to leave behind?"

"That's worse. We were just starting to patch things up. Plessis is just as useful as Jenna, even more so when it comes to strategy. It's just..."

"You don't feel as strongly about her, by our measurements."

"Don't say that."

"You must choose now."

Du Mon clenched his bad fist into a tight ball. He curled it until he was sure his fingernails had to be drawing blood against the dull flesh there.

Plessis is capable. Smart. Self-motivated. She's observant.

"Take Plessis."

The eyes swivelled in her direction, and Plessis sank into the highway of light below her. Du mon couldn't hear her, but he could see she was screaming as the energy surrounded her.

"Don't hurt her!" he yelled.

"She will be given as much comfort as we can manage. Now, you will need our help if you want to secure your throne."

Du Mon saw Plessis' hands struggling to claw their way out from the light, and then she vanished. He looked back at the Administrator, and saw that new tendrils of light were twisting their way up his damaged arm.

"What are you doing?" he asked.

"You aren't fit for fighting, but we will fix that."

Below, Du Mon saw that the other members of his crew were now wrestling with or succumbing to tendrils of energy as well.

"We estimate this new technology will set your species ahead by about five hundred years. That should be more than ample for you to wage effective war against your enemies."

"How long do I have?" Du Mon asked.

"Like we said, one year. One year to change the course of your species' history."

The young prince nodded. Then a warm sensation began in his bad arm. Du Mon looked down, and his eyes widened.

Epilogue

Harmony was reclining against a tall evergreen as the ecosphere's mists washed across her face and neck. The false sun poured through the canopy of leaves. She could feel the flickering shadows as they danced across her face.

"It's so tranquil here," she said. "Are those actual birds I can hear?"

"Some of them are," Savannah replied, baking on a tree branch above. She was the de facto leader of the ecosphere, a creature with wide, feline eyes and downy fur. "Several are sentient species who sing to communicate."

"I can't believe that a place like this exists."

Savannah yawned, mouth stretching wide. "Thank you. It was modelled on my planet."

"You had a beautiful planet."

"Yes, I did."

"What happened?"

Savannah leapt down from her tree branch without making a sound. She stretched, bending backwards and audibly cracking her back.

"The same thing that happens to most planets the Administration finds. It was hollowed out to a husk, the core eaten by some horrific space creature. Then, the Administration rolled through, pulled all of the energy they needed from our sun until it was a cold, red, supergiant. The unluckiest members of my species were taken, cut up, and transformed into monsters."

"Why?"

"So that they would go and do the same to other planets. Its how the Administration sustains themselves."

"Do you think they'll do that to Mars? Eat out its middle?"

Savannah gestured for Harmony to follow. Together, they meandered through the trees, over the rocks and glades, and towards the waterfall that commanded the horizon.

"They'll be cautious if we're nearby. If what you said about Earth is correct, that they have the capability of building ships, and have millions who can fight as soldiers, then I think we have a chance to beat the Administration."

Harmony looked up at the ecosphere's sun, encircled by a rainbow. "I don't think they'll have technology like this."

Savannah's mouth drew up in the approximation of a smile. "We don't need you to provide the technology. We can grow or build anything your species lacks here. What we really need are people like yourself, who are willing to stand up to injustice."

Harmony poked her tongue out slightly. "I definitely think you picked the right Martian for that. I'm a bit of a rebel back home."

"How perfect that Nuk pulled you from space then."

Savannah stopped by the healing trees. They grew straight up from the babbling water, thirty in total. Their roots curled around like an embrace, forming a tiny pocket of still water that was protected from the rushing streams that ran from the waterfall.

"Where's Sheree?"

"Your friend is in this one."

They stopped at the riverbank, and Savannah bent down to examine the base of the healing tree. She parted some fronds that were providing shade to the still waters inside the roots.

Sheree was sleeping peacefully in the water there, curled up like an infant.

"She was hurt a long time ago," Savannah said, looking at the scars atop Sheree's head. With a single claw, she gently traced the pink tissue. Then she studied the lilies and seaweed that grew up and around Sheree's body, cocooning her. "The healing process will end soon, and the plants will release her."

"I'll wait," Harmony said. "She should see a familiar face when she wakes up."

Savannah nodded. "I'll have someone bring you an evening meal." She left the young woman beside the waters.

Savannah skipped across the stones and moss, and climbed her way towards the waterfall. As she went, she saw Nuk laying in his own healing pool. He was sitting patiently, alert, as the plants and seaweed worked their healing on his arm.

"Are you well?" she called.

He gave her a wave with his good arm, and his skin flashed brightly. *Good.*

At the base of the waterfall, Savannah pulled open the exit hatch. When she saw the tunnel out to the outer-shell, she bent down and ran on all fours. A cub-like squeal of glee escaped her mouth and Savannah felt the wind blow across her face. As gravity lifted, her paws left the ground, and she resigned herself to floating towards the outer shell. She unfurled herself then, limbs outstretched like she was paddling down an invisible stream.

The tunnel ahead flared out, and she floated out into the great chamber where Nuk had brought the Martians. *I'd sensed it then. The importance of that moment. No longer are we just picking up the dregs of civilisations, the flotsam left behind from the Administration's raids. This time, we found a species who managed to hold their own long enough for us to arrive. This time, we might be able to stop them.*

It frustrated Savannah to no end that many species like Nuk's had been transformed. Her own people had been spared that fate, thankfully. *The Administration, for whatever reason, selects some species to be mutilated. Others they leave to float through space until they die.*

Above, she noticed a figure who drifted beside the vaulted roof in the greater chamber, looking out through the shifting hull and jellied exits. When she collided gently with the floor, Savannah pushed off, coming in beside the figure. Her paws reached up, steadying herself.

"You've been out here a long time, Peace."

"I supposed I have."

Peace's wounds had been beyond the help of the healing trees. For one, the injuries weren't living, so the plants' chemicals had little effect. He floated with a salve bandaged against the fleshy parts of the wound, and now spent a great deal of time watching the moon approach.

"Have you been here before?" she asked.

"Luna? No. My father was from Earth though."

"When did you last see your father?"

"To be honest, I never met him." Peace gave her a lopsided grin. "When we meet the delegation from Earth, I'd like to get a message to him."

"We'd best play that one carefully," Savannah cautioned. "Now that the Administration has left the system, I'll do the initial contact. We can reveal your presence here later."

"Yeah."

Together, they looked out at the view of Earth's moon, as the ecosphere fell through a crack in spacetime towards it. Its dusty-grey surface was now a hive of lights, movement, and construction. Mountains of factories and cables rose up, distorting the horizon as the moon rushed closer, dwarfing them.

"They've spotted us," Savannah said. She gestured back towards the ecosphere's interior.

Peace nodded. With a sigh, he navigated his body through the zero gravity, back towards the centre of the ecosphere. At the tunnel's entrance he waited for the tunnel entrance to complete a full revolution and return to where he waited. "Our mother is back on Mars."

"The mother you share with Harmony?"

"I'm willing to tear Mars apart, rock by rock, to free her."

Savannah measured the steel in his face, and bared her fangs. "You'll get that chance soon, Peace."

He turned away without another word, and launched himself through the tunnel as it came hurtling back around. He flew through the opening, and landed on his feet.

Savannah looked back towards the moon. *Is this species ready to take part in an interstellar war?*

Tiny runabout ships were detaching themselves from surveyance towers, and heading towards the ecosphere.

They glided up through the chemical smoke that drifted from the moon's factories, and through the void towards her.

About the Author

Jonathan Furneaux (pronounced: "fur-no"), is an author and educator in Brisbane, Australia. In the second grade, his teacher let him write novels in the back of his mathematics exercise book instead of learning his times tables. As a result, he developed a joy of writing and literature, as well as an awkward pause before having to do any kind of counting.

Jonathan was awarded a High Commendation by the Fellowship of Australian Writers (QLD) for his first published short story: *The Second Father*.

Visit **www.jonathanfurneaux.com** to get some free stories, read his blog and reviews, learn about his future projects, and quickly find his social media handles.